Zomerschoon— Beauty of Summer

by

Wendi Dass

Foreign Endearments, Book Two

Zomerschoon—Beauty of Summer

Cover Art by *Jennifer Greeff*

The Wild Rose Press, Inc.
PO Box 708
Adams Basin, NY 14410-0708
Visit us at www.thewildrosepress.com

Publishing History
First Edition, 2023
Trade Paperback ISBN 978-1-5092-4749-3
Digital ISBN 978-1-5092-4750-9

Foreign Endearments, Book Two

Published in the United States of America

Hendrik reached for a book on the shelf. "Since I'm your acting advisor for the foreseeable future, I recommend we take a step back. Has Cayley assigned this?" He extended a thick, green text.

Her breath caught. Advisor? Foreseeable future? In a daze, Anna scanned the book. *Introductory Cryptography*. She shook her head.

"Well, this is a good start." He dropped the book in her hand then turned his back. "Come see me when you've solved all the problems in Appendix A." He faced the whiteboard and ran his inked hands through his hair.

Anna stared, her lips taut with a mixture of rage and dismay. She gripped the book so tightly the cover threatened to collapse. Of course, Cayley hadn't assigned the book—Appendix A or any other parts. She'd read that book when she was fourteen. What a narcissist!

Stomping to the door, Anna let her mind jumble with profanities and various methods of destroying this preschool math book. Maybe she'd smash it over Hendrik's carrot-juice hair. Maybe she'd shred it in a blender and shove the scraps down his throat. Maybe she'd set it on fire and toss it in his trashcan. Yes! Fire would be the perfect crime. No evidence.

With a smirk, she passed through the threshold and turned to slam the door.

Praise for Wendi Dass

"Debut author Dass pens a charming novel that's just as much a story of one woman's journey to find herself as it is a search for love...What truly makes this novel stand out are its vivid descriptions of beautiful scenery, which may make some readers homesick for a place they've never been."

~ Kirkus Reviews

"Let yourself be swept away to Italy in a romantic, engaging adventure that covers a wide spectrum of emotions and will have you cheering for the heroine."

~ Sublime Book Reviews

"Prepare yourself for an entertaining journey of self-discovery full of romance, humor, and drama. ZOMERSCHOON is the story of a young woman's search for purpose and meaning in her life. ... This creates an interesting dilemma that is delicious to devour as a reader. The author's sense of humor also hit all the right notes for me as I found the banter and dialogue to be top-notch."

~Pikasho Deka, Readers' Favorite Review 5 Stars

"In ZOMERSCHOON, Wendi Dass has written a beautiful romance, perfectly capturing the atmosphere of Oxford and its academics. In a world where people tend to write about billionaires and their love lives, an account that is so honest that it could be a true story is refreshing and comforting...I recommend this book to anyone who likes a good romance without sex and nudity. This kind of book is rare and a definite treat."

~Delene Vrey, Readers' Favorite Review, 5 Stars

Dedication

To my writing buddies, Brian and Joe, who read many a "crummy first draft." To my husband and daughter for letting me lock myself in my office to "have some quiet already!" To Irina, Tamara, and Mom for helping me promote my books, even though I preferred to hide in my writer's den. To my besties, Nina and Renee, who indirectly supported my writing by listening to all my hare-brained drama and pretending I wasn't crazy. To my editor at TWRP who also read many a crummy second…and third…and fourth draft but who actually made me fix them. To everyone else, who are too many to name, who supported me through this whirlwind process of completing a manuscript. (And also to those people who drove me so bonkers I escaped to my stories.) I love you all.

Chapter 1

The mathematical likelihood of finding one's life direction by age eighteen is fifty percent. By twenty, sixty percent. And by twenty-five, seventy-five percent. Perched on her tippy-toes, Anna Franklin examined her overgrown bob in a toothpaste-splattered mirror and wondered why in the world was she in the other twenty-five percent.

With hair too long to spike and too short to tuck behind her ears, Anna tugged at her wisps, drawing the strands into a glittery clip—the sparkles matched the streak of purple above her left ear. At six weeks since her last visit to Rome and her trusted hairdresser, both her dye job and cut needed repair. But heck, the hair was the least of her worries. Since her thirteen months in England, not much about Anna had adjusted well to Oxford. The food all tasted like soggy bread, the classes bored her more than a late-night infomercial, and her love life sucked because apparently Brits found her, an American, far less attractive than Italians had.

A heavy fist rattled the door. "I gotta take a leak, Franklin."

Conner's cockney accent sounded thicker than usual. "I thought Brits were supposed to be polite." Anna swept on black eyeliner.

Conner hmphed. "I thought mathematicians were supposed to be precise."

She rolled her eyes, wiped a smudge of liner from her eyelid, and then opened the door. Her scrawny, ruddy-faced roommate stood with ankles crossed as he bounced lightly on his toes. "Precision and timeliness are completely different."

Conner brushed past her into the latrine-sized bathroom without a word.

At least his quiet demeanor rang true to British norms. She stepped over the threshold, and the door slammed behind her. "You, for one, should know the difference in their definitions!" She slapped a palm on the door. "I thought you were an English major—I mean, reading English?" A year in Oxford and she still couldn't keep all their terms straight. Whoever heard about reading English or reading History or reading Maths? The term was more ludicrous than the idea of an imaginary number to an elementary schooler.

"It's creative writing, Franklin. I don't give a sod about grammar. I'm an artist."

Anna stuck out her tongue. She'd heard the artist spiel before—once regarding Conner's inability to trash empty chips bags and half-drunk bottles of beer and another time about the number of women, and the occasional male, who shared his room. Even her employer-provided room at St. Theresa's, which offered about as much privacy as a curtained hospital exam room, topped sharing this shack of an apartment with Conner, *the artist*. The two years she'd spent under Sister Maria's archaic rules in the Italian dormitory offered far more fun than the previous year at Oxford.

Anna slipped into her room and sifted through a pile of clean clothes. Could she stand another year with

Conner, the smooth-talking co-ed, or without Sarah and Sister Maria? She tossed a tattered tee to the corner, her heart sinking. Could she survive another year of Oxford tedium?

Screw mundane. She scrunched a pair of lime-green underwear and hurled it at her unmade bed. She was the smartest math grad student Oxford had this century. She'd finish her coursework this year and her thesis in the next. Then she'd be free to…to?

Running a hand through her bangs, she sighed. Where or what she'd do after graduation she didn't know. Figuring out one's life plan, as it turned out, was trickier than proving Fermat's last theorem.

She yanked on a pair of jeans—too tight. Another inadequacy of her hare-brained idea to return to grad school. Or maybe she'd put on the pudge because she wasn't twenty anymore. Now, she'd tick over the midpoint of her twenties with no steady boyfriend, no plans for the future—at least none she could stick to for more than a day—and not even a good haircut. She had only her friends, the extra five pounds on her waist— thank goodness she'd been a size two before them—and Cayley.

She flicked her gaze to her watch. *Ugh.* She was late again for her weekly check-in with her advisor. Anna slipped a rubber band through the buttonhole of her pants to ease the tightness on her stomach, tugged on a sweater, and hurried out the door.

A short walk away, the mathematical institute building stuck out amongst the century-old stone architecture. While domes and spires graced most of the university, at the Andrew Wiles building, the sun glinted off the metal curves of the patterned pavement.

Anna stepped between the metal arches of the Penrose design which resembled a page from an adult coloring book—everyone knew stepping on the curves brought bad luck. Inside the sliding glass entrance, a slanted glass roof illuminated an atrium filled with sleek furniture. While the paving and roof gave a nod to mathematical feats, like her favorite Roman building, the Pantheon, Anna had her heart set on a dark, stone-crafted building straight out of a wizarding film. When she'd first visited Oxford a year and a half ago as a prospect, that dream had been shattered.

Stifling a yawn, Anna crossed the atrium and nabbed breakfast from a nearby vending machine. Shortbread cookies probably weren't the best choice, but they were better than nothing. Shoving one in her mouth, she took the stairs two at a time to the second level. En route to Cayley's office, she poked her head into an unoccupied grad student office and swiped a piece of copy paper and a pen and scribbled some expressions that had swarmed her mind over the past few days. By the time she reached her advisor's office, Sigmas, Deltas, and a host of parentheses littered the page.

The scent of burnt coffee and expo markers lingered in the air at the entrance to Cayley's office. Black scrawl covered two large whiteboards—pseudorandom generator, PRG. Anna scoffed—baby stuff. An undergrad must have visited him during office hours. Turning her attention from the chicken scratch, Anna was greeted by the bald spot between Cayley's two strips of puffy white hair.

"Half past ten, Ms. Franklin." He held his gaze steady on the paper in front of him. With a shaky hand, he marked the paper in red pen.

Anna slouched into a seat in front of his desk. "Sorry, I overslept." She shoved another cookie into her mouth.

"Does that mean you missed Cohen's lecture?"

Anna cringed, and the buttery cookie in her mouth took on the texture of sawdust. She'd lost count of the times she'd missed the algebraic topology lecture. But why should she have to go if she could ace the tests?

"Again? I can only call in so many favors, Anna. I had to beg them to give you Cs last term. Genius or not, graduating at the bottom of your class doesn't bode well for your future in academia."

Swallowing hard, Anna felt the cookie cinch her throat. So now her future didn't just preoccupy her thoughts, but Cayley's as well. Dropping her chin, she sank into the chair. Cayley thought she'd be as successful as Oxford's most famous mathematician, Andrew Wiles. Her friends in Rome, Sarah, Eduardo, and Sister Maria, hoped for the same. Anna rubbed her forehead. She didn't have it in her to tell any of them how utterly lost she felt. Forcing a smile, she extended the remaining cookie toward Cayley. "Shortbread?"

Cayley furrowed his fuzzy white brows, further accentuating his similarity to the famed English mathematician who shared his name. All he needed was a tie and vest and he'd be an exact match to his great-great-grandfather.

"My physio would detest you." He nabbed the cookie anyway.

Anna grinned. Sweets always appeased Cayley—well, almost always. Shortbread hadn't done the trick when she'd skipped three weeks of complex analysis.

At the time, Anna thought she might not be allowed to return for her second term. But that was before Cayley understood her brilliance, before he realized Anna could decipher complex encryptions faster than she could consume a shortbread cookie. At that moment, he'd let her into his world—let her begin to solve encryptions he'd been given by outside sources.

Solving that first cypher had been like her first month in Rome, when she'd resigned herself to learning the language. She'd needed a few weeks of nonstop studying, incessant eavesdropping in cafes, and even binge-watching Italian soap operas, but she'd done it. The question wasn't whether she could solve the puzzles or not, but whether she could *make* herself solve them. Cayley's puzzles soon became too easy, and she didn't have the motivation she'd had in Rome: hundreds of eligible men to converse with and a plethora of menus waiting to be explored. Not to say she didn't like a good puzzle, she just liked to go out and have fun even more. If only he'd give her something harder to work with—something like he gave his post-doc. These cyphers were easier than point-set-topology, for crying out loud!

"The modulus—did you work out that part?" He moved from his desk and stared at the whiteboard, scratching his head.

Anna approached him and offered the paper. "Actually, I think I did."

Cayley widened his glassy eyes as he took the sheet of mathematical hieroglyphics. As he considered her expressions, he rubbed his chin.

For a moment, Anna doubted herself. Could she have simplified the summation? Had she switched the variable from *n* to *k* by accident? Maybe she should try writing her work a few days in advance of their meetings, instead of a few minutes?

Caley slapped a hand on her back and crinkled a smile. "I knew taking you on as a student wasn't a mistake. If you keep up this work, I might live long enough to see you crack Allerton!"

Anna smiled. Oh, to work on Allerton, wouldn't that be fun? Then she dropped her gaze to Cayley's shaky hand, and she shook her head. "Don't say that, Cayley. You're healthy and strong."

"We'll see what the cardio has to say about that today." He shuffled back toward the desk, his foot catching on the carpet as he did. He steadied himself and cleared his throat. "He probably wants me to increase those damned beta blockers." Cayley reached the desk, picked up a stack of papers, and placed them in an envelope. He extended it to Anna. "Hand these back before you begin the lecture."

"Lecture?" Anna lifted a brow.

Cayley sighed. "Don't tell me you forgot you're covering my class? Intro to Cryptography? PRGs?" He pointed at the whiteboard.

Anna swallowed hard and gave a sheepish smile. She might need to stop at the vending machine—this time for a highly-caffeinated beverage. "Right. Of course." She straightened her posture. "The class meets at one, right? Lecture hall two hundred?"

"Twelve-thirty in the one hundred wing." Cayley spoke in a terse tone.

Anna cleared her throat and then pursed her lips. "Sure thing. I'm on it." With the stack of papers under her arm, Anna headed out the door. *PRGs. Undergrads.*

No problem. She served as a Teacher Assistant for Calculus. How hard could delivering a lecture on her favorite topic be?

As she rushed down the hall, she checked her watch. Eleven-thirty. She'd just spend the next hour reviewing the text, pull out some definitions, examples, and…

Anna stopped mid-descent on the stairs. Did she even have a textbook? Gripping her notebook, she dashed back toward Cayley's office. The door stood open. "On second thought"—she entered the office—"I better borrow your book. I wouldn't want to be un—" Anna gasped and dropped the notebook from her hands. The pages fluttered as it fell to the floor. She struggled against the scream caught in her throat.

Cayley didn't sit at his desk. He didn't stand at the whiteboard, either. He lay on the floor, unmoving.

Chapter 2

The quiet hum of medical equipment and nurses' whispers filled the hospital corridor. Cayley remained in surgery—had been for the last two hours.

"Blood clot in the brain," the doctor said before the surgery. "He's had a stroke."

Anna paced the quiet hall, her combat boots scuffing the white linoleum. How long had his brain been without oxygen? After how long without oxygen would someone's intelligence disappear, would their motor function be destroyed, would—Anna gulped—they survive? She shuddered. No, Cayley would be fine—just fine. He would need to lay off the cookies for a while—okay, maybe indefinitely. But a few statins and a spinach-and-ginger cocktail would make him good as new. *Right*?

Scanning the hall, Anna released a tight breath. Where was the doctor, the nurse, or, hell, anyone with an update? And why hadn't Cayley's family arrived? During the four hours since she found him in his office, only the dean of sciences had emerged.

"Terrible. Just a bugger of a day, I say." The dean had rubbed his gray beard and squinted his hazed eyes. "I was really hoping I'd see the day the old chap retired, not carked it."

Anna narrowed her eyes. "He's going to pull through." Her voice wavered, and she flinched. Didn't she believe he'd recover?

"Yes, you're quite right. I'm sure he will." He dropped his gaze.

The dean, Mr. Bugger, or whatever his real name was, didn't sound convinced, either. What was this pessimist's name, anyway? All she could recall was that Cayley and he had been friends for many years and that he was more than happy to fudge Anna's grades on account of Cayley's trust in her.

"You wouldn't be interested in covering his classes until I find a replacement, would you?" He lifted a brow.

Anna hardened her already stony gaze and lowered her chin. He couldn't be serious.

"I suspected you'd feel that way." Mr. Bugger sighed. "I'll be back this evening. If you receive any more news before then, please let me know."

Anna nodded.

He turned on his heel and started down the hallway.

Dean Bugger strode down the stark white corridor, his fluffy gray hair drifting away like a patchy rain cloud in a murky sky.

A vibration rattled her chest, tugging Anna from the memory. She looked down. Her phone was ringing. She extracted it from beneath her bra strap and stared at the caller ID. Why in the Cartesian coordinate plane was her mother calling? She pressed the green button. "Mom? Are you all right? Dad. Is he okay? Is…" Anna flared her nostrils and pursed her lips. This disturbance better not be about Mom's lab. Because if Mom ranted about an undergrad accidentally nuking her frogs again, this conversation wouldn't last thirty seconds.

"Darling, I've just heard. How are you?"

Clutching the phone, Anna softened her lips and nose. Mom heard about Cayley's stroke? Or had word finally gotten around that Cayley covered Anna's butt for the past year and a half?

"Cayley's illness is absolutely detrimental to your studies—a total derailment. Have you thought about a replacement? Or perhaps you should just transfer schools? Either way, this hiccup will set you back at least a semester—more likely a year."

Mom continued her dramatic spiel, but Anna could barely hear it through her raging pulse. How dare she make such suggestions when Cayley struggled to survive? She stole a peek down the corridor, but still no doctor or nurse emerged. Tightening her grip on the phone, Anna could practically hear the shatterproof cover cracking at the edges. Anna inhaled through her nose and attempted to simmer the rage inside. In the background, her mother chattered on about some nonsense that in no way compared to the gravity of her advisor's situation. But could she really expect more from a woman who spent more time inseminating frogs than with her family? "Cayley isn't even out of surgery." The words tumbled out in a raised tone.

"I know, I know."

Anna clutched the phone tighter. Of course, she knew. Mother knew everything about her academic career—her class schedule, her grades, and, heck, probably what brand of pencils she used to pen her tests. What did she know of Anna's personal life—her feelings? Why couldn't Mother ask how traumatizing finding Cayley unconscious was instead of asking her current average in Abstract Topology?

She leaned her back against the wall, slid up her booted foot a few inches, and dropped her head into her cupped hand. If she didn't get Mother off her back in the next five minutes, the wall wouldn't be the only thing meeting the bottom of her boot. She lifted her head. "Cayley's going to be fine, Mother." And if he wasn't? Well, even if Anna was about to give it a second thought, finding a new advisor would be the least of her concerns. If anything, it might be a reason to walk away from this godforsaken place.

"Anna, you need to be proact—"

"I'm sorry, but I've got to go. I…um…" Anna searched for an excuse. "I've got another call coming in."

"Anna, this conversation is not over—"

Oh yes, it is. Anna pressed off the call and let her head fall back to meet the wall. She stared at the white grid of a ceiling. Of course, no one else had phoned—not Klara, not the Dean, and certainly no one else in Oxford. Did anyone else here have her number? A sting rushed her eyes just as a tightness gripped her chest. To avoid tears, she closed her eyes and took a swift inhalation. The grip on her torso still held fast. Was this pain in her chest because of Cayley's condition or the fact that she'd only made one friend in all of England over the last year?

A surge of resistance rushed through her body, and she stomped her foot onto the floor. *To hell with crying!* Sniffling, she snapped open her eyes and pulled up a contact on her phone—an Italian one.

"Anna," Sarah answered through a yawn, "what's wrong?"

Suddenly, all the pent-up anxiety of the day

flooded to a head. "I…I…" She fought against quavering lips and blinked her eyes to ward off reemergent tears. "How did you know something's wrong?" Her voice croaked.

"You're calling, genius—not texting. I quote you when I say, 'phone calls are for the adulting world.' "

Anna choked out a laugh—a small, dry laugh but a laugh nonetheless. "I said that?" She rubbed her forehead. "Well, I guess I'm having one of those days." If only she knew whether it would end as badly as it began.

****

Across from a wooden bar, Anna slouched in her seat, her chin resting in one hand, while she used the other to alternate between swigs of frothy beer and forkfuls of lukewarm pasty. Still numb from that afternoon's conversation with Mother, she stared at the room. Dim lighting illuminated the knotty pine tables and lead-paned windows. Around the Coat of Arms tavern, co-eds circled, laughter boomed, and tankards cluttered wooden tables. Conner didn't appear among them, although he often hit this bar which sat only a few blocks from their flat. Perhaps he remained at home, monopolizing the bathroom? She shrugged. Had she been home in the last twelve hours, she might know the answer to that question.

"Sorry, I'm late." Klara whisked into the chair beside Anna. "Lab ran over."

Anna raised an eyebrow in her friend's direction and forced a smile. "Thanks for coming."

Klara threw an arm over Anna's shoulders and drew her in close.

The warmth and magnitude of Klara's embrace felt

13

like that of a mother bear. Sometimes, Klara forgot she was a good six inches taller and forty pounds heavier. Anna struggled to breathe under the tight hug.

Withdrawing, Klara smiled. "Has his condition changed?"

Anna shook her head, dropped both elbows to the table, and lifted the tankard with both hands.

Pouting her lips, Klara furrowed her brows.

Her usual bright blue eyes lost some of their luster.

"I'm sure he'll come out of the coma soon." Klara rubbed Anna's back.

Soon? Anna scoffed and guzzled the rest of the beer. Soon as in days, weeks…years?

"At least the brain tests all confirmed he's maintained function."

Frowning, Anna gave Klara a sideways glance. "A lot of good it is when you're asleep."

Klara shrugged and took Anna's glass. "I'll get you another." She strode to the bar.

Anna stared through hazy eyes.

Klara squeezed between two men on stools to reach the bartender. On the right stool sat a dark-haired man with tired eyes. Across from him sat—

Cayley's post-doc? Anna bolted upright. How could she mistake the red-haired, wiry guy who mumbled instead of speaking? The guy who refused to tell anyone what problem he worked on, even though the topic was obvious to everyone in the department. Did he know about Cayley? Did he think Cayley would pull through?

The table shook as Klara wiggled into her seat. "You'll never guess who's at the bar?" She slid a full glass over to Anna. "My Calculus professor and my

English professor. They were talking about Cayley."

Anna jerked her head in Klara's direction. "Hendrik's your Calculus professor?"

"Hendrik? You mean Dr. Van der Aart?"

Across the room, Hendrik smacked a glass on the bar.

Anna focused her attention on him.

"How should I feel?" Hendrik's voice rose above the bar's ruckus. "My research is crap, I haven't had a proper meal in a week, and Cayley is dead."

Anna gasped, and the beer glass in her hands slipped. Had she missed a message from the hospital—from the dean?

"Cayley's dead?" the dark-haired man asked.

She righted the glass, and beer sloshed over the table. It probably dribbled onto the floor, too. But the mess would have to wait; she kept her gaze fixed on Hendrik.

"As good as dead." Hendrik finished his drink. A deep scowl cut Hendrik's pale, freckled face.

Anna heaved a sigh of relief. She sank back into her chair. That apathetic jerk! How could he say such a heartless thing?

"Bloody hell," Hendrik's companion said. "'Ol' chap should've…"

Something jabbed Anna's right side, and she turned.

Klara stared with widened eyes and a frown. "Have you even been listening?"

Anna tucked a stray, black hair behind her ear. "You, um, said Hendrik is the worst teacher you've ever had?"

"What?" Klara flared her nostrils.

Klara's "w" sounded more like a "v," and Anna bit her lip. Her friend's German only emerged when she was agitated. Anna touched Klara's sleeve. "I'm sorry. Today was long and exhausting. And maybe Third-Quadrant Hendrik's lectures aren't as bad as I imagined. I mean, surely they can't be worse than drone-for-a-voice Cohen." She squeezed Klara's arm.

"Third Quadrant?" Klara lifted a brow.

"You know, on the Cartesian coordinate plane? Where everything is negative?"

Klara stared for a microsecond before her glower receded into a smile. She laughed, then rolled her eyes.

Okay, maybe my math jokes aren't as funny outside the Wiles building. Anna tipped back her beer, guzzling the entire thing at once. "C'mon, let's go back to my place and watch some trashy TV and eat chips, uh, crisps." Crisps. She always forgot they called them crisps in Britain. Smacking her glass on the table, she glared in Hendrik's direction. *As good as dead.* She growled the words in her mind. Cayley would improve, regardless of what Third-Quadrant Post-Doc thought. The whole department knew he took the wrong approach to his *secret* research problem, and he made the wrong prediction about Cayley, too.

Anna rammed back her chair, the wooden legs squealing as they drove against the floor planks.

As she sipped her beer, Klara gazed over her broad shoulders and raised a slender, blonde brow.

"The crisps are getting stale, Klara." She yanked Klara's elbow, pulling her to her feet and sending the beer sloshing.

Klara giggled and wiped away the splattered beer on her cheeks. "All right, all right!" She took one last sip from the glass then placed it on the table.

Anna looped her elbow through Klara's and stomped toward the exit, scowling in Hendrik's direction.

Hendrik lifted his gaze to meet hers.

She held his gaze, a mellow somber one. Turning her back to Hendrick, she tugged Klara tighter and rushed out the door. He couldn't be right about Cayley, could he?

Chapter 3

In her pint-sized kitchen, Anna added boiling water to two teaspoons of instant coffee, stirred, and sipped. Ugh. She twisted her face. This brown, bitter water put Italian standards to shame—heck, even American ones. The coffee in England, where tea reigned supreme, was too weak—way too watered down to perk up Anna after last night's fiasco. First, there'd been the sulking over Cayley, then Hendrik's pessimism at the bar, and finally, late last night an email from Dean Bugger. Oh, that email! If only she could strike it from her memory. Growling, she added another scoop of coffee, a splash of creamer, and three heaping spoonfuls of sugar.

A knock in a familiar rhythm sounded on Anna's front door. *Klara.* "It's open!"

Klara entered the kitchen, huffing and puffing.

Pink splashed her broad cheekbones, and beads of sweat percolated on her brow. Purple leggings clung to her long calves, and an Oxford sweatshirt fit snugly on top. She'd been up for hours. Anna awoke about ten minutes ago, at half past nine. She didn't consider nine-thirty too bad since she went to bed after three, and then stayed awake for at least another hour…after she'd checked her email. Klara must have spent all morning doing sprints. Or deadlifts. Or squats. Whatever those gym-attending type did. "You run here?"

As she caught her breath, Klara helped herself to a

glass of water. She gulped it down. "Gotta. Get. In. Race. Form." Her labored breath cut her sentence.

"Five K?"

Klara shook her head as she sucked in air. "I'm trying to qualify for the London marathon."

"London marathon?" Anna stiffened and then sucked in her stomach. "Are you trying to make me feel bad about my figure again?"

"Yeah right, Anna. You know I'd die for your figure. The marathon is another one of Dad's ideas." Klara reached into the front pouch of her sweatshirt and withdrew a scone. "I did swing by the dining hall."

"Klara!" Anna lunged for the flaky baked good. Who cared about having a belly? She still squeezed into her size two jeans, after all. "You're a genius." Biting into the buttery biscuit loaded with plump golden raisins, she silently thanked God for Klara's meal plan. Without these stolen treats, vending machines might serve as her sole means of sustenance. If only Oxford offered the delicacies Rome provided—like gelato or piping hot pepperoni pizza or Eduardo's cooking. Anna had never been so well-fed as she had during her two weeks at Eduardo's and Sarah's home. She tore off another hunk of the scone. Sarah would be so jealous if she knew Anna was eating a British scone, right now. A heaviness rushed her chest, and the bite morphed to a mouthful of cement.

"Genius, no. But I'm beginning to think I might be smarter than Professor Van der Aart. Why didn't he at least come speak to you last night?"

Maybe because he knew he'd be seeing me today. Swallowing hard, Anna blinked away thoughts of her friend in Rome. "It doesn't matter, I'll be seeing—"

"I mean, he must have seen you. You might be petite, but you stand out."

"Stand out?" A piece of scone lodged in Anna's throat.

"You know, the way you bop around a room and take center stage? Or your flashy eye makeup and your purple streak of hair?" She tugged a lock of Anna's hair before biting into a banana. "Haven't you two met before?"

Anna coughed. "We have." She often ran into Hendrik when he was leaving Cayley's office. True, he had been buried in his notes, but Anna always said hello. *And I'll see him again today…hopefully, not anywhere near Cayley's office.*

Klara shrugged. "Then he should have come over then, shouldn't he?"

"Yes, but I will—"

"You chasing away boys again, Franklin?" Conner strutted into the kitchen and winked at Klara. "Maybe they were just chasing Queen Antoinette." He gave an exaggerated bow.

Klara's cheeks burned a shade darker.

Anna rolled her eyes. She'd tell Klara about the email *after* she got rid of Romeo. Anna tugged Klara's arm and chugged the rest of her coffee. "You're such a charmer, Mr. Artist. Is that what you told the girl upstairs, too?"

"I…but…" Conner widened his eyes and cleared his throat. "I never tell a woman…"

Tuning him out, Anna grabbed her backpack in one arm and Klara's sweaty elbow with the other. Klara didn't need to listen to Conner's nonsense, either—a heartbreaker was the last thing Klara needed. Anna plunged into the biting air of the October morning. "I don't know who's the bigger jerk, Conner or Hendrik."

"Conner's cute." A smile lit up her face.

Klara's voice sounded dream-like. Anna scowled.

"What?" Klara raised her brows. "At least he knows who I am, which is more than I can say for Professor Van der Aart."

Anna gritted her teeth. "Hendrik's not a professor—he's a post-doc and if he doesn't remember my name today, then I swear I'll—"

"Today?" Klara stopped in the street.

Anna eased to a stop beside her, throwing back her head as she sighed. With all the excitement of the scone and bloody-freaking-Conner, she hadn't even told Klara about the email. "Why else would I be up so early? I've been called to a meeting with him." With Klara clambering to keep up, Anna stomped down the sidewalk, past the black-posted streetlamps, the rows of parked bicycles, and the hordes of co-eds dashing to their classes.

Fifteen minutes later, having parted ways with Klara at New College, Anna traipsed into the third-floor office and found Hendrik hunkered over his desk. His wiry frame spilled over the chair. His mess of burnt orange hair matched his outfit: disheveled. He wore a faded-blue polo, which was half-tucked into wrinkled khakis. Anna pursed her lips. How nice of him to dress up for their meeting. She cleared her throat.

Hendrik jumped, sending a sheet of paper covered in blue ink pen teetering to the floor. "You're late." Without looking up, he reached for the paper.

Ink covered his fingers, which were long and lean like his body. Anna lifted her cellphone from under her left bra strap and checked the time: nine fifty-eight. Judging by the amount of ink on his hands, he'd probably smeared the time right off his planner. "The dean said ten."

Paper in hand, Hendrik stood. "My email said nine."

Anna rolled her eyes. "The email clearly stated ten. As I recall, the dean sent it at six minutes past nine p.m. Perhaps that's why you're confused."

"No, I…I do think—" His cheeks reddened, and he lost his grip on the paper again. It fluttered to the floor. As he bent again to retrieve it, he muttered something in a foreign language. "Maybe it said ten."

His admission was barely audible, but his flush stained his pale cheeks a shade almost as red as his hair. Grinning, Anna sauntered past him. Now, what language had Hendrik spoken? German? Swedish? No. Dutch, definitely Dutch. Come to think of it, Cayley briefly mentioned a math conference at The Hague. Yes, and he said Hendrik planned on attending as the conference was so close to his home. Holding her head high, she eased into an empty chair beside Hendrik's desk and fixed her gaze on a whiteboard covered in mathematical expressions. She'd solved the puzzle of Hendrik's language, but what about his mathematical problem? Anna peered at the attempts of a proof scrawled on the papers on his desk. "What are you working on?"

Hendrik swiped the papers off his desk into an unruly pile and shoved them behind his back. "This meeting is to discuss your research, not mine. What problem does he have you studying? Bingham? Fieldling?"

Anna exhaled sharply. What an egomaniac. First, he didn't acknowledge her at the bar, and now, he proposed she solved kindergarten problems? If he was any more self-centered, he'd have a moon orbiting his head. "I'm currently working through some of Lovelace's famous cracks." She forced an overly-sweet smile.

Hendrik wrinkled his nose.

"You know, perhaps the most famous woman code-breaker of the last century? The one with a computer language named after her?"

Hendrik frowned. "I know who Ada Lovelace is. I'm not so certain her work is where you should focus your efforts."

Not so certain? Is he implying he doesn't think Lovelace's work is valuable? A force shot through her, the jolt threatening to stand her hair on end. Anna bolted from the chair, sending it teetering backward. Rocking, the chair oscillated before settling in its position.

Hendrik reached for a book on the shelf. "Since I'm your acting advisor for the foreseeable future, I recommend we take a step back. Has Cayley assigned this?" He extended a thick, green text.

Her breath caught. Advisor? Foreseeable future? In a daze, Anna scanned the book. *Introductory Cryptography.* She shook her head.

"Well, this is a good start." He dropped the book in her hand then turned his back. "Come see me when you've solved all the problems in Appendix A." He faced the whiteboard and ran his inked hands through his hair.

Anna stared, her lips taut with a mixture of rage

and dismay. She gripped the book so tightly the cover threatened to collapse. Of course, Cayley hadn't assigned the book—Appendix A or any other parts. She'd read that book when she was fourteen. What a narcissist!

Stomping to the door, Anna let her mind jumble with profanities and various methods of destroying this preschool math book. Maybe she'd smash it over Hendrik's carrot-juice hair. Maybe she'd shred it in a blender and shove the scraps down his throat. Maybe she'd set it on fire and toss it in his trashcan. Yes! Fire would be the perfect crime. No evidence.

With a smirk, she passed through the threshold and turned to slam the door. On the board, the sequence of numbers and letters caught her eye. Hendrik was working on that cypher? Ha! Fat chance he'd solve that hundred-year-old stumper. She puffed out her chest. "Good day, Mr. Van der Aart. And good luck with the Allerton cypher. Although, I'm not so certain that problem is where you should be focusing your efforts."

She yanked closed the door with a loud whack and stormed down the hall to the spiral staircase. To hell with morning lecture. If she didn't let off some steam soon, she'd grab one of Hendrik's fountain pens and give him an "I'm a jerk" tattoo. Exiting the Wiles building, she strode through town. The October sun trickled off Oxford's stony buildings. Cool air whipped through the cobbled streets. Splotches of brown mottled the green grass. As she stalked, she texted Klara.

—*Hendrik was as irksome as last night. No…worse.*—

Pausing by the Radcliffe Observatory, Anna dug her nails into the spine of the book. Why weren't life's decision as clear as stars seen through a telescope? She stared at the smooth, yellow stone of the cylindrical building. It looked much more like a castle than an observatory. Perhaps that's why the university had converted it into a dining hall and common rooms. With a sigh, she dropped her gaze to her phone but found only a black screen. Klara must be in class. She always switched off her phone then.

Anna released her grip on the book, shoved her phone back into her bra, and continued down the road. Students like Klara made Americans look bad. Well, at least this lecture-skipping, homework-missing one. But could she really think badly of her young friend? She'd been much the same during her undergraduate years at MIT. That effort had wound her so tightly, she writhed like a firecracker when she arrived in Rome three years ago. As her friend Sarah often said, Anna returning to school was a miracle.

But what would Sarah, or Sister Maria for that matter, say if they saw her trajectory now? The Autumn term of Michealmas, the first of Oxford's three terms, was supposed to be a time for fun—a time to meet new students and rekindle friendships with students who'd been gone over summer break. This Michaelmas brought nothing but turmoil to Anna. Cayley's illness reminded her further that time slipped past.

At the thought of Cayley's lifeless body, Anna's heart ached. Thank goodness, she returned to the office yesterday morning or who knows how long he would have laid there. Thoughts of her advisor guided her steps, and Anna quickly found herself finishing the two-mile journey to the hospital. She stopped at a vending machine on her way to Cayley's room, this time opting for a candy bar. Flakes of chocolate wrapped in a purple paper—his favorite.

Upstairs, Anna placed the chocolate bar on the nightstand next to the cookies she brought yesterday. Who knew when, or if, Cayley might eat them?

He rested peacefully in the bed. His once-pink flush turned ashen, and his usual balloon of a stomach flattened. He still breathed unassisted, and his pulse beat steadily.

Anna eased into a chair beside his bed, extended her legs, and crossed her feet. "Hendrik is a Class A prig. I can't believe you chose him as your post-doc. You won't believe what he gave me today—the same book you asked me to lecture out of yesterday. He told me to come back when I'd solved all the problems. Can you believe the nerve?" She smacked the book on the table.

"Is everything all right?" a voice asked.

Anna teetered back on her chair, nearly toppling over before she stood.

A nurse appeared at the door.

Anna gave a nervous smile. "Just filling him in on events at the university." Her voice was chipper.

The nurse pursed her lips, held the pose, and then disappeared.

Turning back to Cayley, Anna ran a hand through her hair. She sighed. "Like I was saying, Hendrik's a real ball-cracker. The man has a serious case of stuck-on-problem-itis. He's got nothing on Allerton." She quieted, clearing the air for Cayley to reply. His chest rose and lowered. His hands lay still. His lips remained motionless. Anna slumped her shoulders, picked up the book, and squeezed Cayley's hand. "I'll be back soon.

Tomorrow, or the next day. Promise." She headed for the exit.

Hopefully, he'd be awake—at the very least, still alive then.

Chapter 4

With hands shoved in her pockets, Anna moped away from the hospital. A bus sputtered and lurched down Headley Way. Anna considered hopping on but continued across the road onto a bikepath joining the university with the surrounding community. At just shy of eleven a.m., the path of zig-zag bricks held few riders or pedestrians. Lush evergreens and full boxwoods lined the road. Anna kicked a pebble and let her gaze follow it into a drain where it clinked and clomped its way down. Perhaps if she wasn't so bummed about Cayley and so irritated with Hendrick, she could enjoy this walk. If Cayley awoke soon, she could take him on this path. As they strolled, they could talk about her research and eat biscuits.

Anna stiffened, and her heart ached more than when a student attempted to divide by zero. What if Cayley didn't wake up? And even if he did, what developments in her research might they discuss? She'd barely spent ten minutes on Lovelace's journals in the past week. If only solved problems could hold her interest as long as a thriller flick. Maybe then she would have surpassed Hendrik's efforts who, while he devoted more time and effort than Anna, had gotten nowhere, either.

Pulling the textbook free from her underarm, Anna stared at it with a furrowed brow. What did Cayley have to wake up to? Based on the lack of visitors, clearly no family waited for him. So that left his research and his students. Sure, he enjoyed teaching, but an advisor was closest to *his* advisees and to *his* post-docs. Why would Cayley want to wake up to a deadbeat grad student and a barren post-doc?

Anna grabbed her lock of purple hair and twirled it in her finger. She would give him a reason to wake up. She would make progress on her study of Lovelace or—no…on Allerton! She released her wisp of hair and whisked it back into place. Yes! And not only Allerton, but she would also dedicate herself to her coursework once more—just like Klara.

Sidestepping onto an offshoot of the path, Anna checked her watch. If she hurried, she could still make her afternoon class. In the distance, a bus hissed and groaned. The number fourteen bus drove this road and would drop her straight back at the mathematical institute. Now to make sure she caught it.

After her two p.m. analysis class, Anna never felt so awake. Maybe energy consumed her because she spent half the time texting Klara her plans to be a diligent student—hey, she could multitask. She snapped pictures of everything the professor had written on the board *just* in case she didn't remember it. More likely, though, the giant iced coffee she sipped as she climbed the winding stairwell of the Wiles building to the third floor brought on the surge of adrenaline. She knocked on Hendrik's door and, without waiting for an answer, stepped inside.

"*Verdorie.*" Hendrik cursed under his breath as he crumpled a paper and tossed it in the trash. He kept his gaze downward.

The trash can overflowed with inked papers—some balled and others torn. Ink covered the entirety of Hendrik's hands and even smeared his cheek. While Hendrik's desk and appearance had changed, the whiteboard with the codex hadn't. The Allerton code: twelve rows of letters and numbers locked a message in code for over a hundred years. Dozens—maybe hundreds—had attempted to decipher its meaning, yet none succeeded.

Clearly, Hendrik made no progress, either. No red marker circled digits. No arrows connected different letters. No notes of progress filled the margins.

Part of Anna felt bad for him, but then she remembered the book tucked under her arm. She cleared her throat.

Hendrik jumped up from his seat, sending another paper fluttering to the floor.

"Sorry to disturb you." She strolled into the room and slurped her drink. "I can't stay long, but I just wanted to return this." She dropped the book he'd given her that morning on the desk with a thud. "The problems in this book are for kindergartners. Pick any one of them, and I'll solve it for you."

Hendrik dropped open his mouth. He stared at the book, blinking. He furrowed a brow, then looked up at Anna and then back at the book again.

Anna fought back a grin. Mister Know-it-All didn't know what to say now, did he? She flicked a brow, took an obnoxiously loud sip from her straw, and stepped back from the desk. As she started for the door, a number—first a *6*, then a *3*, and then a *0*—caught her eye. A tingle rushed her spine, and she gazed at the code. In her mind, she shifted the arrangement of the numbers—not from least to greatest, or by number of prime factors, or any other obvious list. But to:

12630156145511300

"Abelian subgroups." The words slipped out in a hush.

"This book, Franklin, is my assignment and not—"

"Have you found the Abelian subgroups?" Anna whirled around to meet his gaze.

Hendrik stood beside her and held the book in his hands.

He must have retrieved the book and stood in the seconds she stared at the menagerie of letters and numbers on his board.

"Abelian subgroups?" Hendrik lifted his brows.

Anna heaved a sigh and stepped toward the board, pointing at the number six. "In the Allerton codex—S1 through S7. Did you know they were there?"

Hendrik gazed over her shoulder toward the board. "S1 through S7?" He rubbed his chin, leaving behind a smear of ink.

His voice was as blank as his face. If he even remembered the Abelian subgroups, then clearly, he hadn't noticed them in Allerton. An energy like she'd just drank five Italian espressos—not this weak, café coffee-flavored milk on ice—rushed through. She let a grin consume her face—not just because she'd solved part of a puzzle in two minutes—which Hendrik hadn't gotten anywhere with in two years—but because maybe now Cayley would have a reason to wake up.

She patted Hendrik on his shoulder. His broad shoulders weren't bony as she'd expected…but lean and defined.

Hendrik dropped his gaze to her hand. He opened

his mouth but only flapped his lips.

A fluttering invaded Anna's belly, and she snapped back her hand. Clearing her throat, she strutted toward the door. "I'll leave you to think about subgroups, Mr. Van der Aart." Still grinning, Anna rushed out of Hendrik's office and down the winding staircase. As she reached the first floor, the trembling in her stomach ceased. She clutched a hand to her stomach. What had brought on the sensation? Her drink? The excitement of the problem? Hendrik? She scoffed, chucked her ice-coffee in the trash can and then let out a laugh. Touching Hendrik Van der *Aarse* had NOT rattled her. The codex excited her—clearly, obviously, QED.

By Friday, Anna found the groove of playing diligent student. She attended all her lectures for three days. Well, she left one ten minutes early, but how could she say no to Klara's offer of treating for afternoon tea? She held her session for Introductory Calculus, and now, she sat at her dingy, basement office hosting office hours. While she hadn't given much thought to Cayley's assigned Lovelace journals, she had chewed over why the Abelian Subgroups appeared in the Allerton codex.

The numbers, each which mapped to S1 through S7, must be a key to deciphering the letters. But to which cypher did the numbers point? She tried a shift first, and the attempt failed immediately. The letters following the S1 number didn't shift forward one position. Nor did the letters following S4 shift forward or backward four positions.

Of course, Allerton hadn't encrypted the message with a simple Caesar shift. He was a mathematician— the cipher wouldn't be easy to find. With chin perched on her hands, Anna drove the code from her mind and concentrated on the very keen—and very attractive—undergrad sitting across. The boy, who happened to look like Christian Bale, questioned her about derivative rules. "What did you say your name was, again?"

"Christian."

Ha! Perfect. "Christian," Anna repeated, grinning. "Remember the product rule is for when you have two things multiplied together. The Quotient rule is for division."

Christian furrowed his brow and puckered his lip. "So for this one, I'd use a Product rule?" He pointed to his paper.

His fierce expression matched any Marvel character. With a selfie-worthy smile planted on her face, she leaned in and let her gaze drop to the problem on his paper. Her smile faltered, and she struggled not to wince. "Actually, that's a chain rule." She'd have to settle for looks over brains.

"Chain rule?" He chewed on his pen.

His jaw, as square as his broad shoulders, glided up and down. As he cocked his head to the side, his thick, chestnut bangs draped over his eyes. His brawny looks compensated for his lack of mathematics ability. And she'd been so diligent in her studies this week, she deserved a little comic-hero fun. She swiped a finger over her watch. "My office hours are over soon. We could continue this discussion over lunch, if you want."

Removing the pen from his mouth, Christian stood and crossed to her side of the table. "How about just lunch?"

Anna opened her mouth to reply just as her office

door burst open.

Hendrik stormed inside.

As he shoved himself between her and Christian, his clumsy movement sprayed the books stacked on her desk into a tumble.

Anna frowned.

"Anna…Abelian…Subgroups." He sucked in air between the words.

Anna widened her eyes and gazed between the two men. Christian's glazed-eyed, lost-Calculus-student expression returned. With the alarm in his voice, Hendrik's Raggedy Andy hair and matching orange stubble looked ready to combust.

"I rearranged the digits in the codex, and"— Hendrik lifted a hand to his chest and took a few audible inhalations—"You were right."

Straightening her posture, Anna pursed her lips. "When haven't I been right?"

Recovering his breath, Hendrick gave a half laugh. "Come to my office. I'll show you what I've pulled together." He reached for her hand.

Christian stepped in and puffed his chest. "Maybe later, Mate. We're going to grab a bite."

Anna cringed. Which was worse, Hendrik ruining her hot-boy hookup or Christian interrupting her Allerton amusement?

Hendrik dropped his hand and snapped his head in Christian's direction. "Am I interrupting something?" His tone matched a low growl.

"Anna's tutoring me in my maths." Christian set his jaw.

"Is she now?" Hendrik narrowed his gaze at Christian, and then Anna. "I need to discuss something with my *advisee* in private." He grabbed her elbow and yanked. "Excuse us for a minute."

Anna flinched. *My advisee.* Was it necessary for him to always treat her like a subordinate? She went willingly with Hendrik, but a rage burned in her belly. As they entered the hall, Anna wriggled out of his grasp. "What in the hell do you think you're doing?"

"What am *I* doing?" He thumbed his chest. "What are you doing is the question. What you do in your personal life is up to you, but don't do it in your university office."

Anna jutted her chin. "Christian is my student."

"Your student?" Hendrik jerked back. "Your student!" His voice echoed through the hall. "Having personal relationships with our students is against university policy, as is a relationship with anyone under our supervision." His cheeks reddened, and a twitch below his eye disrupted his stern countenance. He glanced away then back again. "Is that clear?"

Anna struggled against the anger seething inside. Her pulse raged, and she clamped her hands into fists. If only she was tall enough—and not on the verge of expulsion—she would punch his smart mouth. Without a word, she nodded. But her glower didn't waver—if she'd had superhero powers her stare would have turned him to dust.

Hendrik flinched, stepped back on wobbly legs, and then spun on his heel. He scurried down the hall until he disappeared into a stairwell.

Anna stomped into her office.

"What was that all about?" Christian stood beside a grimy window.

"Nothing." She flopped into a chair.

He stepped closer. "Well, that guy was a real dolt."

Anna snickered. "You got that problem right." Her stomach twisted, and her forearms ached from clenching. "You know, I'm not feeling up to lunch. You go ahead."

Christian screwed up his lip before releasing an audible exhalation. "All right, Anna. I hope to see you soon."

"In class, of course."

"Oh, right." Christian rubbed his forehead. "In class." He rushed out the door.

Anna blew a stray, purple strand from her face and collapsed her chin into her hands. Christian was definitely a few circuits short of completing a loop, but he did have one thing right. Hendrik was full of himself. Anna perched a brow. If only she knew why Hendrik was so upset. Because she wasn't helping him on Allerton right now? Because she was going out to have some fun? Or because she was having that fun with someone other than Hendrik?

Chapter 5

In the dungeon of the Wile's building, Anna paced her office as much as the tight space allowed. Four wooden desks, which looked as ancient as St. George's tower, crammed the room, and she knocked her hip into their corners as she milled about. Christian's woodsy aftershave lingered in the air, and images of Hendrik's tightened jawline filled her mind. She supposed she pissed off both men: Hendrik for…for….? Well, that reason was to be determined, and Christian for bailing on lunch. But she hadn't been in the mood. Hendrik's chastising soured her stomach. Stopping in front of a wall covered in four whiteboards, she picked up a marker and scrawled the first line of the codex on the board.

"I'll show you what I've pulled together," Hendrik had said.

Had he found something more than the abelian subgroup connection? A warmth tinged her elbow—the same place where Hendrik grabbed her. She scratched through the writing on the board. How dare he judge her flirtation with Christian? So what if their interaction became more than a flirtation? Everyone knew grad students fooled around with undergrads. Hell, if Hendrik weren't so caught up in his mystery numbers, he might get in on the action himself.

She tossed the marker onto the sill of the board so

hard it bobbled and fell to the floor. Kicking it to the side, Anna slid into her chair. Stiff and creaky, the wood drove into her backbone. No wonder she never wanted to stay in this office. The office was old and dusty, and nothing good ever happened in here—ever.

With her foot tapping at lightspeed against the floor, Anna snatched a sticky note from inside the desk and wrote: *OFFICE HOURS CANCELED*. She'd attended her classes. She'd held her discussion. And she'd even made it through five-sevenths of her office hours. She deserved a break. Taking nothing with her from her office, Anna smacked the note on her door.

Twenty minutes later, she found Klara at the gym. Unlike the thousand-year-old, stone and stained glass that decorated most of the campus, the main gym offered state-of-the-art equipment and setting. But at a fee of fifteen dollars per a month, Anna couldn't be bothered to join.

As usual, her young companion busied herself burning more calories than were possibly consumable. This afternoon's torture session included sprints on a treadmill. Anna stood beside the treadmill, leaning against the wall. She chomped on a bag of chips as she filled in Klara on the afternoon's events. "Can you believe the nerve? He's such a jerk." Her words sent chip crumbs flying. She wiped her lips with the back of her hand.

"Christian or Hendrik?"

Anna pursed her lips, and salt stung them. "Both. Hendrik is stuck in the matrix, and Christian has bigger biceps than brain. Hell, his pinky toe is probably bigger than his brain!"

Klara glanced at Anna out of the corner of her eye,

lost her balance, and grabbed the handrails as she regained her composure.

Anna smirked. Klara's innocence was another of her faults. Anytime Anna mentioned sex Klara acted like a student in junior high sex-ed class. "Geeze, Klara, settle down. I'm speculating here."

"Right." She eased back into her run.

Anna reached her hand into the bag of chips. Empty. For crying out loud! This day couldn't get any worse. With a shrug, she tipped back the bag and poured the crumbs into her mouth. Some landed on her cheeks and shirt, and she dusted them off.

Nearby exercisers shot her dirty looks.

Haters. What those sweaty kids wouldn't do for a bag of chips instead of gut-wrenching workouts. Hendrik was no better than them. He was envious and frustrated. Not just with the Allerton codex, but sexually, too. When had Anna ever seen him with a woman? Never. The man hardly made an appearance outside his office.

A tightening grew in her belly, surged up through her chest, and pulsed down her arms. If she stood in the weight-lifting section, she would let out a scream. Only she and Klara would know the shout was out of frustration and not exertion. She stared down at the empty bag. Okay, maybe the chips—er, crisps. Brits called them crisps. The crisps might be a dead giveaway. With a sigh, she crumpled the bag and tossed it into a nearby bin. Screw Hendrik. Screw the Allerton problem, too. "Are you almost done?"

Klara didn't reply.

With eyes straight ahead and chest heaving, Klara ran faster than someone chased by Jack the Ripper.

Anna waited. Klara neared the end of her workout—sprints always concluded them.

"Why don't you join her?" a voice asked.

Anna turned her head.

Conner stood beside them, his gaze moving up and down, tracking Klara's legs. "That's right." He grinned. "You won't ever look as good as Klara." He winked at Klara.

Fortunately, Klara didn't see, or else this time she would definitely have fallen flat on her butt. Anna gritted her teeth, going into helicopter-mom mode. "Just remember whose name is on the lease, smarty pants."

"Yeah, yeah." Conner kept his gaze on Klara.

His greedy, hungry gaze persisted through Klara's deceleration. Anna's pulse soared. Where was that lunk of a boy, Christian, when she needed one? He could clock Conner over the head with a dumbbell.

"Drinks, anyone?" Conner flicked his brows.

Klara stumbled off the treadmill. A flush painted her cheeks, and she wriggled her hands.

Anna resisted the urge to palm her forehead. Why was Klara such a lovestruck puppy? Bonehead Conner couldn't be the only reason. The fact that she ran farther than Anna had in her total existence must be distorting her reasoning. Regardless, this madness needed to stop. As she flared her nostrils, she stepped between Conner and her friend. "Klara and I already have plans. Thanks."

"Actually, drinks sound great."

Klara's wavering voice sounded behind Anna. As Anna glowered at Conner, she imagined her friend biting her lip. Anna held Conner in her glare—Conner deserved a death-stare more than Klara needed a scolding.

Conner wiped his sweaty brow, broadened his grin, and stared over Anna's shoulder. "McGrady's? An hour?"

"Sure," Klara said.

Anna crossed her arms over her chest and released a tight exhalation. "Fine"—she snapped her chin to the right and glowered over her shoulder at Klara—"but I'm coming, too." Now, if only she could convince Klara that Conner was the biggest jerk this side of the Atlantic before then.

On the third floor of the New College dormitory, Anna joined Klara for her date-night preparations. With bare, white walls, the room housed little more than a bed, desk, and a nightstand. At least the gingerbread-trimmed windows and non-functional fireplace gave the room some character. On the desk, a tabletop mirror sat atop a stack of chemistry books. As she waited for Klara to get ready, Anna paced the room.

Seated behind the mirror, Klara swept on a pink shade of lipstick, smiled into the mirror, and then frowned. She wiped it off with a tissue and selected another tube.

Anna rolled her eyes. "I swear, Klara. We're only talking about Conner Bloom, not eat-your-heart-out Christian Bale." Anna grimaced at the thought of Christian—her student, not the actor—and clenched her hands. If not for Hendrik, she would probably be out with protein-powder-for-brains Christian. But no, Hendrik put her in a mood where she couldn't even enjoy a carefree, flirtatious lunch.

Klara swept mascara through her blonde lashes.

"Please. Conner is a modern-day Shakespeare. Don't tell me you haven't read his poetry. It's published online, you know."

"Published, smublished." Anna sighed. "I bet that boy's sonnets are as weak as his biceps. Besides, what do you care about poetry? You're a chemist, for crying out loud."

"Maybe I want some chemistry in my own life." She puckered her lips and stared in the mirror.

Anna smacked a palm to her forehead and shook her head. Of course, Klara was goo-goo, ga-ga. She didn't have parents who treated each other like arch enemies.

Klara lifted her long, golden hair—first into a ponytail, and then pulled to the side, hanging over her shoulder. She frowned, removed it from the band all together, and swept the front into a clip.

"Enough!" Anna shot a tight palm midair. Even if Klara intended on finding love, she didn't have to be a ninny about it. Klara looked beautiful soaked in sweat at the gym—she didn't need to spend an hour doctoring her face. Grabbing Klara by the hand, Anna yanked her from the mirror and straight to the door.

Outside, lamps lined the circular courtyard and stone walkway. The sun dappled the Norman windows and gothic arches. Above, a cloudless sky provided a picturesque background to Oxford's famed dreamy spires. Bad mood or not, Anna couldn't help but admire the university's campus. If only Klara could focus on the beautiful setting and not handsome Conner.

A short walk later, Anna entered McGrady's with Klara. Low ceilings and tiny windows darkened the room, even though the sun had yet to set. A warm glow bloomed from stained-glass lamps hanging from the ceiling. Co-eds, locals, and undoubtedly tourists crowded the bar. Smoke lingered in the air.

Anna hadn't been to McGrady's since the night of Cayley's stroke. She scanned the bar, half wishing Hendrik might be there. How could she get back at him for ruining her afternoon? Smash a tankard of a strong stout on his head? Better yet, she could find the youngest boy in the room, plant a wet kiss on his lips, and watch Hendrik seethe. Screw Hendrik. Neither he, nor his silly problem, was worth a worry.

Anna shoved through the crowd and ordered an English porter for herself and a light American beer for Klara. Her lovestruck friend would fare better with the weaker drink. Beers in hand, Anna found Klara in a booth tucked under a window. Her friend adjusted her shirt collar and peered out the window. Anna flared her nostrils and considered dumping the beer over Klara's head. Perhaps the dousing would snap some reason into her. But seeing as Klara was her *only* friend at Oxford, she probably should play it safe. As she slipped into the seat across from her, she handed the light beer to Klara. "Any sign of Romeo?" To avoid scrunching her face, Anna sipped her porter.

"You mean the Bard of Avon?" Klara's gaze remained fixed on the window.

"That's the one."

Klara shook her head and shifted her gaze from the glass.

With her glassy-blue eyes, pale blonde hair, and mile-long-legs, Klara was as different from Anna as their contrasting beers. Their studies in sciences were about all they had in common—that and their shared love of beer.

Klara sipped her drink and spat it out. "Ugh. What is this?" With a soured face, she stared at her drink.

Anna laughed. "An American classic."

"It's awful. You drink this stuff?" Klara lifted her glass.

"Yeah, right. Only girls on diets *and* ladies staying sober to fend off poetic advances drink that stuff."

Klara lowered her chin. "I'm Austrian, Anna. I can hold my liquor. Besides, I don't think your roommate's going to show." She reached for Anna's drink. "Gimmee."

Tugging back her drink, Anna sloshed beer onto the table. "No way."

"You two fighting over me, again?" a man's voice interrupted.

Anna shot up her gaze. Conner stood beside them. Freshly shaven, he wore a crisp, button-up gray shirt that matched his eyes. Clearly, he hadn't nabbed his outfit from the pile of laundry spilling out his doorway, something Anna often suspected he did. Anna ticked a brow. Maybe he was interested in Klara, after all.

Klara gave a giggly laugh, and pink erupted on her cheeks.

Anna took a deep inhalation to prevent herself from laughing. "Klara didn't think you were gonna show."

Conner grinned, stepped closer to the table, and placed a hand on Klara's shoulder. "I didn't realize I meant that much to you."

Klara's blush deepened.

"Relax." He squeezed her shoulder. "I'll buy you a drink." Conner swept Klara toward the bar.

"Nothing too strong!" Anna called after him. "And get her home before midnight."

"Yes, ma'am," Conner said over his shoulder. He winked at Anna, then turned his attention back to Klara.

Chasing after the lovebirds, Anna snagged a bowl of pretzels from the bar and found an empty seat with a clear view of Klara and Conner. They stood by the bar, chatting. Whatever Conner said, Klara ate it up. She gazed with pathetic, lovestruck eyes. Conner probably recited Wordsworth or Tennyson, or some other froufrou phrases she'd heard him use through the thin walls in their apartment. *Please don't let Klara be one of those girls he brings to his room…because not one of them ever makes a reappearance.*

Why couldn't Klara see Conner was a bigger player than Henry the VIIIth? She knew one thing for sure, if she saw Conner so much as move a hand anywhere below Klara's waist, she'd wring his neck.

Anna watched them carefully, counting the number of times Klara laughed and the number of times Conner tried to refill her drink, but Klara pulled back her glass. She noted the patrons in the bar change, as well. A young student dressed in robes grabbed a pint of frothy beer. A rowdy group of rugby players, still dressed in muddy uniforms, smacked bills on the table and hollered, "Another round!" A skinny guy with circle-rimmed glasses slid onto a stool.

Remembering the man, Anna paused. He was the same man Hendrik met for drinks last week. Anna passed her gaze between the stranger and the door and back.

The man in glasses ordered a glass filled with a dark liquid.

Anna guessed whiskey.

He lifted the glass to his nose, closed his eyes, and sniffed. As he sipped, the man checked his phone. Then he looked up at the bartender and raised his glass.

The bartender filled a glass and set it next to the man.

Anna tightened her shoulders. Was he meeting Hendrik?

A moment later, the door to the bar swung open, and Hendrik stalked in.

At the same time, a man's voice shouted, "Anna!"

A familiar face stepped forward from the crowd of rugby players. Anna's breath caught. Christian and Hendrik both stood in the same room. She didn't know if she should run or cry.

Chapter 6

Anna flicked her gaze between Christian and Hendrik. *Just great.* Who could she slip past easier, brainless co-ed or crabby post-doc? As she released a heavy breath, she found Klara and Conner again.

He rested a hand on Klara's waist.

Anna scowled. Poetry Boy beat Christian and Hendrik in the jerk department by a long shot.

Across the room, Christian chest-bumped his friends.

Anna sank into her seat. Why was she so disappointed to see her hot student? She should have some fun, like old times.

Hendrik took a seat next to his friend, gave him a half smile, and picked up his glass.

Anna sighed. Hendrik spoiled everything. Her stomach dipped…hadn't he? She tracked the three men of interest. If she sandwiched Christian's looks with Hendrik's intelligence and tossed in a dash of Conner's charm, would this near-perfect man hold her interest? Heck, could anyone?

Still seated beside Conner, Klara seemed content. With a broad smile and stargazed eyes, Klara was ready to accept a marriage proposal. While Anna had her doubts about Conner's sincerity, she could only baffle at Klara's. *Have I ever been head-over-heels for a guy?*

Anna looked away from Klara and Conner. The

answer to the question was as simple as the solution to a linear equation. Of course, she never had, and she probably never would, either. Love resided only in the movies or, as in the case of her best friend, Sarah, was only achieved with the help of meddlesome nuns. Anna's parents weren't ashamed to admit they'd never been in love. Heck, sometimes Anna wondered if they even loved her. Or were they in love with the idea their name might be tied to a new mathematics theorem?

"Well, if it isn't Miss Calculus." Christian grinned and slid onto the stool beside Anna.

He swung a muscular arm over her shoulders. Anna sighed, recalling Cayley's rebukes for skipping class and his fuzzy, furrowed brows as he explained how he'd cooed the department chair's concerns. Maybe, Hendrik was right on this one. At this point, even if she held any interest in a relationship—heck, even another fling—Christian offered no viable option. Without Cayley around to cover her tail, she needed to walk a straight line. As things were, Hendrik had probably already filed a grievance with the Provost. She flared her nostrils. He better not have!

"I figured out those problems." Christian squeezed her shoulders. "Well, my mate did, at least. I've still got time before the test to learn the rules."

Anna nodded but kept her gaze alternating between Hendrik, Conner, and Klara.

Klara sidled up to Conner, leaning her head close to his face.

On the other side of the room, Hendrik's friend chatted away, but Hendrik didn't seem to hear him. He stared blankly at the glass in his hand, lifting it to his mouth from time to time.

"When's the test again?" Christian snatched some pretzels from Anna's bowl and shoved a handful into his mouth. "End of the month?" he spoke through chewing.

"Try Tuesday." Anna shot him a glare.

He scrunched his face.

Anna winced. In the crumpled position, his handsome face looked more like a B-rate movie actor's than a superhero's.

"Well, I've got three days to figure it out then." Christian downed his beer, whacked the empty tankard on the table, and then scanned his gaze up and down Anna. "You wanna get out of here?"

Anna bristled and shook her head.

Christian lowered his arm from her shoulder. "No? But…" He tilted his head to the side and rubbed his chin. "No? Really?"

Anna closed her eyes. Had this meathead never been turned down before? She snapped open her eyes. Well, he clearly never had hit on the likes of Anna Franklin before. She stood, and as she did, she caught Hendrik in her gaze.

He stared, but then his gaze drifted to Christian. Red painted his cheeks, and he jerked back in his seat, sloshing his drink out of his tankard and onto his shirt. He grabbed a napkin and dabbed at the stain.

Anna froze. If Hendrik hadn't blown the whistle, he certainly would now. The room seemed to shrink around her. Christian's hot, alcohol-infused breath lingered in the air. Hendrik's glare, even from across the room, seemed to cut deep into her body. Klara and Conner—couldn't they get a room already? She needed to get out of here…and soothe over things with Hendrik before he went mad-mathematician bonkers.

With her chin held high, she stepped back from Christian, staring dead-on. "I apologize if I gave you the wrong impression, but you're my student, and this"—she gestured with her eyes between them—"isn't allowed."

Christian unscrunched his face.

His perfectly spaced gray eyes sagged under arched brows. How sad she wouldn't gaze into them before a kiss, but wow, did a relief wash over her! A weight lifted off her shoulders. Cayley would be proud. And Hendrik? She cleared her throat. "Feel free to stop by my office, for questions—on math, that is. Now, if you'll excuse me." *I need to convince my would-be advisor not to have me expelled.*

Anna started toward the bar, toward where Hendrik and his friend had been sitting. Only they weren't there. She scanned the room. *Shoot.* Hendrik was already gone.

****

The walk to Cayley's hospital seemed longer than usual. Maybe the distance seemed longer because two miles was a lot for Anna's short legs. Or maybe the walk dragged on because of the lack of sleep—not that Anna stayed out late last night. No, just after Hendrik's departure, Anna snagged Klara by the wrist, barked a curt, "Date's over," to Conner, and delivered her romanticized friend back to her dorm. Anna made a swift entry into her own apartment where Conner was nowhere to be found—no doubt using his Shakespeare mind-tricks on another undergrad—and flopped into bed. She intended on getting a good six hours of sleep, but her restless mind capped her rest at four.

Turning a corner, the crisp, November air whipped down the alley, sending Anna's already bedhead hair into further chaos. The chill also jostled her thoughts back to the worry that kept her up: Michaelmas term, the first of Oxford's trimesters, would end in another month. Without Cayley here to defend her, would this be her last term at Oxford? Certainly, if Hendrik had any input, she'd lose her post before the second term, Hilary. She shuddered and zipped up her *Italia* hoodie.

Anna kicked a loose stone and gave a noisy yawn. Worries weren't the only thing that kept her awake. Hendrik's famed problem, the Allerton cypher, lured her back. What were the abelian subgroups doing in the text? Were they part of a polyalphabetic cypher or the key to a Caesar shift?

Huddled in her sweatshirt, Anna sped across the main thoroughfare, Headley Way, and weaved her way through hospital buildings until she found the one which housed Cayley. Inside, cool air, not so different than outside, greeted her. She frowned. Who wanted to wake up to a chill? Yet another reason Cayley hadn't woken. She jammed two coins into the vending machine on the ground floor and said a silent prayer for her advisor. *Please let him be awake. Please let him be unharmed.* The words weren't just for her own survival, but also Cayley's. What if he didn't wake up? Would his family—if he had any—pull the plug?

Pocketing one packet of shortbread cookies, she ripped open another, crunching on the cavity-inducing breakfast as she found her way to the elevator. She couldn't recall seeing any family at his bedside—no faculty or students, either. If no family turned up, who made decisions about life and death?

Shuddering, Anna entered the elevator. Her stomach seemingly stayed on the ground floor as it rose. On the third floor, she followed the now-familiar path to Cayley's room. As she approached, a soft, male voice drifted from inside. Her breath caught, and the shuddering ceased.

A son, an uncle, heck maybe a cousin three times removed had arrived! Surely, this visit would awaken him. Not denying the smile which crept to her lips, Anna neared the door, and the gentle voice inside materialized—a mixture of accented English and Dutch emerged. Anna froze. *Hendrik?* What was he doing here? Tiptoeing closer to the door, Anna pressed her back against the wall and leaned an ear in the direction of the room.

"We're all hoping you're back soon. Me, Don Goddard, and the freshers barely know how to get on without you. And your grad-student…Anna." Hendrik paused.

Anna smoothed her palms against the wall and held her breath. *I've reported her to the Don?*

"She misses you, too. She's a bright one, but a *pijn in de kont*."

Anna released the stale air with a whoosh. *Pain in the…?* Even without the Internet's help she could fill in that blank. *Pain in the butt.* She shoved another cookie in her mouth and munched harder. *Pain in the butt?! Who gave you your first break on Allerton in forever?*

"If she could stop acting like a twelve-year-old, we might actually work well together. Maybe we could make some progress on Allerton together."

Together? She loosened her hands and allowed a smile—a flicker of a smile, yet still genuine—to brush her lips. She let it morph into a grin. Post-doc extraordinaire wanted to work with her—not just assign her pointless problems from a dusty text or forget her name in public? She might even forgive his "pain in the butt" comment—his maturity jab, too.

"Maybe even," Hendrik continued, "have it worked out before you awaken—give you something to wake up to."

Anna furrowed her brows as a warmth crept into her fingers. Perhaps she had more in common with him than she thought? They both frequented McGrady's. They both were fascinated by puzzles. And they both held endearing conversations with a sound asleep Cayley. But was it enough to work with him? When had she last worked with someone on a math problem, anyway? First year at MIT? High school? Maybe now was the time to start again…maybe. Dusting cookie crumbs from her lips, Anna stepped away from the wall and marched into the room.

With his back to the door, Hendrik stood over Cayley's bed.

His long fingers covered Cayley's wrinkled ones.

"Don't sleep too long, Cayley. All of us want…need…you back." Hendrik released Cayley's hand and turned.

Anna grinned and ticked up a brow. "Morning, Mr. Van der Aart."

A flush seared his cheeks, and Hendrik jumped back. With widened eyes, he stared. He relaxed his eyes and formed his lips into a hard line.

Anna stepped past him, digging the extra package of cookies out of her pocket and adding them to the pile on the nightstand. "How is he? No change?" She studied Cayley's gray face. The crevices on his cheeks seemed deeper than when last she visited. His wisps of white hair had grown, as well.

Hendrik stared at the stash of junk food on the nightstand and softened his expression. He looked back at Anna. "Not yet. I…I wish I could say there was."

His voice was tender. His eyes were, too. Perhaps he now realized she brought the food. Perhaps he realized she was more than just an annoying, first-year grad student. Maybe they could work together. Anna rubbed her hands. "I've been thinking about your cypher. The abelian subgroups, do you think they are a—"

"The commands for a shift?"

Anna furrowed her brows and tucked back her chin. She nodded. Hendrik wasn't flushed any more.

"But it's complicated." He rubbed the back of his neck and paced in a small circle. "The repeated digits? The fives. The zeros. Do they point to S4 or S7? S5 or S6?"

"No fun in solving easy problems, is there?" Anna smirked.

Hendrik stopped pacing and looked up, blinking.

"Besides, with two people working on the options, we'll figure it out twice as fast." She lifted her chin and raised an eyebrow. "Actually, with me as one of those people, four times as fast."

Hendrik stared. He furrowed his eyebrows before relaxing them, and a smile eased onto his face.

During the split-second he took to realize she joked, she took in his appearance. Did his eyes always display flecks of gold? Did his lips hint at a smile? Was it her imagination or did he look almost handsome?

Almost.

"You're not too busy with"—he dropped his smile and cleared his throat—"office hours?"

Anna held his gaze. "No." She deepened her grin. "I don't have office hours on the weekend." She turned her back toward Hendrik, returning her attention to Cayley. "Besides, as you said, relationships with our students aren't permitted."

Hendrik gave a deep exhalation.

She could sense him questioning his next move.

"I usually work alone, but…"

But I'm smarter than anyone you've ever worked with? But I'll crack this case wide open?

"You are technically my advisee now. If you want to assist me, I won't object."

Assist him? Anna rolled her eyes. She lifted the sheet on Cayley's bed closer to his chin, tucking it tight around his shoulders. At least working with Hendrik would provide something promising for Cayley to wake to and, better yet, provide a reason for her not to get expelled.

"When do you want to start?"

Anna gave Cayley a quick kiss on his forehead. *We need you back, Cayley. Me and Hendrik, too.* She turned back to Hendrik. "How about now?"

Chapter 7

Later that day, Anna paced around Hendrik's office and chewed on a whiteboard marker. Behind her, slumped in his chair, Hendrik scrawled on paper with his ink-stained hands. Anna stared at the array of numbers and letters on the board. The first line read:

6TMWXC0YMOEYNTRC

For the past four hours, she and Hendrik had tried all possible shifts. They'd gone forward and backward. They'd shifted by $n-1$ and $n+1$ and $n+27$ for crying out loud. But still, she had found nothing. "What are we missing?"

Hendrik sighed and threw his pen on the desk. "The same thing I've been missing the last three years working on this damn project."

Anna stared. Three years? The longest she'd spent on one topic was an all-nighter for freshmen geology. Of course, she'd spent a few hours on the Voynich manuscript and the Shugborough inscription, but she'd never been serious about figuring them out. But three years? No wonder Hendrik was so frustrated—sexually and otherwise. She raised an eyebrow at Hendrik.

He ran a hand through his unruly ginger mop, yanking as he reached the end. The movement left it standing more on end than before.

Anna suddenly had an urge to tame it. She stepped toward him, caught herself, and stopped, twiddling the marker in her hands. "We'll figure it out."

Hendrik gave her a sidelong glance and frowned.

"Before the end of Michaelmas." She grinned.

Hendrik held her in his glare.

"Okay, maybe Hilary?" Anna shrugged.

Standing, Hendrik crossed his arms. "Don't you have some algebraic topology homework or something to work on?"

"Homework, shmomework." Anna swatted the air. "Who knows? But I do know one thing, if I don't get a proper meal, I'll keel over."

Hendrik checked his watch. "I guess you're right. You wanna grab a bite?"

Anna smiled and lifted a brow. "You buying?"

Hendrik's cheeks reddened, and he cleared his throat. "Well, I…"

"What? Post-docs make double my stipend, for sure. Probably triple." She stuffed her phone into her bra strap and sauntered toward the door, brushing Hendrik's shoulder as she passed. God forbid he should think she suggested this outing was some sort of *date*. "Are you coming, or what?" She turned.

Hendrik lowered his chin and rubbed his jaw. "Fine." The word came out with a sigh. "But you record what we've tried so far today."

Anna rolled her eyes. No wonder this guy hadn't gotten anywhere on Allerton. Scowling, she yanked out her phone, snapped a shot of the board, and then started down the hall. "Easy, peasy," she called over her shoulder. "Record made."

Nearby, Balliol Hall offered dining for non-college affiliates. As a post-doc, Hendrik held no college affiliation. And since he'd pay, Anna saw no point in taking him to her college's dining hall, which she hadn't visited all term, regardless. Inside, a quietness settled over the magic castle-like dining hall. A domed ceiling covered the long, narrow hall. Large, ornate windows covered the top half of the walls. Portraits of renowned Oxford figures decorated the lower portions. Seated at a long wooden table, Anna stared across at Hendrik.

His gaze rested on his food—a grilled cheese sandwich which he methodically dipped into his tomato soup before each bite.

Apparently, he wouldn't be much for conversation outside the confines of the mathematical building either. Anna shrugged, popped open her soda, and dove into her pizza. The slice tasted nothing like one found in Rome, of course, but at least here she didn't have to listen to lectures on her junk food tendencies. If she saw soda, Sarah would slap Anna's hand for sure.

Anna pulled a string of cheese from the slice with her teeth, slurping it through her lips. *Pish to Sarah's health food.* Anna didn't have a bunk mate like Eduardo to prepare five-course dinners every night. Besides, Sarah needed to impress her tot. When last Anna saw Gianluca, Sarah introduced soft foods—rice cereal, mashed peas, and other usual suspects. If a mother expected her kid to eat vegetables, she better set the standard. A heaviness set into Anna's gut. Sarah's mothering was so sincere—unlike her own mother's stringent meal requirements, designed solely for control.

Cayley's illness is absolutely detrimental to your studies—a total derailment. Have you thought about a replacement? Or perhaps you should just transfer schools? Her mother's voice played in her mind. Over a week had passed since her mother's last appeal. When would she call again? *Too soon.* Anna pushed her half-eaten pizza to the side and leaned forward on her elbows. "So, three years on Allerton, huh?"

Hendrik glanced up, his gaze stopping at hers, and then lowered it to his food. He nodded.

Anna exhaled sharply. Could Hendrik converse normally? Or was he one of those nerd-cross-mute types? She sipped her cola and thought of another conversation starter. "At least we figured out the subgroups. That's a start."

"You figured out those." Hendrik flicked his gaze to her before returning it to his food. He sighed. "And I'm beginning to wonder if the subgroups appeared out of coincidence."

"Coincidences are rare in science, Hendrik—especially in cryptography."

Hendrik dunked his sandwich again and took another bite. He shrugged.

Did he have to be so impartial? Did this dude contain an ounce of grit aside from that used to take mammoth bites of grilled cheese? Anna picked up her soggy slice of pizza, gave a passing thought to slapping his ruddy cheeks with it, and then took a gargantuan bite. "If you've been working on the problem so long, you're bound to have studied the history. Why don't you fill me in?"

Hendrik put down his sandwich, wiped his mouth, and straightened his gaze. "Well, historians attribute the passage to a British mathematician named Allerton, but no one knows if he wrote it or not. But the hundred-year-old existence, and the fact they discovered the document here at Oxford, seem to point to him. They say Allerton left the puzzle as a test for his students, which no one has since cracked."

"I'm guessing he didn't graduate too many students then, did he?"

Hendrik lifted a brow. "Probably not."

"At least he didn't ask his students to solve all the problems from the back of an antiquated textbook." Anna gave a grin.

Hendrik's lips twitched up at the ends. He shifted his gaze from Anna's eyes to her mouth, and he flushed. "I guess not."

"He's up there with the jerks at Langley, leaving codes on statues for its employees to solve. As if they haven't got anything better to do."

"You mean Kryptos?"

Anna nodded.

As he smiled, the color on Hendrik's cheeks mellowed.

The unease on his face melted away, leaving behind his cocky, post-doc prince demeanor. *What will he throw in my face now?*

"When I cracked the third passage, they gave me an open invitation to any of the intelligence agencies. CIA. DIA.—"

"What?" Anna shot back on the bench so hard the feet squealed against the floor. "Kryptos—the statue outside of the CIA building in Langley with four encrypted messages? You cracked the third passage? *You*? I thought an operative found the solution."

Hendrik flicked a brow. "Prospective operative. I made no commitments." He scanned the room.

She followed his gaze. A scattering of people

around the room stared. Had she just yelled that last statement? Heat crept to her face. Did her jaw hang open? She snapped it closed. Mr. Made-No-Progress-In-Three-Years was smarter than he let on. When was the last time she'd been so flabbergasted? When was the last time she'd been so…impressed?

Hendrik widened his smile.

With full lips and straight teeth, his smile *might* be suitable for kissing. Might. Anna ripped off a bite of crust with her teeth. "Being an operative would be one commitment I wouldn't mind making. I'd love to work as the secret spy. My parents thought I should follow in their footsteps…academia." She frowned.

"Beats tulip bulb farming." He shrugged off his smile, used the last of his sandwich to wipe the sides of his bowl, and popped the bread into his mouth.

Anna stopped mid-chew. *Tulip bulb farming?* First Kryptos. Now tulips. What surprise would he drop next? "You'll have to fill me in on—" Anna'a phone buzzed and burst into an upbeat techno beat. *Klara.* "Excuse me." She removed her phone from her bra strap and pressed the screen. "Wazzup, Ms. Capulet?"

"*Um Himmels willen!*"

Oh, boy. She'd really struck a nerve if Klara cursed in German. Anna grinned.

Klara sighed. "Where are you? And more importantly, did Conner say anything about last night?"

Crud. Anna dropped her grin. She hadn't even heard him come home last night. That could be a good thing—at least he hadn't brought home another girl. Unless that meant he'd gone home with her instead. Anna covered the receiver and stood. "Thanks for lunch. I'm sorry to cut our chat early. I found the conversation interesting,"—*Interesting, indeed.*—"but I have to take this call. Work again Monday?"

"After your Algebraic Topology class, of course." He smirked.

Anna widened her eyes. *Holy Fathers of Calculus, does everyone at this University know I ditch?* Maybe Sister Maria employed an informant at Oxford.

"Anna? You there," Klara said.

Anna placed a hand over the microphone. "Sure thing, Mr. Kryptos." Then she lifted her chin, turned her back on Hendrik, and removed her hand from the microphone. "I'm here. But I have no idea what Shakespeare's been up to." As she exited the dining hall, she cast her gaze over her shoulder at Hendrik. She had no idea what infinite surprises Hendrik had for her, either.

As she chatted with Klara, Anna returned to her apartment. Her blue door with glass inset greeted her, and Anna smiled. "I made it home." She broke off and hesitated to turn the knob. What if she found Conner here with someone? "Let me scope out things, and I'll call you back."

Klara muttered something in German under her breath. "All right, but call me right back."

"As sure as the square root of four is two." Anna bit her lower lip, ended the call, and entered the apartment. The kitchen was quiet—too quiet. With no sign of Conner, she scoped out the place for evidence of whether he'd been home yet. No steam lingered in the shower, and no water splattered the sink. No dirty dishes sat in the kitchen sink, and laundry piled on the floor. Unless Conner had returned and left unchanged, unbathed, and unfed, he hadn't come home last night.

And that could only mean one thing.

Anna's ears burned. *Poet, my butt.* Who had he stayed the night with this time? A first-year? An insecure transfer? Anna found a half-empty bottle of soda in the fridge and twisted the cap. It didn't fizz— who knew how long it had been in there? She took a swig anyway. What would she tell Klara? That Conner had probably shacked up with someone else? Swallowing hard, she tried to harness the sugar rush. No. She didn't need to tell Klara if she didn't ask. Besides, maybe Conner had fallen asleep on a buddy's couch. She scrunched her nose. Maybe if he had any male friends, that might be a possibility. Anna picked up her phone and called Klara. She held her breath. One ring then…

"Yes?"

Klara's voice sounded anxious. Anna took another swallow of cola. "Conner's not here. He must have gone out." Not a complete lie. "Wanna do it like the Brits and get afternoon tea?" That diversion would cheer up her bestie Sarah. Maybe it would work on Klara, too?

Klara sighed. "Fine. But I'm getting a *kaffee*."

Anna smiled and dumped the rest of the cola in the sink and tossed the bottle in the recycle bin. "Me, too," she replied. "But we can still order the tower of cakes, right?"

Klara laughed. "*Ja,* of course."

Now if only she could keep Klara in as sweet a mood as those cakes…especially once she realized Conner's true MO.

Chapter 8

In Mabel's café, a flowery tablecloth covered a table holding two dainty cups. Anna added three packets of sugar to her cappuccino and swirled the coffee with a spoon.

Across the table, Klara raised a blonde brow as she sipped her coffee—straight black.

Anna cringed. How could someone so conservative and rigid in her ways as Klara be attracted to someone as outlandish as Conner Bloom?

"He said nothing about last night?" Klara lowered her cup.

Anna shook her head. "Like I said, I haven't seen him." *Maybe if he'd come home last night...* To keep herself from blabbering, she swallowed a gulp of cappuccino—not bad like the sludge her father brought back from the donut shop in Boston but not great like the drinks from a *caffè* in Rome.

Klara clapped a hand to her mouth, squeezed her lower lip, and then released. "I thought he'd say *something* to you. We did exchange numbers."

Anna choked on her drink and coughed. "You gave him your number?" She whacked her chest with a palm.

"Why not?"

Why not? WHY NOT? Because Conner Bloom must be a booty-call kind of guy, and I'll hand write detailed solutions to all the problems in Hendrik's dusty kindergarten cryptography book before I let Klara receive one of those calls. Wait—had he already called? Anna thwacked her cup to the table, and it met the saucer with a heavy clank. "Did he call you yet? Like…last night?"

Klara shook her head.

Her friend's glassy eyes and tilted head meant she spoke the truth. Anna threw her head back with a sigh. Well, thank the Shakespeare Gods! At least Conner had the decency to hit up someone else before Anna talked her friend out of this grave mistake. She returned her head to its usual position, found a rogue purple strand of hair, and loosely wrapped it around her finger. Now…exactly how could she stop Klara from joining his graveyard of one-night stands?

"I really hope I made a good impression. I just think he would be such a smart match."

Anna wound the hair tighter, her frustration replacing the blood in her veins with magma. Were they talking about the same person? Mr. Lothario. Mr. Don Giovanni. Mr. I-Want-To-Get-Into-Any-Undergrad's-Pants. With a deep inhalation, Anna cooled the rising tide inside her, sidestepping an eruption of Mount St. Helen's proportions. As she placed her palms on the table, she stared Klara dead-on. "Klara, Conner is a literature major, and you're chemistry. Conner is an idiot, and you're brilliant. Conn—"

"He is most certainly not an idiot!" Pink painted Klara's cheeks.

Anna waved a hand. "Fine, he's eccentric, and you're practical."

Klara leaned back in her chair and folded her arms over her chest. "I thought opposites matched."

"I'm not saying they don't. I just don't know if Conner's your match."

Klara pursed her lips.

Unlike when Anna consoled Sarah through her divorce and the Eduardo breakup, this conversation was going nowhere. Anna sighed and kicked back in her seat, extending her legs under the table. Her stomach growled. "How about we close the curtain on Shakespeare for today?" She picked up a menu. "You in for a meat pie?"

Klara snatched the menu from Anna and studied it. "Mmmm—strawberry salad with walnuts."

Bringing her hands to her face, Anna made a gagging gesture. Must all her besties be health conscious? "Fine. But I'm getting a pasty and one of those." She pointed at a towering rack of plates filled with scones, teacakes, and other bite-sized treats she didn't know the name to, but which melted in her mouth faster than the limit of one over x approached infinity at the origin. Without waiting for an argument from her friend, Anna snagged Mabel's attention and drew her to the table.

If only she could convince Klara that Conner was worse for her than a meat pasty.

****

By Monday afternoon, Anna still made no headway on the Conner situation, nor had she and Hendrik progressed on Allerton. In his office, she stood, tapping a finger to her forehead.

Hendrik rubbed his chin and stared at the board where he'd written the first line of the codex:

6TMWXC0YMOEYNTRC

"Let's summarize what we've tried," Hendrik said.

"We used the 6, which appears in the abelian subgroups A3 and A5, as a shift three places right and left. No luck. We then tried shifting the letters five places right and left—still nothing."

Anna nodded and tried to tune out Hendrik. She knew what they'd tried; she'd replayed all the translations in her mind a thousand times…even the ones she'd gone through without him. She chewed a nail. She'd never been this stumped before.

"We tried listing the alphabet backward and performing the shift." Hendrik paced in front of the board and rubbed the back of his neck. "Maybe we should list the alphabet in rows of varying length and perform the shift vertically. But that's getting complicated. We might as well get a coder."

"Well, where's the fun if you're using a computer? Besides, I tried those transpositions, and they didn't work."

Hendrik jerked back his head. "You did that already? How did you do it so fast?"

Is he serious? Anna sighed. How was it Hendrik still underestimated her abilities? She might also say the same thing about him. "How did you crack Kryptos?"

"What?" Hendrik stepped back. "What's that have to do with Allerton?"

Anna shrugged. "I don't know. I suppose that depends on your answer."

Hendrik turned and strode to the window. "Elliptical curves," he whispered.

"No way." She stared. Hendrik knew how to use elliptical curves? Hell, only a few dozen brilliant mathematicians in the world knew how.

Hendrik still faced away from the room. "The

summer after I graduated from University, I wanted to go to grad school, but my folks urged me to stay on the farm. I worked on Kryptos—in my mind—all summer as I yanked up the tulip bulbs in the field. I knew finding the solution would be my ticket out." He faced her and lifted his gaze. "And it was."

A tiny spark erupted inside her. Hendrik's story sounded so familiar. As if taking the job at St. Theresa's was anything but escaping her parents'—perhaps just her mother's—demands. Anna stared, wanting to know from what he escaped. But his story entranced her...or maybe the glow of his amber eyes did.

Hendrik grabbed the eraser, wiped the board, and hurried toward his desk. From the back of his chair, he grabbed his coat and rustled through the pockets and withdrew a vape stick. "I'm going out for a few. Done for the day?"

While they shared common interests in math, bars, and junk food, when it came to unwinding, apparently his methods differed. "Same time tomorrow?"

Nodding, Hendrik opened the door and held it.

Anna swept on her jacket and stepped through the doorway. "You know, if you don't give up that nasty habit"—she fingered his vape stick—"You'll be done and dead sooner rather than later."

Hendrik flushed but then grinned. "Why, Miss Franklin, does this mean you care about my well-being?"

"Don't read too much into it, Dr. V." She spun on her heel and started down the hall. Of course, she didn't care about him...did she?

****

Over the next few days, Anna diligently attended her classes during the day, spent her evenings working on Allerton with Hendrik, and in between did her best to sidestep any and all of Klara's questions about Conner. By spending most of her time at the mathematical institute, she got the best of two worlds—keeping her promise to Cayley and ensuring she didn't run into loose-drawers Conner.

On Thursday evening, Anna spent another three hours with Hendrik on fruitless endeavors to decipher the code.

Hendrik balled an ink-soaked sheet of paper and tossed it into the trash. "It's late." He rubbed his forehead.

Black ink smeared above his firecracker brows. Normally, Anna would have smiled. But she just stared and tugged on her purple streak of hair. Was she helping Hendrik or leading them on a numbers chase? She chewed her lip and scrunched her brow. Her Abelian subgroups might be a mistake. Maybe she was wrong. Maybe the numbers existed in the code by coincidence.

Anna shook her head, jostling her hand free of her hair. No, she was never wrong. She just couldn't see the connection…yet. And she was tired. Getting up for nine a.m. classes put a damper on her sleep schedule. She just needed more sleep, then the cypher would come to her. Standing, she yawned. "You're right. Let's call it a night."

Hendrik lifted a brow, and the black streak creased in his forehead.

All week Anna urged him to stay an extra hour, which always turned into three or four—sometimes five. "We'll work again." Anna gave him an easy smile. "Tomorrow."

Nodding, Hendrik lowered his brow. He shoved papers into his leather shoulder bag.

Her smile deepened. So Mr. Works Alone now enjoyed her company? She packed her backpack and followed him out the door. Outside, a chill swept through the November air. Anna trotted down the steps, drew her jacket tight, and started for her apartment.

Hendrik fell into step beside her. "I'll walk you back."

Anna made a sideways appraisal. He hadn't walked with her before, but his company couldn't hurt. At least she'd feel safer making the half-mile jaunt in the dark.

He removed the vape stick from his pocket.

Seriously? If he wanted to walk with her, he'd have to avoid subjecting her to carcinogens. Anna flashed him a glare.

"Right…umm…" He returned the e-cigarette to his pocket. "It calms my nerves."

Anna frowned. "I can think of plenty of other things to help you relax. Wine. Yoga. Sex." She flicked a brow.

Hendrik caught his foot on an uneven patch of pavement and stumbled. "*Stront*." He struggled to regain his balance.

Anna chuckled. Male mathematicians were the most awkward people on the planet.

As he rubbed his forehead, Hendrik muttered foreign words under his breath.

"Dutch, huh?" Anna asked. "What other languages do you speak?"

Hendrik took a deep inhalation then released it, his

breath clouding in the frigid air. "English, German, Dutch, a little French. You?"

"English and Italian. And enough Spanish to order a burrito without sour cream."

Smiling, Hendrik sucked in the air.

He breathed the night air as if it were a cigarette. Perhaps the cool air, which burned Anna's lungs, produced a similar feeling in him. Hendrik sure was a typical European. He smoked, drank, and could speak half a dozen languages. Americans and Brits rarely spoke other languages. Well, unless you counted math a language, which some did.

Anna stopped dead in her tracks. *Other languages.* A shiver swept through her, and she snapped her head in Hendrik's direction. "Do you think Allerton spoke other languages?" The words spilled out faster than she could scarf a candy bar.

Hendrik stared before blinking three times. "Oh, Allerton? Other languages? I doubt it. He's a Brit."

Anna scrunched her face and tugged on her lip. Dammit! She hoped Hendrik would surprise her with some outlandish fact, like Allerton spoke Hindustani or Flemish or Greek. Anna gasped. Allerton was still a mathematician, and all mathematicians knew one language better than most. She grabbed Hendrik's elbow. "But he would at least know the Greek alphabet."

"Yeah, I guess." He took a step forward before careening to a stop. A haze washed over his eyes as he let his mouth fall open.

Anna didn't need to ask what he was thinking, because she saw the same thing in her mind. Jitters rushed to her fingers and toes. A new window opened to cracking the code—a new alphabet to explore. The lines of the Allerton codex streamed through her mind like Hendrik's cold breath floating through the air. "How many of the English letters map directly to the Greek ones?"

Hendrik blinked away the haze and gazed down. "I…I don't know. *A*—alpha. *B*—beta. *C*—gamma? Maybe? Maybe not?"

Anna nodded. "No gamma is for—"

"*G*, definitely *G*."

"Yes." All Anna's tiredness vanished in a heartbeat. Her pulse soared, and her thoughts raced in a thousand directions. "But what letter does map back to *C*? Chi? Or perhaps nothing at all."

Hendrik smiled, grabbed Anna's hand, and squeezed. "Let's go find out."

****

Anna followed Hendrik to the nearest location offering a blank whiteboard: his flat. On the first floor of a thimble-sized attached house, the entrance to Hendrik's flat greeted her. A lantern illuminated the front door, and green paint peeled at the corners.

Hendrik shoved a shoulder into the door, and it opened with a whoosh. He rushed in.

Anna raced after him, stepping inside. A blizzard of inked papers flooded the entry. The penned sheets lifted from a pile on a cluttered desk which sat…in the kitchen? Behind Anna, the door snapped shut, taking the light from the front porch. As Anna took a second to adjust to the darkness, she stared again at the desk. Yes, it plainly sat where a kitchen table should.

Somewhere in the flat, Hendrik flicked on a light.

The rest of the room came into view. Behind the

desk parked smack in the middle of the kitchen, a wheeling office chair haphazardly sat. Cereal boxes and empty bowls covered the four square feet of counter space in the galley kitchen. More bowls and cups filled the sink. Hendrik's flat looked as much like a home as Anna's untidy room did. At least no cigarette butts littered the entry, nor did the smell of them linger in the air.

Hendrik headed to the area opposite the dual-purpose kitchen.

A dingy couch and a beat-up coffee table crammed against a wall. Instead of facing a TV, the couch sat opposite a large whiteboard. The twelve rows of the Allerton code were neatly drawn on it—the letters in black, the numbers in green or red.

Anna rushed to the board, joining Hendrik.

He grabbed the black marker.

Anna snatched the red and green.

"*A* maps to Alpha, *B* to Beta, and…" Hendrik started.

"If *T* maps to Tau then where does Theta fit in?" Anna said simultaneously.

Hendrik stared for a hanging second then dashed through a door behind the whiteboard.

What the hell? Anna had never seen him so alive…so animated. They were on to something here…she just knew it!

With another whiteboard in his hands, this one clean, Hendrik returned. He propped it on the coffee table and started to write the Greek alphabet. "Tell me what we know, Franklin."

Anna rattled off the Greek alphabet and the mappings. Of the twenty-four Greek letters, twenty corresponded directly to English letters, leaving six letters in the codex with multiple options. "Go ahead and write in Chi for *C* and *Y* for Psi. I'm almost certain those work."

Hendrik furrowed his brows and opened his mouth again but wrote the letters.

Anna stared between the devised mapping and the first line of Allerton. Letters and numbers swarmed her mind. *Five left. T M B N...Not it. Three left. R K V N...Nope.*

"I think we should start with the first shift, and—"

"Shush!" Anna chewed on her nail. *Five right. C D M P. Ugh. C'mon, Allerton.* She mentally applied the last option: three right. *C O N G R...* Anna's heart thumped. "Three right!" She bounced on her toes.

Hendrik stared.

With head perched to the side, and amber eyes alight with wonder, Hendrik wasn't following her. "Map the English letter to Greek: *T* goes to Tau, and then shift right three: Chi. Now map back to the English alphabet." She darted to the whiteboard with the original codex. "And, yes, Allerton did use Chi for *C.*" Under the first line of encrypted text, she wrote: *CONGRATULATIONS.*

"Congratulations," Hendrik said.

His voice spilled out in a whisper—a shudder. "Congratulations." Anna nearly squealed. She whipped around and danced on her toes.

Hendrik shifted his gaze between the board and Anna. "Congratulations." His mouth hung open.

Paleness replaced the color on his ruddy cheeks. The black marker in his hand quivered under his shaky grasp. His lips twitched into a smile.

"The first line says congratulations," he said.

They'd cracked it. They'd really cracked it! Anna jumped and nodded so fast she might suffer from whiplash.

Hendrik reached for her, tugging her into his chest and squeezing her tight. *"O mijn God,* you did it.*"*

Within his strong grasp, Anna's breath caught. Heat tinged her cheeks. Why in the world was she so flustered? Was it because they'd just cracked one of the world's most hyped, unsolved math problems? Or that Hendrik was giving her all the credit? She swallowed hard, looping her arms around his broad shoulders, and returned his embrace. Or was it that Hendrik's closeness revealed he didn't smell at all like cigarettes; rather he smelled like an expensive, department store cologne?

Hendrik released her and held her at an arm's distance. "We did it. I can't believe we—you…you figured it out."

With his amber gaze on her, Anna could only think about his warm woodsy scent. She didn't know which cologne he wore—a department store staple or some Dutch brand she'd never heard of—and it didn't matter. The scent did its job; she wanted to yank him back, close her eyes, and take a deep inhalation.

Hendrik stared, smiling. A dimple marked his left cheek.

Where else on his body might he have a dimple? Heat rising again, this time in her belly, Anna looked away. *We've just made history, Anna. Stop thirsting.* She lifted her chin. "We figured it out." She emphasized the word 'we'. "But we're not done yet. We've got eleven lines left."

"It's late—really late." He tapped the marker to his lip.

On the wall behind him, a clock hung haphazardly. Eleven-thirty p.m. *If the clock was accurate.* "Eleven-thirty isn't late at all…if I'm skipping my nine a.m. class." She smirked.

"We could wait until tomorrow."

But the excitement in his voice and the glow in his eyes told her he didn't want to wait, either. As she mentally began the potential shifts of the next line, Anna shook her head. "Make us some coffee."

Hendrik exhaled sharply, shrugged, then stomped into the kitchen.

She hadn't a doubt in her mind she'd solve the rest of Allerton tonight. She did have serious doubts, however, as to her feelings for her temporary advisor.

Chapter 9

Anna awoke to the quiet hum of a space heater, and she couldn't recall ever feeling so hot. Something hard poked her side. Squinting, Anna adjusted to the light of the room, as the whiteboard for a TV and desk for a kitchen table came into focus. Apparently, she'd crashed in Hendrik's living room last night. Throwing off the not one, but two blankets, she scrambled to her feet. The clock on the wall read ten a.m.—so much for Analysis seminar. What time had they called it a night? Where exactly was Hendrik? And had they finished deciphering the codex?

As she stretched up her arms, Anna scanned the whiteboard. All but the last two lines were deciphered. Her heart pounded. They'd done it! Cayley would be so proud. Maybe he would wake up? Maybe he was already up? Maybe—

A door off the right of the living room squeaked open, and Hendrik, dressed in only boxers, stepped out. His carpet of red hair looked more shag than Berber, and his cheeks colored more rouge than pale. His bareness revealed the chest she felt the previous evening during their embrace was anything but flab. Strong, wide shoulders framed a lean torso with a line of muscular definition down the center. Warmth blossomed again, and she smoothed her hair, which was sure to be equally as tangled as Hendrik's. "Morning."

She folded her arms over her chest, in case she'd stained her shirt with coffee during their all-nighter.

"*Stront.*" Hendrik jumped, flicked his gaze in her direction, and then scurried back into his room. He emerged a minute later, wearing a T-shirt and sweatpants. He cleared his throat and tipped his head in her direction but didn't look her in the eyes. "Sleep okay?"

Anna nodded.

"I…ummmm…" He waved a hand in the direction of the whiteboard. "I stopped working after you fell asleep. Figured you'd want to be a part of finishing it."

"Wait—I fell asleep first?" Anna bolted to her feet.

Hendrik laughed. "I don't know. We both faded in and out there at the end." He ran a hand through his hair, got a finger stuck, and furrowed a brow. As he withdrew his hand, his cheeks reddened. "Anyway, when you rolled on your side and closed your eyes, I figured you were done for the night."

"So you covered me in blankets?"

He shrugged. "You looked cold all curled up like a wounded bird."

Anna laughed. "A wounded bird, huh?"

Hendrik rolled his eyes. "I'm going to freshen up." He pointed to his hair. "You know, do something with this bush on my head."

"It beats not having any."

"So they say." He entered the bathroom.

Anna rummaged in the kitchen. The rumbling in her stomach reminded her she hadn't eaten in nearly twelve hours. After popping some bread in the toaster, she shimmied around the desk/dining table to the coffeemaker and started a pot. She spread butter over the toast, placed them on chipped plates she found in the cupboard, and brought them to the coffee table in the living room.

Hendrik returned to the living room.

With hair slicked back and face freshly shaven, he suddenly resembled Christian Bale more than her student.

He lowered himself to the couch. "Thanks for breakfast." He crunched into the toast, devouring it in two bites.

"Thanks for letting me crash on your couch." Anna added a spoonful of sugar to her toast before taking a civilized bite.

"Anytime." He took a gulp of coffee.

"Oh yeah?" Anna grinned.

Hendrik choked on his coffee. "I mean…" He shoved another bite of food in his mouth, stood, and crossed to the board.

Clearly, he wasn't comfortable with her flirting, even though she stayed the night and saw him in his boxers.

He cleared his throat. "Shall we?"

Anna glanced at the clock on the wall. "As long as you're okay with me skipping Seminar, Mr. Advisor Extraordinaire." She winked.

"I suppose this once." Hendrik smiled and winked back.

They cracked the second line by the time Anna finished her toast. Toast with butter and sugar couldn't compare to a proper English Breakfast or a Sarah and Eduardo brunch, but it sure beat vending machine snacks.

Hendrik didn't complain, either.

His face shone brighter, if that was possible for a fiery-cheeked redhead who already emulated a wizarding twin. After second helpings of both the toast and coffee, the process quickened, and Allerton's secret message stood before them on the whiteboard.

"*Mathematics, now and forever*," Hendrik read from the board.

"Ha!" Anna jumped to her feet. "Allerton should have made the puzzle easier if he wanted the message to be *now*."

Hendrik laughed. *"Now* is a subjective term." He snatched his coffee mug off the table and lifted it in the air. "To Allerton and…to a dynamic duo."

Anna took her mug and toasted. The coffee was cool, but a warmth burned inside. Had she ever solved such a prestigious problem? Had she ever been part of a 'dynamic duo'?

"Cayley's never going to believe we did it." Hendrik stared at the whiteboard and beamed.

"Cayley." She gasped and lowered her mug to the table so fast coffee spilled onto the table.

Hendrik raised a brow.

"I've got to tell him." Her heart raced, and she jerked her head side to side, scanning the room for her belongings. "Where's my jacket?"

"Wait." Hendrik placed a hand on her upper arm. "I'll go with you…but first, I need to email the society."

She sighed. "Right, the society." Heaven forbid he didn't inform the proper authorities—didn't stake a claim to their solution. Hendrik seemed almost as eager as her mother when she'd made her last discovery. She chatted on the phone with half the department before she even finished writing up her results.

Hendrik frowned. "We can't be too careful, Anna. We've just solved one of the most famous problems in all of mathematics. Do you know what people would give to be the first with a solution?"

Anna slumped her shoulders. He was right, but it didn't make her angst to tell Cayley—to see if their revelation might awaken him—any weaker. "Fine, but make sure you write that email as fast as you can eat a piece of toast."

"Deal." He squeezed her arm then dashed off to the bedroom and emerged with his laptop.

As Anna waited for him to finish the message, she wondered if he would include her in the email. Ultimately, it didn't matter; what Cayley thought about their discovery did. He would wake up and tell her, wouldn't he?

****

When Anna and Hendrik arrived at Cayley's room, she rushed to his side, taking his hand in hers. "Cayley, you won't believe what's happened. Hendrik and I did it—we cracked Allerton!" If the news didn't rouse him, her squealy voice surely would. She shook his hand as she stared, her breath unsteady and her heart pounding.

But Cayley lay still, his quiet breaths the only sign of life in his listless body.

Anna squeezed his hand. "I noticed the numbers came from the Abelian subgroups which described the Caesar shift, but it didn't work. Then last night, we had a breakthrough. We realized we needed to map to the Greek alphabet. Genius, right? A mathematician using Greek—so epic!" The words tumbled out as fast as her racing pulse. Anna held tight to Cayley's hand, hoping—willing—her energy would pass through.

For several long moments, Cayley's chest rose and lowered.

Then she focused on his eyelids, waiting for them to spring open. A hand touched her shoulder, and Anna jumped. She spun on her heel.

Hendrik stared down and squeezed her shoulder.

With her attention so focused on Cayley, she half forgot Hendrik stood with her. But now, his sympathetic gaze made her stomach turn. Maybe Hendrik really did think Cayley was as good as dead? Maybe he'd given up hope?

With a strained smile, Hendrik removed his hand and withdrew a piece of paper from his pocket. "You were wise to put your faith in Miss Franklin, Professor Cayley. She's proved her intellect, her ingenuity, and her devotion to you." He rested a hand on Cayley's chest. "I'm sure Anna would like to tell you the decoded message"—he winked— "but I'm not letting her do that today. I've written it for you and am leaving right here. You only need to wake up to read it." He patted Cayley, and then placed the paper on the nightstand.

Hearing Hendrik speak, she felt the unease in her stomach vanish, replaced instead by a soft glow in her chest. Hendrik did believe Cayley would recover. He also believed giving him a reason to awaken might cure him. In a swift movement, Anna enveloped Hendrik in a hug, feeling his warmth and inhaling his woodsy scent. "Thank you," she whispered before she stepped back.

Somehow, in the last two days, Hendrik had become so much more than the grumpy post-doc. How much more she didn't know.

****

The autumn sun dipped behind the horizon as she strolled with Hendrik back from the hospital. The wind whipped through the winding roads of Oxford, and giggling co-eds dashed along, their robes whirling in the wind. Crossing the bridge over the river Cherwell, Anna spied couples, huddled under blankets and holding lanterns, punting their gondola-like boats along the water. Anna could imagine Sarah enjoying the romance of it all, nuzzling under Eduardo's chin as they admired Oxford's dreamy spires. Had Anna ever slowed down enough to notice? Somehow, with Hendrik by her side, as time seemed to slow, she thought she could now.

In front of Anna's place, Hendrik faced her. "I've been thinking about my email to the academy and how we should list our submission to the journal. You cracked the cypher, Anna. When we submit, I think we should list you as first author."

"What?" Anna froze, and warmth tinged her chest. "That's ridiculous. The advisor is always before the student—always."

Hendrik released a long exhalation. "Strictly speaking, you're my advisee, not my student."

His voice softened. If she wasn't his student, then why did she have an uncomfortable feeling staring at the honey-colored specks in his eyes? Or for having the urge to bury her face in his neck and inhale the scent of his cologne? And why should she feel uncomfortable having those thoughts? Men didn't make her feel uncomfortable before, so why should this one? Raising her chin, Anna stepped toward him and stared up into his eyes.

Hendrik tightened his jaw but didn't drop her gaze.

The long, deep stare made his freckles sprout on his cheeks, and his breath became haggard. Anna grinned. No matter how much Hendrik tried to hide his feelings, his attraction was evident. She lifted her lips closer to his ear. "I don't care about being first author. It's more important for your career than it is for—"

Hendrik placed a hand on her arm. "This proof will make you famous—will open any door."

"I don't need any doors opened. What I need is…" What did she need? A master's degree? A boyfriend? A job? How about a freakin' clue about what she would do with her life?

Suddenly, from inside the house, a muffled laugh escaped—not Conner's laugh nor a floozie first-year's, either. The laughter belonged to Klara.

As Anna jumped back from Hendrik, a fire burned in her chest. Conner better not have passed first base, or he could consider himself homeless. "You're first author," she said to Hendrik. "End of discussion. But I call dibs on the poster for presentations." Without waiting to hear Hendrik's response, Anna heaved her shoulder into the door. "Klara," she called, "there better be a darn good reason why you're in my apartment alone with Conner. And don't try to sell me that you're taking British Lit. I helped you pick your schedule, remember?"

Either Anna needed to work on her shout or lusting caused partial deafness, because on the couch, Conner and Klara sat so close, they might as well have shared the same outfit. If Anna hadn't entered when she had, they probably would.

Conner's arm emerged from behind Klara, and his mouth locked on hers.

Anna cleared her throat loudly.

Flushing, Klara leered back and bolted to a stand. "Anna, what—" She straightened her shirt. "What are you doing here?"

"I live here, remember?"

"Don't remind me," Conner said through a moan.

With nostrils flared, Anna unleashed, "Jerk. Scumbag. Tosser." Each word erupted with increasing volume.

Conner threw up his hands. "She even knows the British lingo."

At the same time, Klara's blush deepened, and her eyes went wide. "Anna!"

In that moment, Anna didn't care if Conner was the Prime Minister himself. She still wouldn't let him screw over the only friend at Oxford she had. She held Conner in a glare and grabbed Klara's hand. "My room. Now. *Alone*."

Klara might have protested, and Conner might have shouted obscenities, but as Anna tugged Klara to the back of the flat, she heard only her pulse rushing her ears and the voice in her head saying, *Take her virginity, and I'll go Tybalt on you*. Reaching her room, Anna slammed the door behind them. "Have you lost your mind?"

"No, of course not." Klara wriggled her hands. "Why?"

Klara's voice sounded unsure. Anna released a sigh. "Conner practically has Oxford Pimp tattooed on his forehead. Girls, guys, heck maybe even some medium-sized mammals, are in his room practically

85

every night. The guy must be a walking STD."

Klara furrowed her brows, and tears welled in her eyes. She blinked them back, folded her arms over her chest, and held her chin high. "Stop making up lies, Anna."

Her friend spoke in a clear and straight tone. Whatever nonsense Conner placed in her head, she fell for it. "Klara, please? I didn't want to tell you this, but that night at the bar…your first 'date,' Conner didn't come home."

"So?" She widened her eyes.

"So?" A fire stormed in her chest, and she thrust out her hands. "He was out knockin' the headboard with someone else. Just hours after—"

"Stop," Klara shouted. "I don't know why you're saying these things. Are you jealous because you haven't had a hookup all term?"

"What?" Anna reeled back, catching herself on the bed post. "This has nothing to do with me. I'm trying to save you from getting hurt."

"Maybe I don't want to be saved. Maybe, for once, I want to be the one who has a little fun." Klara stormed out.

Anna stood, dumbfounded. What had just happened? Had she just lost the only real friend she had at Oxford? She winced and dropped her head.

A door slammed, then another, followed by thuds and creaks from Conner's room. Anna sighed. At least she succeeded in separating the two for the moment. Why wouldn't Klara listen? Maybe he was a better actor than a poet. In the distance, another door closed with a bang—the kitchen door. Conner had left, too. Was he going to meet Klara? Or another Juliet?

Anna flopped on her bed. An eerie quiet consumed the room—so quiet even the muffled squeak of the mattress resounded. She scanned her room. The space was so much less a home than her room at St. Theresa's had ever been. A dingy blanket covered the secondhand bed—an item she scrounged off a student who'd transferred to Cambridge. Across from the bed sat the only other item of furniture in the room, a beat-up dresser she'd found on a nearby street-corner with a *free* sign taped to the front. She barely ever used it, living instead out of the oversized suitcase she never properly unpacked from her visit to Rome two months ago.

Her phone buzzed, and Anna jumped. Klara! She dove for the phone and swiped the screen. But she found only a message from Sarah. She released a sigh again as her heart dropped. The message contained another picture of Giac. He smiled with pudgy cheeks and mismatched teeth. As she stared at the photo, Anna slumped back to the bed. If only she and Sarah could weave Giac's stroller through the crowds in the Piazza Navona today, could let him smear a spoonful of creamy gelato on his cheeks, or dip his feet in one of the many fountains as Anna and Sarah tipped back their heads and soaked in the sun.

Blinking back tears, Anna scanned the other messages she'd neglected the past week during her Allerton-immersion—the last week which in some sense she'd devoted entirely to Hendrik. The inbox contained messages from Mom and another from Dad, both inquiring about flights to Boston. With a perturbed exhale, Anna tossed the phone on the floor. Going home sounded about as much fun as being stuck in a boring city with NO FRIENDS. Except, she had a friend other than Klara, other than beefstick Christian, and other than her slumbering advisor. A shimmer blossomed in her chest, and she flicked back her gaze to the phone. In no way would she spend the rest of the night moping about her apartment, especially when she had such an accomplishment as Allerton to celebrate. Picking up her phone, Anna stood. She pulled up Hendrik's contact and typed, *celebration drinks?*

As she waited for his reply, she changed into skin-tight, black leather pants and a purple tube top. With some gel, she smoothed her bangs into a shimmery clip and dusted her purple streaks with glitter. A thick coat of mascara, purple eye shadow, and lip gloss finished the look. As she wrestled on her black leather jacket, she heard her phone buzz again. Hendrik.

Already there. Coat of Arms.

Anna smiled. Tonight, she would have some fun. How much, she didn't know.

****

Anna walked the distance to the Coat of Arms which sat on the east side of town, a little farther from her apartment and nearer to Hendrik's. Inside, dark, wooden beams striped the ceiling. A matching, coffee-colored bar, flanked with stools, stood at the back. Anna unsnapped the buttons on her jacket, the warmth of the cozy pub hitting her chest, and twisted her way through the crowd until she reached the bar.

On the right side of the L-shaped bar, Hendrik sat.

Changed from his previous outfit, Hendrik wore a red Utrecht University shirt—his alma mater, she supposed—and jeans. While nothing special stood out from the outfit, the brightness of the shirt brought a gleam to his face. Beside Hendrik sat a dark-skinned man with a buzz cut and a clean shave. Both men drank from lowball glasses. As she sucked in her gut so her pants would comply, Anna hiked herself onto a stool and crossed her legs. "Evening, boys."

Hendrik looked over and smiled. "Anna, so glad you could join us. This is Rashaad." He nodded to a man beside him.

Dressed in a tweed coat with corduroy patches on the elbows, Anna instantly recognized him. He was the same man Hendrik sat with after Cayley's stroke. She extended a hand. "Anna."

Rashaad took her hand and shook. "Hendrik's had more to say about you than he did all of last Trinity."

Anna cocked her head in Hendrik's direction and held his gaze. "Has he now?"

"Oh yeah, it's always 'guess what Anna did today?' or 'let me tell you what Anna figured out now.' Isn't that right, mate?" He elbowed Hendrik in the side.

Hendrik opened his mouth, furrowed his brows, and then snapped closed his mouth. He gave a sheepish smile and raised his glass.

Even hidden behind the dark liquid in the glass, his searing blush showed through. Anna grinned and sat tall on her stool. Bashful Hendrik was much more endearing than bossy post-doc. Excitement brewed inside. Maybe Klara knew one truth. Maybe Anna needed a hookup. And now that she completed her work on Allerton, Hendrik seemed the obvious choice. They were both adults—they could keep things confidential. What harm could come from encouraging him? She removed her jacket, revealing her midriff shirt beneath, and draped it over the back of her stool.

Hendrik's gaze swept over Anna's bare arms and shoulders. His Adam's apple revealed a deep swallow.

Rashaad waved a hand in front of Hendrik's face. "Eh, Henry. You lost all your brains after your big discovery?"

"Huh?" Hendrik shook himself from his stare. "I've kept Rashaad informed of our progress is what he means. Naturally, I called him first to celebrate." He raised his glass to Rashaad's, and the glass clinked. Then Hendrik extended his glass to Anna and furrowed his brow. "I meant to order you a…what would you like?"

The red in his cheeks deepened. Anna tapped her finger to her lips. "What would I like? How about sex on the beach?"

Hendrik jostled his drink, splashing whiskey over his shirt. "Excuse me?"

Rashaad roared with laughter and slapped his palm on the bar. "It's a cocktail, mate—not an invitation."

"Right." Hendrik yanked at the collar of his shirt then hailed the bartender and ordered Anna's drink.

"Don't mind him." Rashaad leaned across the bar, blocking Hendrik. "He's lived a sheltered life."

"Ah, yes. Tulip farming."

"Tulip bulb farming," Hendrik corrected. "But we're not here to talk about our stinted childhoods." He raised his glass again. "To Allerton. To Cayley. To Anna!"

The guys clanked their glasses again.

Anna grinned wildly that not only had Hendrik toasted to her, but he'd definitely said her name with the most enthusiasm.

The bartender returned with Anna's drink, a tall

glass filled with orange and red liquid, with a slice of orange resting on the lip.

"To sex on the beach," Anna toasted before sipping the fruity, vodka mix.

Rashaad laughed.

Hendrik dropped his gaze to her skin again.

"Henry tells me you're the code-cracker-extraordinaire. You figured out the Abelian subgroups and the Greek alphabe—"

"Sh!" Hendrik cut in. "Not so loud. We don't need someone else stealing our work."

As she watched Hendrik scan the room, Anna pursed her lips. An elderly duo—no doubt tenured professors whose students wished would retire—sat in a pair of club chairs and stirred their drinks. A couple, half hidden in shadow, embraced each other in a corner. A group of chittering ladies exited from the etched glass door, the autumn wind whipping echoes of their conversation.

"Let's try McGrady's," one said.

"Or the piano bar," chimed another.

Not one person in the building noticed them. Not even the bartender, who Anna wished would add a splash more vodka to her drink. "Relax, Hendrik. Or should I call you Henry?"

Rashaad smiled and flicked a brow in his friend's direction.

Hendrik still searched the room.

No doubt, he suspected the bar contained an ex-CIA, rogue hacker who might steal their work. Anna's urge to drag Hendrik into the shadows for a make out session began to morph into a desire to join the unfamiliar ladies for a night of barhopping. She exhaled audibly. "For gawd's sake, we're here to celebrate, are we not?"

Hendrik snapped back his gaze to Rashaad and gave a tight smile. "Indeed, you're quite right, Rashaad, I couldn't have done it without Anna's insight. I was beginning to think I'd end up a tormented and crazed mathematician. Or worse, out of a post-doc, out of a job, and back plucking bulbs from the farm."

Rashaad finished his drink and stood, tossing a wad of cash on the bar. "You two continue the celebration without me. If I don't get home before ten, DeAndra's gonna push out the kid just to spite me." He gave Anna a wink and smacked Hendrik on the shoulder. "And cheer up, ol' chap, everyone knows the best mathematicians are the crazy ones."

Anna grinned. If Rashaad wasn't Hendrik's wingman, he couldn't have asked for a better one. She waved as he left, then slid onto Rashaad's stool, closer to Hendrik.

The bartender made his rounds.

Anna tipped her head in his direction, ordering another. "You sure I can't tempt you?" she asked Hendrik. "Sex on the beach is great."

This time, Hendrik didn't even flinch. He just stared at the bar, his brows knit. "Tomorrow I'll call the conference to see if I can change my presentation. Then I must write it all up, or we can write it up together."

Anna opened her mouth to say she'd love to help him, to suggest that they start first thing tomorrow, after, of course, their *celebration*.

"No, no, no," he rambled on, "it's best if I write it up first, then you review it for edits. Besides, I'm a LATEX wizard. No point in you troubling yourself with the heinous insipidities of mathematical typeset."

Anna frowned. Okay, he was *a little* preoccupied by their discovery. Well, maybe 'a little' was an understatement. But, at least, he no longer fretted over their professional relationship, and besides, she found the divot that appeared between his brows cute. She'd just have to help him along. With one hand dancing along her exposed collarbone, she placed the other on Hendrik's thigh. "Well, I'm quite the LATEX master. Why don't you let me help you?"

"*Ben je gek geworden?*" He jumped to his feet. "Have you gone completely crazy?"

Her pulse thumped, and she set her jaw so tight, she could have cracked a tooth. Squaring her shoulders, she sat tall enough to stare him dead-on. "We're here to celebrate." She spoke through gritted teeth. "To have fun. Certainly, you're not so daft not to notice Rashaad intentionally left us to have some fun on *our own*."

Hendrik stared, a fog setting on his gaze momentarily before it lifted. He pursed his lips. "Rashaad always retreats early."

With nostrils flared, Anna's chest burned against her boiling blood inside. Why must he pretend no attraction existed between them—because of his beloved proof? His career? Her breath caught. Had he just used her to solve his problem? Was that all *this* arrangement was, another superior taking advantage of a student's genius? She picked up her coat, wrestled it on, and jumped off the stool. "Screw you, Hendrik." She shoved his chest.

He stumbled back, grabbing the bar stool to steady himself. "Anna, wait. Stop."

She stormed away, calling over her shoulder, "And

I hope you do go insane." She rushed out of the bar, with no intention of stopping, not until she'd hit all the bars and nightclubs on Walton St. Because if she couldn't find her fun there, she couldn't find it anywhere.

Chapter 10

The buzz of Anna's phone roused her. She opened her eyes, and blinding light streaming through her bedroom window sent a shot of pain through her forehead. She groaned and slapped the phone, silencing the ringer, but the sound still bounced between her ears. Throbbing pounded her head, and waves of nausea flooded her stomach.

While her hedonistic lifestyle had its perks—the alcohol dulled her senses, the incessant disco beat drowned her racing thoughts, and the darkness hid any of the feelings that broke through—she paid for these luxuries with hangovers from hell. Not to mention the damage to her studies. Homework? Office hours? Exams? She squeezed shut her eyes. She'd worry about those tomorrow.

The phone sounded again—this time not the buzz of a message but a mellow seventies song. Her father. Anna stared at the phone. Darn it. She never answered his question about visiting over break. For the past two weeks, she'd been too busy visiting every nighttime establishment within a ten-mile radius. She drank alone at bars, letting the strong whiskey burn her throat and dim her perceptions. She danced with unfamiliar faces and brushed against sweaty bodies she would never know the names to. She even let some of those bodies tow her into a dark corner and knead her flesh as they kissed her. Not that she kissed them back with the same fervor, nor rubbed their chests with the same salacity as they did hers. But she hadn't pushed them away, either—at least not until the song changed, and she hurled herself back on the dance floor.

The ringer stopped, and Anna rolled back over, relieved. When was the last time she'd spoken to her parents anyway? Just as the fuzzy memory of a conversation about Anna's failure in academia began to resurface, the phone rang again. Anna threw off the covers and snatched the phone. "Hello," she growled.

"Anna, dear. It's your father."

Anna rolled her eyes. How a Ph.D. in psychology didn't understand caller ID baffled her.

"We've been trying to reach you about your flight details."

Flight details? When did she agree to coming home?

"I just sent you the itinerary. I have only twenty-four hours to cancel, so can you let me know if the times work?"

Anna thought for a second—maybe a fraction of a second, whatever microcosm of time might be deemed as a legitimate consideration to his request. "Actually, I have a final that day."

"Two weeks after end of term?"

Damn it! Apparently, Dad's persistent technology deficiencies didn't extend to finding Oxford's academic calendar.

"Anna, your mother and I haven't seen you in a year. She's even coming home for your visit."

Anna perked up. Her mother was coming home? That would be a first in...in...? Since her mother took the job at Harvard, she rarely went across the Charles River. The ten-mile commute from Anna's childhood home near Dad's post at Northeastern was, in her mother's words, "too hampering on her academic life." Heck, her mother barely made the one-mile trip to visit Anna at MIT when she studied there.

"Can we go see the Christmas tree?" A wistful smile crossed her face, and the pounding in her head reduced to a dull knocking. Seeing the lit tree in Boston Common highlighted the Christmas season. Not to mention, a visit to the tree remained the only holiday tradition Anna enjoyed with her family, even if the annual trip past the tree was merely a consequence of using the adjacent parking garage. Northeastern University held its annual Christmas party nearby.

"Well, we haven't been to the Christmas party in a few years, but…"

Anna dropped her smile to a flat line of listlessness, quite like the numbness in her chest. Of course, her parents didn't want to see the Christmas lights. Dr. Seuss probably tapped her parents' psyches when he wrote *How the Grinch Stole Christmas*.

"…I'll ask your mother."

Anna frowned. Asking her mother confirmed a "not a chance." But even without a trip to the tree, Boston still offered more than gloomy Oxford. Klara wouldn't be here—not that Anna had heard from her in the last two weeks—and neither would all the other students. The bars would be empty, and the clubs closed. Snow would fall on Oxford's dreamy spires, making a picturesque scene for romantics to enjoy. Anna's heart ached, and she huddled back under the covers, the backlight of her phone illuminating her cavern. She didn't know if Hendrik would be in town either. She'd done a stellar job of ignoring his professional and curt emails, asking whether she wanted to proofread the submission before he sent it off. He was such a jerk. He could have at least sent a heartless text, asking if she was all right or, heaven forbid, a thank you for saving his career.

If Anna stayed in Oxford, she'd be stuck at Cayley's bedside where she'd munch on shortbread cookies, getting fat as a spoiled kitten while she contemplated plans for the next term—heck, the meaning of life. "Okay," she breathed into the phone. "I'll see you…"

"December twenty-second."

"Right. See you then."

"Love you," her father said.

Anna opened her mouth to repeat his sentiment but stopped. His words seemed more out of obligation than genuineness. Did she really want to preserve any more inauthentic relationships? The call ended with a gentle click, sparing her from answering the question. A hollowness crept into her chest. Perhaps after twenty-five years of existence, the absence of sincere affection began to bother her. A sudden urge to visit Cayley sprung to her mind, and she checked her phone. Three p.m. Visiting hours ended an hour ago. She missed him, just like she skipped her office hours and her Algebraic Topology class, too. She slumped her shoulders. When she bombed this trimester, how would she tell her parents? How would she tell Cayley?

****

Happy hour at McGrady's started at six. With thoughts of Hendrik and another hollow Christmas with her parents, half-priced drinks and burly men shouting at the TV never sounded so appealing. The commentary for the World Darts Championship was as dull as Anna imagined it would be. But no one else in the pub seemed to find throwing pointed objects at a target boring.

"Look at that archer!" a man with an overly hairy chest, arms, and—EW!—back shouted from his spot on a stool.

"He doesn't want it!" yelled a tall man dressed in a football jersey.

Anna sat hoisted on the shoulders of a broad-chested man who looked on the other side of twenty. By attaching herself to an older—and definitely the most attractive of the lot—she needn't worry whether he was one of her students. Judging by the calluses on his hands, which steadily climbed from her feet to her knees, he probably worked as a landscaper.

She stared down at his mound of dark curls. Was the sprinkle of gray in his coils natural color or ashes? Anna leaned in and took a whiff. A smoky scent drifted into her nostrils. Huh—maybe he worked as a boiler operator. A furnace technician? Did it really matter? She didn't even know his name. He wanted her and after Anna's rejections—of both the Dutch and Austrian variety—she longed—no, needed—someone to desire her.

"Bullseye," Smoky Hair shouted, jumping slightly as he raised a fist in the air.

The motion shook Anna's unsteady position on his shoulders, and she struggled not to fall. She jostled the beer in her hand, splashing it on his hair as she gripped his thick bicep with her free hand.

"You all right, sweetie?" Smoky tightened his hold on her knees.

"Flying high." Anna drained her beer—best not to spill on him again. She passed down her empty cup.

A man dressed in clothes like Smoky's, a dark navy jumper and workbooks, refilled it.

Enjoying the buzz between her eyes, Anna guzzled the new beer. The men with their funny arrows suddenly seemed so silly with their determined gazes and rigid stances. They made such a fuss to hit a round piece of cork. And the dart throwers wore the most hysterical outfits! One donned a bright orange shirt, which matched his mohawk, and star-printed pants. Anna giggled, an uncontrollable laughter that buckled her over and sent her headfirst over Smoky's head.

"Whoa there, sweetie." He caught her in his bulky arms, cradling her like a child.

Weightless, Anna stared straight into Smoky's chest. Only Smoky wasn't his name. Stitched in white letters across the chest of his jumpsuit his real name appeared: Butch. Anna giggled again, flung her tankard to the floor where it landed with a crash, and looped her hands around Butch's sturdy neck. Built like a barrel, Butch boasted a belly as broad as his chest. With arms like tree trunks and legs sturdier than those beneath a pool table, "husky" would have been an understatement raised to the power of fifty.

Yet Anna found something about the ox of a man attractive—the gentle wave of his hair and the shadow of stubble on his chiseled jaw. Of all the men she tangled with that week—of which, there had been many—Butch seemed the most likely candidate to take back to her place for a tussle under the sheets. He didn't attend Oxford. He knew a thing or two about taming hot things. And he didn't look a thing like Hendrik. In fact, the only concern that ran through her presently soupy thoughts was whether Butch would crush her when she lay beneath him. She drew his face to hers. His stubble scratched her chin. His breath, hot and yeasty, spilled over her lips. "So, Butch"—she paused to kiss his coarse lip—"do you think you can hit the target?" Butch kissed her back—a hot, wet, jackhammer of a kiss that matched the strength of his arms gripping her. Smoke tinged his hoppy breath.

He shifted back to answer. "I ain't never missed yet."

His mouth covered her smile. She could only think how good it would feel to wake up next to Butch, to run her hands through his sure-to-be hairy chest, and to just feel wanted. Except she couldn't dwell on those thoughts, at least, not entirely, because in the back of her mind, a tiny voice called out, *Anna! Anna! What are you doing?*

Anna tried to drown out the voice—tried to focus on Butch's stubble and his forceful tongue. But the voice persisted, louder now.

"Anna Franklin, what in the hell are you doing?"

Anna suddenly realized the voice had a distinct accent—not an American accent, nor a British one, either. No, this accent was entirely German. She yanked herself back from Butch's lip-hold just as Klara's hand tugged her elbow.

"Anna!" Klara sounded more exasperated than before. "What are you doing with—" her gaze dropped to Butch's nametag, "Butch?"

She might be drunk, but Anna wasn't completely

oblivious. Klara had some nerve showing up now. She could have at least called—texted even. She leaned her head into Butch's chest and stroked the back of his neck with her fingers. "Butch and I were just about to leave."

Klara pursed her lips, grabbed hold of Butch's arm, and wrenched it free.

Tumbling to the floor, her butt hitting hard, Anna palmed sticky linoleum. "Klara!" she shrieked. "What the h—" She caught sight of Klara's point.

With her gym-buff arms, Klara held Butch's left hand splayed. A thick ring, partially covered in soot, wrapped around his ring finger. She ticked a brow. "Did you invite his wife?"

Bile rose in her throat as Anna struggled not to drop her jaw. Could anything go right this term? Even a benign hookup?

****

Inside Mabel's café, Klara brought two cups of coffee to a table. She placed one beside Anna along with three packets of sugar.

"I can't believe I didn't notice the ring." Anna ripped off the tops of the sugar with one tear, added the contents to her drink, and sipped. The caffeine sent a jolt through her, and the surroundings settled into focus. Dim bulbs strung in glass shades illuminated the tight quarters of Mabel's. A tiny, hole-in-the wall around the corner from McGrady's, Mabel's stayed open twenty-four hours, and many of Oxford's night-owls frequented it to sober up—Anna being one of them.

"Apparently you didn't notice my phone calls either."

"Wait—you called?" Anna stared at her phone, perplexed.

"And texted. I even dropped by your office. I only found Hendrik there though. Apparently, he's looking for you, too. Some hunky rugby player was there, too." Klara stooped over her coffee, cupping the mug in her hands.

Anna took another swallow of coffee. Holy Fathers of Calculus! How had she missed so much…and acted like such a melodramatic schoolgirl? Over a guy—a guy! Not to mention she'd wasted half a month's grocery money on beer. What was she thinking? And poor Klara. With dark circles under her eyes and slumped shoulders, she didn't appear her usual NCAA athletic self. Anna dropped her gaze to the table. "I'm sorry…I…" She fidgeted her hands—first rubbing her forehead, then balling the sugar wrappers.

Finally, she picked up her phone and scanned through her messages. Sure enough, texts, emails, and even voicemails remained unopened. Who left voicemails these days? Shaking her head, she dropped her phone to the table with a thud and released a tight exhalation. Obviously, she could no longer pass for a vampire, as Sarah so fondly referred to her. Hell, she couldn't even cut it as a functioning drunk, because moonlighting as a furnace operator's sidepiece was definitely not functioning. With another slow draw of her drink, Anna cleared her head and settled her gaze on Klara. "I'm so sorry, Klara. I don't know how I missed your texts."

Klara sat silently, her gaze on her coffee.

Anna furrowed her brow. She'd really done it this time—pushing away her only true friend in all of the UK. Fortunately, she knew Klara well enough to know what she wanted: an explanation. Every scientist, Klara included, needed to know the why—why Hendrik sought her out, why Anna avoided him in the first place, and most importantly, why Anna jumped off the deep end.

Such discussions required more caffeine.

Anna downed the rest of her coffee, letting it slowly wash away the effects of one too many liter-sized beers…and Butch's smoky taste. She stood and approached the counter.

Mabel, a gray-haired woman with a sunny disposition, filled the cup and offered more sugar packets.

Anna politely declined—nothing could sweeten what she had to say. As Anna sipped her hot cup, she filled in Klara on the events since their blow-up: breaking Allerton, coming onto Hendrik, and traipsing through bars, plastered. Finally, Anna arrived at the end of her soap opera of a story.

Klara opened her eyes.

Her blonde eyelashes could have attached to her brows. Anna swallowed and tugged on a tendril of hair.

"Well," she said through an exhalation, "that sure tops writing a research paper on the seven functional groups."

"Oh yeah? Did you get Conner to edit it?" Anna smirked.

Klara snatched up an empty sugar packet, balled it, and tossed it at Anna's head.

"Hey!" Anna dodged it. "I merely asked a question."

"A snarky question." Klara stuck out her tongue. "But since you ask. Yes, he did."

"Really? Now, that revelation is surprising. Did

you pay for those services with sexual favors?"

In a swift maneuver, Klara swiped the rest of the strewn sugar packets and chucked them Anna's way.

One caught Anna square between the eyes. She winced, but somehow the abuse felt good—she totally deserved it.

"I swear, Anna Franklin, sometimes I wonder why I'm friends with you."

I'm beginning to wonder myself. Anna forced a smile and shrugged. "Because you know if Conner ever screwed you over, I'd put him in a half-nelson?"

Klara giggled.

Finally, she'd eked a smile out of her friend. Perhaps she'd partially fixed the havoc she'd wreaked on their relationship.

"You don't have to worry about Conner. I told him I want to take things slowly. We're just friends, no benefits. Well, maybe a little necking but no *Geschlect.* I told him I want to wait until after I get back from break."

Anna smacked a palm to her forehead. "It's no wonder you're a virgin, Klara. The German word for sex sounds like some sort of torture maneuver."

Klara flared her nostrils and crossed her arms, but she still broke a smile. "Can we stop with cracks at me? This little intervention is supposed to be about you."

Sighing, Anna braced herself for the rebuke. She leaned back in the stiff café chair and stretched her legs under the table. "How'd you find me, anyway?"

Klara picked up her phone and waved it. "There's an app for that."

Anna clucked her tongue. Sheesh, she really wasn't on her A-game. She'd forgotten they'd sign up for that people finder app. Why hadn't she thought to check it the night she'd walked in on Klara and Conner?

"What about your classes, Anna? What about Hendrik? What about Cayley?"

A giant hole formed in her chest and threatened to swallow her. Suddenly, Anna remembered why she'd chosen a week of insobriety. Hendrik pushed her away. Cayley remained asleep. Why was her life so absent of meaningful relationships? Beyond Klara and Sarah, she had no one.

Klara reached across the table and squeezed Anna's hand. "You've got to salvage this. Cayley isn't here to bail you out. But when he wakes up—"

"If he wakes up," Anna corrected her, the hole inside widening.

"When," Klara countered. "When he wakes up, do you want him to learn you flunked out?"

Anna shook her head. The thought of Cayley waking—to seeing his misty, gray eyes—tugged at her heart. But to even begin to imagine his eyes filled with disappointment? That image broke her heart. Klara was right. She didn't have to get her act together for her parents, for Hendrik, or even for herself. But she did need to for Cayley. Anna glanced down at her phone and groaned.

"What now?"

Anna grinned, pocketed her phone, and stood. "It's ten p.m. which means I have Partial Differential Equations class in eleven hours." How in the world would she get up on time?

Chapter 11

Anna snapped her gum and flipped through the pages of her Algebraic Topology text for a final time. Alone in her office—thank goodness, examinations preoccupied her office mates—Anna drew a fuzzy blanket around her shoulders. When November waned into December, a draft overcame the office, and since Klara insisted Anna stay at the Mathematical Institute until she completed her courses each day, Anna had taken matters into her own hands. She flipped on the space heater beside her and settled into the beanbag chair—also a recent addition.

Often, over the past month, Anna took to studying in the common area—a bright space with modern furnishings. On many occasions, Klara joined her.

While their college memberships afforded them entry into more quaint study rooms and libraries than the glass-covered atrium at the Mathematical Institute, Klara insisted the proximity to lecture halls encouraged Anna to attend her classes.

And she'd been right; Anna hadn't missed a lecture the whole month of November. She popped her gum. Hopefully, her instructors paid attention to her recent attendance and ignored her negligence from earlier in the term…especially Quinton. His synopsis—or whatever they called their syllabi here—specifically indicated more than four absences warranted failing the course.

Her heart thudded in her chest, and Anna drew in her knees, focusing her attention on the symbols on the page. *If I ace this exam, he'll have to pass me...won't he?* This pass/fail course structure had its perks, but absences weren't one of them. At MIT, if she missed four classes, she dropped a letter grade—not failed! She drew in a breath, snapped her gum, and released a shaky exhalation. *Relax, Anna. You're gonna nail this.* But in the back of her mind, she knew Cayley was the main reason she survived this long. He bailed her out of her messes...and now? Now, she held out hope her achievements would bail him out of his coma.

A knock sounded on the door, and Anna jerked upright.

At the entrance of the room, Hendrik stood with a furrowed brow and his chin buried in his hand.

Her breath caught, and she fought against dropping her jaw. In the past six weeks, she went to great lengths to avoid seeing her *advisor*. She ignored emails, she offered ridiculous excuses on why times didn't work, and she even went so far as to hide in the ladies' room to avoid running into him. How had she, on this most important of days, slipped up?

"Anna." He shuffled into the room. "You're a hard person to pin down. I've been trying to speak to you for weeks."

Anna held up a hand. "You can speak from there."

Hendrik froze, and his ruddy cheeks fired. At the desk nearest the door, he leaned a hand on its top and withdrew a sigh.

"But make it quick. I have an examination in ten."

Nodding, Hendrik swallowed hard, his Adam's

apple rising in his neck. "I've heard back from the cryptography conference in The Hague. They've agreed to let me change my presentation to Allerton. The conference convenes just as Hilary term begins. I want you to come with me. This proof is as much yours as it is mine—more so yours."

Anna pursed her lips and stood. Of course, he'd come about Allerton—always Allerton and never her. "No," she snapped. She threw the blanket on the beanbag and crossed to the coat rack where her *sub fusc* hung. She hated the formal robes, but she couldn't jeopardize her academic career anymore by refusing to wear them to exams.

Hendrik sighed. "Anna, please. All the top researchers attend—NSA and MI6, too. This will be good for your future."

As she yanked on the robe, Anna scoffed. Hendrik didn't care about her future—he only wanted to secure *his* future…his fame, not hers. "I have an exam, Hendrik," she said through gritted teeth. Lowering her gaze, she slipped past him.

He caught her by the arm. "Please come. I want you to come."

His voice, soft and gentle, sounded sincere, and his touch sent a shiver up her spine. Anna cringed. Of all the hotties, uber-athletes, and filthy-rich men she'd dated, why did Hendrik unravel her? She stepped forward, setting her lips in a hard line. "I have to go."

He released her arm. "Okay."

Defeat resonated in his listless voice. Anna rushed down the hall, casting aside the thought of him. Apart from NSA and M16, this exam would secure her future. If only she knew Quinton would view it the same.

****

Later that afternoon, Anna placed a shiny red-wrapper packet of cookies on Cayley's bedside table. Someone removed the ones she left last week. Had a nurse eaten them? Hendrik? A knot formed in her stomach, and she struck the thought from her mind.

"This week has been epic. Exams, projects, packing for break…" She filled him in on her recent actions, focusing on the mundane and leaving out the hooting on the shoulders of Butch and dodging Hendrik. "I finished my algebraic topology exam in twenty minutes—even wrote a short essay on Poincare's contributions. I noticed his framed picture hanging in Quinton's office so I figured he must like him. Think he'll pass me?"

Cayley responded with a steady whistle of his breath, not a pat on the knee, or a crinkled smile, or an "I'll take care of it," like Cayley used to say. No, she stood on her own now. If she managed to pass her classes—which was an if even bigger than string theory—she would be on academic probation at the minimum. What would Hendrik say? What would Mother say? Anna dropped her head, an ache in her chest swelling. "Cayley, I wish you'd wake up." A desperation consumed her voice as her throat tightened. He couldn't lie like this forever. Eventually, the hospital would—

She lifted her head, tears welling. Anna couldn't finish the thought. What would happen to Cayley if he didn't awaken soon? Two months had passed, and he made no progress. Were there timelines on such matters? Surely, there must be. "Cayley"—an urgency consumed her voice—"if you wake up, I'll bring you all the cookies in the world. I'll even bake you a batch. They might not taste great, but I'll have made them with my own hands."

Cayley's hand tightened around hers.

Anna gasped. "Cayley?" Standing, she clutched his hand, stiff and cool, as she fought against her heart lodging in her throat. "Cayley, can you hear me? It's Anna, Anna Franklin, your dingbat advisee."

His face remained motionless—his body still.

"Cayley." Her voice pinched. With her free hand, she shook his shoulder.

Cayley loosened his grip, and his hand became limp.

Anna's insides drooped. If he squeezed her hand, why couldn't he open his eyes? Why couldn't he say something? She pulled back her hand and sighed. Would he ever awaken? She stared. This new movement was a good sign—a great sign. Maybe he would awaken while she visited Boston. Now that would be one great excuse to shorten her stay. If only she knew it would come true.

****

The train hiccupped and shook as it bustled from Oxford to London. Anna tucked her knees beneath herself and stared out the window. The only other times she journeyed into London were for fun—a flight to Rome or a night in Piccadilly. But today, twelve days since her Algebraic Topology exam, the trip seemed like a one-way ticket to purgatory. Beside her, Klara nudged Anna's foot with her clunky running sneakers. At least her friend's flight to Austria coincided with Anna's flight to Boston so they could share the journey.

"You look like you just came in last in a

marathon."

Anna pursed her lips and gave a side-long glance. "I did—the Algebraic Topology marathon where I crossed the finish line first, but the referee disqualified me for technicalities."

Klara arched a brow. "Technicalities will get ya."

Anna sneered.

"I mean." Klara rubbed her hands over her shoulders. "I can't believe Quinton failed you. You said you aced the final."

"I did. I killed it." Anna's voice boomed.

Around her, strangers shot knowing glares over their newspapers.

Anna heaved a sigh. God bless the quiet British. Back home in Boston, a raised voice wouldn't warrant a double take. Anna stared out the window. Layers of fog and mist covered the countryside. "I've never failed a class. I've never failed at anything." *Except, maybe, pleasing my parents.*

"It's just one class." Klara smiled. "I'm sure it's no big deal."

Anna wanted to believe her, but she knew Klara's smile was forced. She also knew Hendrik emailed her that morning to discuss completing her Graduate Assessment. What would her assessment of herself be? What would his be? Was she even eligible to apply for transfer to DPhil status now? Or was she stuck with the door-prize MSc degree? Hell, she'd need to turn in her building entry card and vacate her shared office.

"We're talking about a pass-fail class, Klara. I failed a pass-fail class." She dropped her head between her knees. If he knew, Cayley would be so disappointed.

Klara placed a hand on Anna's shoulder and rubbed. "My mother always said everything happens for a reason."

A shiver climbed Anna's spine. Anna's mother would give her the lecture of the century, would threaten to disown Anna, and would go completely ballistic. Anna tipped her head to the side and looked up at Klara. "My mother always said, only idiots fail classes."

Klara laughed. "I'm sure she'll understand. I mean, just the name Algebraic Topology says it all."

Anna chuckled. Klara had a point there. Who in their right mind had a clue what Topology was, even a rock-star biologist like her mother?

As they approached the Heathrow Terminals, the train wheels squealed. Anna drooped her shoulders. Maybe the dean would make an exception due the traumatic event of the hospitalization of Cayley? Or maybe Anna could justify her poor grades with her contributions to Allerton. The train jolted to stop, and the doors slid open. Anna stood and clutched the handle of suitcase. But convincing her parents? That might take a Christmas miracle.

****

After losing a day to travel and jetlag, Anna settled into her former room which Father recently converted into a hobby studio. A large, rectangular table, cluttered with delicate model boats, dominated the room. Printed labels marked the shelves and drawers of storage cabinets lining the walls. A blow-up mattress with a pile of sheets on top sat in the corner of the room—the one spot unfilled with craft-shop galore.

Sighing, Anna stashed her bag on the mattress and

picked up an unused piece of a diorama. What would she do here for a week? The thought of sitting next to Dad for a few hours, attaching pieces with glue and tweezers, made her forearms ache. She couldn't sit still that long, even if glue stuck her butt to a chair. At least he owned a big-screen TV—not a whiteboard. A heaviness seized her chest, and with a listless hand, Anna replaced the discarded piece. She wouldn't mind the whiteboard if the company was sincere in his sentiments.

"Anna!" Father yelled from the living room. "Your mother's home."

Great. She rolled her eyes, smoothed down her hair, and straightened her posture. Mother was sure to have the rest of her week planned. The events would include a lecture on the necessity of publications, which would undoubtably include a rundown of Mother's recent ones, and then the parading of Anna amongst her parents' colleagues and—

"Anna!" Mother's voice rang out.

"Coming!" Anna rushed to the living room.

In the sunken living room, an underlit and decorated with dated furnishings space, her mother stood resting a hand on her rolling suitcase—a small suitcase, an overnight-sized suitcase. Anna's stomach sank. So much for a family holiday celebration. Mother would be gone before Santa made his rounds.

"Darling" —Mother pulled her into a hug— "we've missed you."

The hug felt close enough not to wrinkle Mother's suit. Mother still smelled the same—a flowery department store perfume Father always bought her on her birthday. In some small way, the scent welcomed her. It didn't smell like Hendrik's cologne or the staleness of Cayley's hospital room. This scent came with every memory of Mother—the first time she visited her office at Harvard and the time they shopped for Anna's dorm-room supplies. "I've missed you, too." Anna squeezed Mother before teetering back.

Mother smoothed her blouse and gave a smile.

Was her smile genuine? Was she really happy to see her?

Father handed Mother a glass of wine and kissed Mother's cheek.

"Tell us, darling, how is Oxford? How is Cayley? Have you found a new advisor? I put in a few plugs for you at Harvard…Yale, too."

Anna struggled not to wince. Every part of Mother's question hit so deep—Cayley, Hendrik, and her future. Every aspect made her want to snag Mother's glass of wine and drain it. "Cayley is getting better. I'm sure he'll be back soon." The words came out in a groan.

Mother sipped her wine, maintaining a flat expression.

Clearly, she didn't buy it. "But"—Anna perked up her tone—"I made a major contribution to a post-doc's research." *Major contribution as in essentially had my knowledge stolen.* "I should have my first publication soon." Her parents' faces lit up.

"That's our girl," Father said.

"Oh, darling, I just knew you would be our shining star," Mother added.

A glow blossomed inside, and Anna had a sudden urge to have a group hug. Maybe they would have a Merry Christmas after all.

"And how about your classes? I hope you didn't make any B's this term."

Mother's question snuffed the light inside. Anna dropped her shoulders. "Not exactly…" Fortunately, Mother seemed to have forgotten the UK's classification system of first, upper second, lower second, and third, plus the fact that most graduate classes were Pass/Fail. So as long as she steered clear of "fail," Anna should be okay.

"Oh good, your studies are improving, and you're beginning to publish." Mother cast a glance at Father. "See, Charles, I told you she'd pull things together."

A coolness washed over her. Was this why they wanted her to visit—to have a scholarly intervention? Not to see THEIR OWN daughter on the holidays? Lowering her gaze, Anna sank into a nearby sofa. She rubbed her fingers over her brow. How had she got up her hopes this visit would be anything more than that? That they'd wear fluffy mittens on their walk to the Boston Common Christmas tree, then come home and drink hot cocoa and play board games?

Across the room, her parents sipped their wine and chatted about some academic nonsense, seemingly content with life and ignorant of Anna's inner turmoil. Normal families spent quality time together on the holidays because that's what a family—one not bound together by scholarly citations and robes and mortarboards—did. They thoroughly enjoyed each other's company. They loved each other regardless of their academic rank, the length of their curriculum vitae, and most certainly, their GPA.

Anna straightened her spine. She should have gone to Rome or to Vienna. Even staying in Oxford would have been better than this. Sister Maria and Sarah wouldn't harangue her on her studies. Klara, neither. They might badger her about her life intentions, yes, but only because they wanted the best for her—wanted what would make her happy. They wouldn't dictate her life because of some selfish endeavor for a prodigal child.

Setting her chin, Anna scrunched her hands into fists and stood. "My GPA hasn't gone up." Her tone was as rough as the winter's whipping wind. "I didn't make any first classes. I didn't make any upper seconds, either. I didn't even pass all of my classes."

Mother's cheeks tinged red, and her glass slipped from her hand, splashing wine down the front of her shirt, as it tumbled to the floor. Burgundy splotched the carpet. "But…but…" Mother pressed the back of her hand to her brow and started to sway.

Father rushed to her side. "It's all right, Ruth. Everything will be fine, Ruth. We'll call the dean, Ruth."

Mother let out a guttural cry and shoved Father's chest. "How will she secure a post-doc? A tenured faculty position? My God, she might as well just sign a contract with a blasted community college."

Her parents continued to argue as if Anna wasn't there—as if she was her five-year-old self again who refused to practice her piano drills. Why should she practice? She never had any interest in playing the piano, just like she had no interest in staying here with two parents—no, people…strangers, really—over Christmas. As her parents continued to quibble, Anna plotted her escape. She could change her ticket. She could stay in a hotel. She could take Father's blow-up mattress and sleep in Fenway Park. She didn't care, so long as she was away from them.

"Let me see your transcript."

Mother interrupted her thoughts. "What? Why?" Anna scrunched her face.

"Maybe you're mistaken. Maybe you misread."

"For gawd sake, Mother. Did you forget I'm a bloody mathematician and not a psych major?" Anna glanced at Father. "Sorry."

Father didn't register the blow. He seemed used to taking the supporting role in their academic theatricals.

Mother didn't speak—only stared at Anna.

Her fierce look remained unwavering. Anna set her jaw. Fine. She would show them how royally she messed up. She would show them how, for once, their prized daughter wouldn't have a four-point-o. For once, maybe they would let her free of their incessant scholarly dreams. "If you insist." Anna huffed and jabbed her phone's screen. After a series of "accepts" and "renders," the virtual transcript loaded on the screen. "See for yourself." As Anna passed the phone to Mother, she glossed her gaze over the term's grades, specifically her Algebraic Topology grade. Her breath caught, and she furrowed her brow. She yanked back the phone. "What the hell?" The words slipped out just as the phone nearly fell from her softened grasp.

"What is it?" and "Let us see," sounded from her parents' mouths.

But Anna was too stunned to respond. She blinked, refocusing on the transcript, wondering when the letters would return to what they were when she left Oxford. But no amount of blinking changed the result. No F marked her transcript, not for Quinton's class or any other, either. Her grades now all showed as Passes.

Her heart leapt to her throat. Who could have changed her grades? Who could have gifted her this grace of all graces? Goose bumps rushed her arms, as she fought against her gaping jaw. Only two possibilities existed: Either Cayley made a miraculous recovery, or she suddenly had a new benefactor. Either way, she knew who could tell her the answer…if he hadn't left for the Netherlands.

Chapter 12

Anna wouldn't describe the walk from her father's rowhouse to Boston Common as particularly safe. Streetlights dimly lit sidewalks. Frigid beggars huddled on park benches. Swaying bodies, who staggered out from bars, stunk of alcohol. Others still roamed the streets like Anna, with heads buried in fuzzy scarves and hands stuffed deep in coat pockets. She entered the metal gate to Boston's version of Central Park. The wind picked up, sending flurries into a whirling dance, and Anna drew her coat closer. Yet somehow, a warmth brewed within—an excitement, not just at the anticipation of seeing the Christmas tree but of hearing Hendrik's gravelly voice and finding out if he cared about her for more than her contributions to Allerton.

As the tree came into view, Anna pulled up Hendrik's contact on her phone and pressed the green button. A dial-tone filled her ear, and then a click followed by a throat clearing.

"Anna, erm, what time is it? Are you, erm, okay?"

Hendrik's voice was gristlier than usual. Anna bit her lip. Why hadn't she considered the time difference? It must be the middle of the night in Oxford. She yawned. Whatever? Her flight left her so jet-lagged she was no more awake than Hendrik anyway. She smiled, though. Hendrik answered...and he'd asked after her, too. "I'm more than okay."

"More than okay warrants a two a.m. phone call?"

The lights of the tree flickered, and the dark evergreen glowed under a blanket of shiny bulbs. Was it really two a.m.? No wonder she had the urge to curl up on the park bench and drift off to sleep. Stifling a yawn, she let the glow of the tree wash over her. "Either the three ghosts of Christmas visited Quinton, or *someone* has been busy on the other side of the pond."

Hendrik chuckled. "I guess you saw your grades. And no Ebenezer Scrooge enlightenments for Quinton, I'm afraid—just a little bartering by a lowly post-doc."

Anna drew in a quick breath, struggling to settle her fluttering heart. Hendrik worked this miracle—for her. A sudden warmth grew in her chest, and a smile played on her lips. "How did you manage that deal? Did you sell your rights to Allerton?"

His laugh echoed through the line. "Not quite. Let's just say I'll be doing some extra grading next term."

"Oooh." She let the sound dangle on her lips. "Don't worry about marking mine."

"As if you'll turn yours in."

"Oral presentation?"

Hendrik laughed again.

His husky growl prickled Anna's ears. Anna let the silence swallow the line, then sobered her tone. "Thank you, Hendrik."

"I told you, Anna. I don't want you to throw this accomplishment away. Your contributions to Allerton are enough to make your name in the field, but if you want a professorship, you have to back it up with academics."

Anna shivered. With her coat pulled tight around her, she circled the tree until the state house appeared in the distance. The golden dome glistened under the lights of the city—not as grand as St. Peter's Basilica in Rome but still beautiful. Would Sarah and Sister Maria tell her the same thing as Hendrik and her mother—to join academia? "And what if I don't want a professorship?"

"Don't want?" He paused, then exhaled audibly. "Well, a graduate degree still wouldn't hurt for field positions."

Wouldn't hurt? What about the fact that attending Quinton's class slowly drove her insane? If she heard one more lecture on the isomorphisms of a torus, she would bring an inner tube to class and strangle him with it.

"You know," Hendrik said, "lots of field reps will be at the conference."

"And now we learn the true nature of your gratitude." She hmphed.

"The thought might have crossed my mind. Come on, Anna. I'll take you to see the windmills and even buy you some cheese."

"Nothing like cheese to win a girl over." She rolled her eyes.

"And the Escher gallery. You could practically spit on it from the conference hotel."

Nothing like mind-twisting sketches to go with her gouda. She'd best not pair the two together; that combination would be a recipe for a cheese-chunk explosion.

"As long as it doesn't cut your visit to the States too short," he added. "Family is important."

"Says the man who's still at Oxford over Christmas."

"How'd you…?" He sighed. "Right, the time change. I'll stop home after The Hague. My family lives only a few hours from there."

"Oh really? Am I invited?"

Hendrik yawned again. "That depends."

"On what?"

"Whether you wear those combat boots of yours to the conference."

Anna laughed. Perhaps she could dress appropriately if she had a chance to shake hands with someone from MI6. For an interview with NSA, she'd wear heels.

"So what do you say, Franklin? Should I book you a ticket?"

Anna chewed her lip. She'd return to England in time, for sure. And attending the conference didn't obligate her to anything—applying for her doctorate or otherwise. "I'll think about it." *Think…just think.*

****

The chill of the floor woke Anna from a restless sleep. Her butt met the cold floor, and she stared downward. Darn it. The blow-up mattress in her room had deflated. She yawned a growl and stood, careful not to knock her head on the hobby table as she had done last night. The spot on the back of her head throbbed, and she rubbed it.

Good-for-nothing boats. Couldn't her father have moved the table to the side? She kicked the leg of the table. "Ow!" She grabbed her toe. The blasted table weighed more than Big Ben. She shrugged. Perhaps the weight was reason enough to keep it smack in the middle of room.

Stretching up her arms, bones in her back popped, sending a firecracker of snaps through the room. Maybe she'd camp on the couch tonight. At least then she wouldn't wake with her butt frozen to the carpet. She'd also have a TV and…easy access to the kitchen. Her stomach rumbled. Darn if she'd find any vending machines around Dad's rowhouse. And judging by her parents' taste, she'd find nothing but bran flakes in the cupboard. But she had to start somewhere.

The kitchen and living room sat empty and quiet. Mother and Father had probably already eaten and now worked in their offices. Anna rummaged through the pantry and found the usual suspects—Bran flakes and Oat O's. And…score! Toaster pastries—strawberry, too! Bonus points for Dad. He must have eased up on his diet since Mother moved out. Anna threw two pastries into the toaster.

"Coffee?" Dad appeared, clad in a robe and slippers. He lifted an accordion door beneath a cabinet to reveal an espresso machine.

"Wow"—Anna raised a brow—"you really have upgraded since Mother left."

Father scowled and tugged on the tie of his robe. "Sometimes it's the small things."

The toaster chirped, pushing out two steaming-hot toaster pastries.

"One of those for me?" he asked.

"You're not worried about Mother's lecture? *Sugar isn't good for productive research.*" She spoke the last sentence with an upturned nose and nasally tone.

"I'm not concerned about my research. Besides, your mother's not here."

Anna fumbled the pastry, dropping it to the counter. "But it's only"—she caught sight of the time on the microwave—"nine-thirty."

"Trouble at the lab." He kept his attention on the espresso machine, pressing a button here and adding coffee there.

Anna took a mammoth bite of pastry, and hot filling nipped her tongue. The roof of her mouth burned, and her eyes watered, but Anna kept chewing. Mother's stupid frogs called...again—on Christmas Eve Day, of all times. Swallowing hard, Anna's throat singed under the heat of the partially chewed pastry, burning all the way down to her stomach. "When will she be back?"

His attention still on coffee, Father smashed a button on the espresso machine. It hissed but didn't drip. "Damn machine." He scowled. "I should have gone with the standard model."

"When will she be back?" Lifting her chin, Anna repeated the question louder.

Father jiggled a lever. He pressed another button. Then he groaned and slammed shut the door. "I don't know, Anna." He hung his head and slumped his shoulders.

The burning sensation in her throat returned, but it had nothing to do with the pastry. "But aren't we having Christmas Eve dinner? And the tree? We never went to see the tree together."

Father turned.

His black eyes washed to a heathery graphite.

He pinched his eyebrows and opened his mouth. "Anna...I..." He rubbed Anna's shoulder and sighed. "Let's go get some coffee."

Two blocks away, the local donut shop welcomed Anna and her father with steamy windows and a foyer wafting with the smell of freshly fried dough.

"Two coffees and two crullers," Father said to the cashier.

Anna gazed up at her father with a lifted brow. First toaster pastries and now donuts? Everyone knew all New Englanders worshiped donuts—all of them except the Franklins. But today Anna couldn't complain. "Can you make that three crullers?" She tipped on her toes to see the trays of donuts. Fluffy, round donuts gleamed with glaze and pink icing. Voluptuous, twisted donuts tempted her with their cinnamon sugar. And the pièce de résistance, the Euler Formula of the lot, a mound of fried dough filled with gooey custard and topped with glistening chocolate glaze. Anna's mouth watered. "And one Boston crème, too, please." Her stomach growled. In Britain, lunch time had long since passed. And since her stomach remained hard-wired to that time zone, she needed a pick-me-up. A few donuts could stifle her appetite. If only they could snuff the unsettling caused by Mother.

The cashier nodded.

"Boston crème, huh? You're branching out." Father paid the tab.

Anna gave the beginnings of a smile. At least Father remembered her partiality to crullers. Not that his attention made up for her Grinch mother. She sighed. "I have to eat one while I can—toaster pastries, too. I can't get them across the pond."

Smiling, Father took their order and headed for an empty table. "I remember the days when I studied at St. Andrews. You had to sell your leg to get a spoonful of peanut butter."

"Don't even get me started on the sandwich cookie shortage. It's worse than living under Mother's tyranny."

Father stumbled, his smile vanishing, before he shuffled his way into the seat.

Anna slid into the seat across from him, studying his worn face. Mother's behavior not only began to give Anna an aneurysm, but it also exponentially increased Father's wrinkles. Anna removed her Boston crème donut from the box and swept up a glob of chocolate glaze on a finger and popped it in her mouth. Maybe the gooey topping would keep her from sticking her foot in her mouth. She watched Dad.

He tapped fingers against his cup. He scrunched a napkin—then another. He extended his hand to the cruller, furrowed his brow, and then withdrew his hand. "About your question about Mother…when she will be back…" He darted his gaze around the room and tensed his shoulders. "She didn't say when she was coming back."

From her side of the table, Anna clamped down her teeth on the bite of donut in her mouth. *Didn't say? What did that mean?* Flaring her nostrils, Anna glared across at Father, and the once-lighter-than-air donut now tasted like fried rubber.

Father cleared his throat and dropped his gaze to the table. "Her suitcase is gone, so…so…I wouldn't expect her return."

Anna swallowed, the donut chafing against her dry throat. She opened her mouth, but words didn't come. What could she say? What kind of mother doesn't come home for Christmas? A hollowness crept into her chest.

How bad of a daughter was she that her mother didn't want to spend time with her? Sarah couldn't get a break from her mother, even by moving halfway across the world. And her mother wasn't just nagging about Sarah's career. No, Ms. Miller was concerned about Sarah's art, Sarah's desire to have a family, and Sarah's happiness. Anna sniggered. As if she ever needed to worry about her mother overstaying her welcome—that would be the day. A hollowness formed in her chest—one long since carved out, yet slow to fill. She replaced her donut in the box and shoved back from the table.

He reached across, taking her hand. "Your mother's work at Harvard is important. She has more opportunities and more responsibilities, too. She's in charge of the lab—eight, maybe nine employees. The grant applications are endless, and if she doesn't—"

"You don't have to defend her decisions." She whipped back her hand. "If she really cared how I feel, she would tell me herself. She wouldn't leave her only daughter alone on Christmas." Her voice came out louder than she'd intended.

The hustle-bustle in the shop paused.

The cashier looked away from his customer and stared.

A whining child ceased her bellows.

Father sipped his coffee, his hands shaking. "Anna, I know you wanted to spend time together. And I will spend time with you—I want to spend time with you. Your mother is…just…"

"Not much of a mother?" She stared into his eyes. Rounded and dark, they dampened with tears. Anna's breath caught, and her throat tightened.

Dropping her gaze, Father stood. "We should get

back." He picked up his coffee and the box of donuts.

Right. They should get back to what exactly? Because heaven forbid, they actually have a real conversation.

****

Alone in the makeshift bed in her room, Anna napped, scoped out places to visit in The Hague, and stared at the walls all through the day. She could call up some old Boston friends. While many had moved away, a few remained in town—some slogged through dissertations, while others already secured tenure-track positions. Two friends, including her college roommate, had married and started families of their own.

Anna studied her childhood room. What part of the table-tennis-length hobby table covered in sticks and plastic storage containers said family? She stood, hugging her arms to her chest. No part of them. She'd never worked on a boat with her father—never built any model she could think of. With head lowered, she squeezed past the table to the closet and pried open the door. Perhaps inside held traces of family.

The closet housed a box of books—organic chemistry, university physics, and operator theory. These books she'd read while huddled in the corner of Mother's office, while she waited for her to finish drafting an article. A dusty game box sat on the floor— a game she used to love playing with her parents. Her parents smiled genuinely when she found one of the harder matches in play. They patted her on the knee when she corrected their incorrect sets, although she suspected they tested her, anyway.

Anna replaced the box and searched among the other objects for anything not designed to enhance her intelligence. Wedged between a stack of books and a board game sat a stuffed animal—a faded, pointed-ear dog. Anna removed it and hugged it close to her chest, burying her face in the velvety fur. The stuffie didn't feel as soft as when she'd first gotten it, and it smelled musty. She'd won the dog at a carnival at Northeastern. The sun had shone that spring afternoon. The university held a celebration of sorts for the students and faculty.

On the car ride over, Mother sighed. "Do we really have to go?"

"It's a colloquial obligation, dear." Father glanced over from the driver's seat. "All the others in the department will attend."

More conversation ensued, but that part of the memory was fuzzy. She could fill it in with others, though—a snide remark from Mother about only Social Science faculty attending such events or a snooty comment that Science faculty only showed up to donor-sponsored events. Anna pushed away the thought and returned to the carnival. Images swirled in her mind: cotton candy, a dunk tank, and a man handing out balloons. Not that Mother allowed her to partake in any of the food or fun, but she smelled the salty popcorn, imagined the clouds of pink melting on her fingertips, and stared at the giant, black-and-white huskie dressed in a red T-shirt—the university's mascot, Paws. As Anna took in the sights, Father and Mother dove into conversations with Father's colleagues. Upcoming talks, conferences, and publications were among the topics of discussion. None of them kept Anna's attention. She kept returning her gaze to the ball and pins game—knock down the pins and take home a stuffed animal version of Paws.

Anna tugged on Dad's elbow. "Can I play?"

Father smiled down but didn't answer.

Anna asked again…and again.

After the third attempt to sway Father, Mother knelt. "We're not here to play silly games, Anna."

Her tone was sharp. Anna stuffed her hands in her pockets and resigned herself to the fact that at eight-years-old, she still wouldn't own a stuffed animal.

After a while, Mother excused herself to use the bathroom. "When I get back, we're leaving." She gave a knowing look to Father.

An electricity charged through Anna's veins, she tore her hands from her pockets and yanked on Father's elbow.

He cast his gaze downward.

Anna pouted her lip and gave him the most pathetic puppy eyes she could muster. "Pleeeeease?"

He exhaled audibly before brandishing a smile and tugging on her pigtail. "All right." He winked. "Just don't tell your mother."

Aside from mother's scowl when she saw Anna's prize, the rest of the afternoon was a blur. Who had won the dog? Her father? Herself? Anna didn't remember—and she didn't care.

In her room, she squeezed the dog, its belly fur matted from the years of wearing the T-shirt since lost. She stroked the pleather nose and muzzle, now absent of the black thread which once formed the mouth. A lump formed in Anna's throat, and the smile fell from her face. Was this the only memory of genuine happiness with her family she had?

A knock rattled the door, followed by the squeak of its hinges.

"Anna?" Father entered the room. "Do you want to watch a movie?"

Anna tossed the stuffed animal into the closet and yanked shut the door. She shrugged. "What's on?"

"*It's a Wonderful Life.*"

She cringed. Even if her father had been a Jimmy Stewart fan, the suggestion would have been a stretch. At least he was trying. "There's a Finnish thriller series streaming I've been meaning to watch. You could psychoanalyze the killer."

Father laughed. "Sure. How about we order a pizza? Pepperoni, right?"

Anna returned his smile and nodded. "And extra cheese."

Seeing Father disappear from the doorway, Anna slinked her way through the cramped room. When she came to the half-constructed boat-model, she paused. A tiny, plastic tree trimmed with snowy-white branches sat along the diorama's shoreline. Anna picked it up. The tree didn't have a shiny star atop it, nor did it have bright, colored strings of lights. But the model tree held more promise of holiday memories than Boston Common's evergreen landmark.

"Dad," Anna called into the hall. She returned the tree to its spot on the table and picked up an unassembled piece of the model. The piece was as thin as a bobby pin and as fragile as a toothpick. As she examined the ship for where it might belong, the squeak of a floorboard announced her father re-entering the room. "When did you take up model building?" she asked, still studying the model for where the piece fit.

"Sometime between when your mom moved across the river and when you left for school."

Anna furrowed her brows. He'd started building models when she was still in high school? She couldn't recall ever noticing them before. Perhaps Mother wasn't the only neglectful member of the Franklin family. "After the series, do you think you could show me how it works? Maybe, we could…work on it together?"

Father crossed and placed an arm over her shoulder. "I think that sounds like an excellent idea." He took the piece from Anna's hand and brought it close to his eyes. "Part of the hull. We'll need tweezers to put it on." Squeezing her shoulder, he placed the piece on the table and started for the door. "Let me get the pizza order in."

As Father's footsteps faded in the hall, Anna stared at the hobby table. This Christmas she might not have all her family together, but perhaps Father was the only family she really needed. She retrieved the stuffed dog from the closet and left it on the blow-up mattress. Then she raced out the door, eager for a piece of cheesy pizza and the beginning of new holiday traditions.

****

Pizza grease dripped off Anna's lips and down her chin, but she didn't reach for a napkin. She couldn't—she might miss the next line of subtitles. She used her crust as a napkin, then gnawed on it as another grisly attack played out on the TV.

"Inari. It's definitely Inari," Father said as the credits to the fifth episode scrolled across the screen.

"Inari? No, it has to be Veeti. Didn't you notice the ring on his neck? That symbol was on one of the victims."

Father shook his head and snagged another piece of

pizza. He slathered it with garlic dipping sauce. "Anna, Anna, you have so much to learn about the criminal mind. I'm positive it's Inari."

Anna grabbed the remote. "Let's just see for ourselves. There are only three episodes left."

Father nodded, a grin on his face, and bit into his slice.

Anna pressed a button on the remote, and the next episode whirred to life on the TV. Engrossed and equally challenged—it couldn't be Inari, could it?— Ana snuggled back into the couch, drawing a throw blanket close to her chin. The intro faded, and the episode opened with a shot of Veeti dead on the floor. "What?" She sprang forward to the edge of her seat. "No!"

"Ha! I told you." Father cheered through a mouthful of pizza.

"No." Anna raised a finger. "Maybe he's not dead? Maybe there's a twist, a—?"

A door slammed shut.

Anna jumped.

Father whipped his neck in the direction of the door.

"What in God's name is going on here?" a shrill voice called.

Mother appeared in the entry, a stack of papers shoved under one shoulder and her suitcase clutched in her hand.

Father choked on his pizza, and a coughing fit ensued.

Mother glared, her nostrils flared.

Mother's charcoal eyes were wild with anger. Anna released hold of the blanket, and her stomach dropped. The blanket slipped to the floor. The TV blared.

Father darted across the room; his words muffled by the indecipherable Finnish screeching in the background. He took Mother's suitcase and rubbed his hands over her arms in a soothing fashion.

Anna's heart sank. With Mother here, would she ever watch the end of the series with Father? Would she ever learn how to put together a model boat? Or would he always put her mother first?

Chapter 13

Anna awoke Christmas morning to the buzz of her cell phone beneath her pillow. She adjusted to the light of the room, shadowed by Dad's hobby table which stood between her and the window. Unclutching Paws, she peeled back the covers and unearthed the phone lodged between the deflated mattress and pillow. She swiped to accept.

"Merry Christmas, Anna!"

Anna yanked the phone from her ear, softening Sarah's cheery voice. "Arrumph" was all she could muster.

"Oh, c'mon. Even vampires get up early on Christmas morning."

"Only vampires expecting a stocking full of blood." With a yawn, Anna curled back under her blanket. Seeing as she didn't expect a stocking of any sort from her parents, Anna was inclined to stay in bed indefinitely.

"Must you be such a curmudgeon? Today is Christmas!"

If only Sarah could tell that to Mother. "I know, I know. And Merry Christmas, I mean *buon Natale* to you, Eduardo, and Giac. What's the little man getting this year?"

"A kitchen set. Lucia played restaurant with him nonstop since daybreak. She's such a doting sister."

"Why does that gift not surprise me at all?" If Eduardo chose his career again, Anna would guess he'd opt for chef as opposed to lawyer. Apparently, he instilled this in his son as well. "And how is Sister Maria?"

"Very well. We saw her last night at mass."

The warmth of the blanket suddenly ceased, sending a shiver over Anna. Even Sister Maria, who hadn't a family member in the world, celebrated Christmas Eve properly. After Mother's dramatic interruption, everyone went to bed within the hour. She even trashed the last piece of pizza. To think, the last piece of pizza!

"Is everything all right with your visit? I don't think I've ever heard you so tight-lipped."

"That's because we're not texting." She grinned.

Sarah laughed.

Anna let out a deep exhalation. Why she hadn't shared her family's inability to love each other, she wasn't sure. Perhaps because Sarah's whole world seemed wrapped in love? "I miss you," Anna blurted out. *I wish I was there with you and Sister Maria instead of here*. "And thanks for calling. Give my love to everyone." *Love. Ha! As if I know a thing about love.*

"I will. And I miss you, too, Anna. I hope we can go to Al Forno's soon."

As she ended the call, Anna smiled. Hopefully, she could visit Rome after Hilary term—maybe even take in some sights with Sarah while she visited. Anna tucked Paws under the blanket. It would be nice to feel loved for a change as opposed to a pawn in academic chess.

In the kitchen, Anna found Father fighting with his

espresso machine. "You better get that thing fixed before Mother gives a live demonstration on nuclear fission." Anna fished out the box of toaster pastries, noting one more absent than yesterday morning. Huh, maybe Father had a late night, after all.

He frowned. "Your mother means well." He jabbed his finger into a button, making the machine hiss. "But don't get caught with that hunk of lard in your mouth. Christmas or not, she will discipline you."

She jutted her chin. "I'm not thirteen anymore, Father. What exactly is she going to do? Refuse to talk to me? Because, hell, she does that half the time, anyway."

His fingers fumbled on the machine, and his face flushed. He dropped his gaze to the counter.

A twinge of guilt rushed through her. What exactly was Father scared of losing with Mother? She didn't live with him. She barely even spoke to him. Heck, what remained of their relationship? Did he hang on to Mother for Anna's sake? Because she long passed the age of pretending things were okay.

"Morning." Mother swept into the kitchen and stopped near the espresso machine. "What in God's name is this monstrosity?"

Father flushed.

Dressed in slacks and a cardigan set that accentuated her petite figure, Mother looked ready to scuttle off to work. Anna heaved a sigh. It wouldn't surprise her, if she was…even on Christmas. But maybe that would be better. Maybe then she and Father could finish watching the mini-series and maybe even start the boat.

"I made us a reservation for a late lunch at

O'Neals." She glided past Father, flicked two buttons on the machine, and it whirled to life.

Father rubbed his chin and widened his eyes.

Anna rolled her eyes.

Mother turned, dropped her gaze to the toaster pastry, and snatched it from Anna. "I'll make us all some oatmeal."

Anna inwardly gagged.

"With raisins," she added.

Anna dropped her head and moaned. She'd sneak one later. Could she stand up to her mother about anything? Even a toaster pastry?

At the dining room table, Mother and Father made idle talk about lunch plans. Should they drive or take a taxi? Would they order from the menu or do the buffet? Anna drew figure-eights in her oatmeal, her stomach gurgling. What was Hendrik doing for Christmas? Was he alone in his apartment eating toast and butter as he prepared for their—er, *his* presentation in The Hague?

"So, darling, I bought you a little something." Mother dabbed at her lips and stood from the table.

Anna eyed Father. Since when did they exchange Christmas gifts? Perhaps Mother had reverted to Anna's school years and bought a textbook or puzzle or some other heartless nonsense.

Father shrugged and scrunched his face.

Mother returned to the table with a small box and extended it to Anna.

As she took the box, she felt a sudden shiver rush through her hands. Small and dainty, the box held something which clinked inside. Had Mother bought a piece of jewelry? Her heart fluttered. Had she *ever* gifted her jewelry? She'd never even let Anna *borrow* a piece of jewelry. "Thank you, Mother." Her voice shook. "You didn't have to get me anything." She removed the lid. Inside, a small key rested. As she tightened her fingers on the box, Anna looked up with a furrowed brow. "Wh…what is this?"

Mother beamed and stared down with gleaming eyes.

Father chewed his lip and left his gaze on the table.

"Now don't get too excited," Mother said. "It's just a studio, and it's only a rental, but I've paid through to the summer."

Her breath caught, and the key slipped from her hands. "I…I don't understand." She stared at Father.

He wrung his hands and flicked his gaze between Anna and the floor.

"The Math Chair at Harvard agreed to take you midyear. Come home, Anna. You have nothing left at Oxford."

"Nothing left?" Like hell she didn't. Anna bolted to her feet "What do you mean I have nothing left? I have Cayley. I have Klara. I have Hendrik!"

"Hendrik?" Mother shrieked and stepped back. "Who's Hendrik? Please tell me you haven't gotten yourself caught up—"

"I meant Dr. Van der Aart, my advisor."

Mother heaved a sigh, pursed her lips, and placed a hand on Anna's shoulder. "You don't have an advisor, Dear. That's precisely the problem. And you're nearly twenty-six. I had my doctorate by then."

Mother stared as if they were talking about which brand of toaster pastries to buy, not how Anna should live her life. What reason did her mother have for sticking her nose in her business, anyway? Anna fought to slow her thumping heart which shook her breath and her lower lip. Heat rushed her cheeks, and she clenched her hands. Stepping back, Anna shook free from Mother's grasp. "No."

"No?" Mother dropped her jaw and widened her eyes.

Father shot up his gaze.

"No." The word tore from her lips.

Father stood with his brows pressed together.

Was he astonished or fearful? Perhaps both. What he felt didn't matter now. He hadn't stood up for her about the thriller series or the toaster pastry or Paws. He wasn't going to now, either. She stormed out of the dining room, raced to her bedroom, and slammed the door. Alone in the corner of her room, she nuzzled her face into Paws. Tears, cool on her hot cheeks, seeped into the stuffed animal's matted fur. Seconds, minutes…hours passed. Mother didn't come—neither did Father. If only she could talk to someone. But today was Christmas. Both Sarah and Klara were busy with their families. She couldn't disturb them over something non-life threatening.

Leaving Paws on her mattress, Anna rose, paced the room, and hugged her arms around her waist. If only she had someone to hug—a deep, warm hug with no ulterior intentions of sexual favors. A hug like Hendrik gave her after they cracked Allerton. Anna removed her phone from her back pocket. *He said he wasn't going home until after the conference.* Maybe he spent Christmas alone, too. Anna pulled up his contact and swiped the screen.

"Anna?" Hendrik's voice rang clear through the phone. "I thought about calling you."

Anna furrowed her brow. "You did?"

"Yeah...well...you were on my mind."

His voice sounded hesitant. *I was on your mind because of the conference or because you care about me?*

"I wanted to wish you a Happy Christmas, but I didn't want to interrupt your time with your family," he said.

"Ah. Well, one would assume I'd be spending time with my family on Christmas, but I prove that hypothesis false." Anna heaved a sigh and returned to her bed.

"Is...um...everything all right?"

Anna dragged her knees to her chest and curled up on the deflated mattress. "Let's just say my holidays took a nosedive. I predict a divergence to negative infinity."

"Ouch, that bad, huh? I'm sorry. The holidays are supposed to be about fun and family and friends."

"Yes, they are." Her voice came out in a whisper. She stared at the models on the table, wondering if she and Dad would ever build one.

"If it makes you feel any better, I only have a whiteboard and inked papers to keep me company."

Anna smiled. "With a feast of buttered toast and coffee?"

Hendrik laughed. "Yes. I took dinner at Rashaad's last night. That will keep me full for a while."

As Anna pictured Hendrik in his sparsely furnished flat, a lightness filled her chest. He might not have an espresso machine or a TV to stream a thriller series, but more warmth filled his place than this house would ever have. "Hendrik?"

"Yes?"

"If I came back sooner, tomorrow or the following day, would you like to meet for coffee…to work on our presentation, of course?"

"I'd love to." He cleared his throat. "I mean, that would be a great way to prepare for the conference."

"Excellent." Anna smiled. "I'll call as soon as I'm back." As she ended the call, for the first time all day, it felt like Christmas.

Late that night, a knock sounded on her bedroom door. Her eyes blurred from hours on her phone and crumbs from stolen toaster pastries covered her shirt. She cringed. Please let it be Father and not Mother. "Come in."

The door squeaked open, and Father emerged, carrying a steaming mug. "Your mother's gone to bed."

"Here? Or at *her* place?" Anna didn't hide the cynicism in her tone.

Father frowned and crossed. He handed her the cup.

Hot cocoa steamed from inside. The chocolaty sweetness permeated her nose, and Anna couldn't help taking a gulp of the goodness. The sweet warmth threatened to melt away the anger and resentment she held inside for her parents, but she wouldn't let them push her around anymore. She lowered the cup. "I rebooked my flight. I'm taking a red-eye tomorrow."

Sighing, Father sank into the mattress beside her. His knees popped as he bent. His sandy brows buckled.

He looked as though he might burst into tears. Anna's heart leapt to her throat.

Father placed a hand on her knee. "Do you have to go so soon? You just returned."

The warmth of his hand seeped into her, and Anna scooted away. She tried to open her heart to him yesterday, and he thoroughly rebuffed her. "I see no reason to stay."

"But we haven't gone to Boston Common yet or finished the series or started constructing a boat."

Her heart ached and at the same time felt hollow. *No, we haven't, Father.* She swallowed hard and hardened her heart. "I don't think Mother would approve of those." *Which means you won't be doing them.*

Father heaved a sigh and ran a hand through his hair. "Your mother is just trying to help."

Anna scoffed and jumped to her feet. "Help me? Ha! Funny how her way of helping always improves her image, her career, and her ambitions, not mine. Mother's agenda—whether through her interactions with me or you—always comes back to her. Why can't you see that?"

Father hung his head. "Anna, stop this. Your mother—"

Anna slapped a hand on the hobby table, and the pieces trembled. A boat shook and fell to the side. "No, Father, I won't stop. I have every mind to leave here and *never* come back."

With a reddened face, Father stood and crossed to her. He gripped her upper arms as he gazed down. "Anna, please. Your mother only wants what's best for you."

"What's best for me, or what makes me happy?" With a set jaw, she held his gaze.

Father quirked a brow. "Is there a difference?" He released her and stepped back.

Relaxing her jaw, Anna took care to soften her tone. "There shouldn't be."

Father strode to the door. He slumped his shoulders and crinkled his brow.

He looked ragged; he looked beat. Anna wanted to feel sorry for him. She wanted to run to him and say she was sorry. But she couldn't let him continue to crush her heart.

"No," he said, finally. "I suppose there shouldn't." Then he opened the door and walked out.

Anna stared at the empty doorway. Did he finally understand? Would things between them finally change? Or was it too late to repair their fractured relationship?

Chapter 14

Mabel's seemed the ideal choice for a first meeting with Hendrik to discuss the upcoming mathematics conference. The café held no memories of turned-down advances nor did it offer a chance encounter with a local hookup, like Butch. Unlike the last time Anna met Hendrik for a drink, she didn't dress to lure him. Rather, she chose a simple pair of corduroys, a chunky sweater, combat boots, and, of course, an infinity scarf because what mathematician in their right mind wouldn't wear one in the winter?

Still jet-lagged from her flight back to Boston, Anna yawned as she entered the café. The warm, mellow glow of the pendant lighting offered a welcome escape from the bright, winter sun. In the back of the café, far from where Klara and Anna usually chose to sit, Hendrik sat alone at table set for four. With his laptop propped on a side chair, Hendrik tapped the keyboard with one hand, and used his other to alternate between sipping from a cup and munching on a scone.

Anna approached. "Coffee or tea?"

Hendrik bobbled his scone, lifted his gaze, and smiled. "Coffee." He furrowed his brows.

He looked as if she'd asked the most ridiculous question in the world. Anna clucked her tongue. What did Mabel think when he ordered that drink, which from her vantage point she could see he'd taken black.

Clearly, he didn't gather they dined in the tea-drinking mecca of the world. Mathematicians. They always had their heads in the sand.

Standing, Hendrick reached out a hand but stopped just short of touching her. Blushing, he cleared his throat. "How was the rest of your visit?"

Anna stiffened. As if coming back a week early didn't speak for itself? The tension squeezed her chest. Maybe Hendrik assumed she made a dramatic reconciliation with her parents, and they celebrated the holidays in grand splendor. If her family actually held feelings for each other, maybe they would have. Swallowing hard, she plopped down into the seat across from him. "My visit was just peachy."

Hendrik tipped his head.

Did he not know the phrase, or did he want to know why she hadn't had a good visit? It didn't matter. She was too tired and hungry to explain why she never built a replica of *HMS Victory.* As she leaned forward to place her chin in her hand, she tossed him a box she brought back from Boston.

Hendrik jerked back, juggling the box before it settled in his hands. "What's this?" He stared at the bright blue box.

"A Christmas present."

As Hendrik flushed, he dropped his gaze to the box. "Toaster-Tarts?"

"You're holding a quintessential American breakfast there."

"Better than toast and butter?"

Recalling the toast she'd prepared them as they worked on Allerton, Anna smiled. "One hundred percent."

Hendrik chuckled and dropped the box into his backpack. "Thanks. I got you something, too." From his pocket, he withdrew a small box. "It's…just…" He stammered and bit his lip. "Just a little something to sway Quinton…if you ever decide to take another one of his classes."

"That's a big if." She smiled, letting a warmth replace the tension in her chest. The feeling inside didn't match the firecracker of excitement she experienced when Juan gifted her the diamond studs lost somewhere in her room. The sensation coursed deep within her—a feeling of acceptance and of safety. She took the box, careful not to touch his fingers as he passed it across. Somehow, without even knowing what the box contained, she knew the energy that pulsed through her veins would only intensify if she touched him.

She lifted the lid, and a shiny metal bracelet glinted inside. Not just any bracelet—the twisted band of a mobius band. She grinned. "You're right. Quinton would love it." As she slid it on, her grocery store gift diminished in both price and thoughtfulness. She smoothed her fingers over the cool metal, knowing she could traverse both sides of the band in a single pass without lifting her hand—a characteristic of the topological object. "Thank you."

"You're welcome, Anna." He held her gaze.

His voice was soft and sincere. His amber eyes glowed. And the warmth in her chest expanded. She was wrong. She hadn't needed to touch him to intensify the energy within; he'd done it with his voice and eyes.

His face reddened, and he shifted his attention to his laptop and rubbed the back of his neck. "Did you get a chance to view the presentation? I added some slides to the beginning on the history of—"

Anna grabbed his hand. Her insides melted at the warmth of his hand against her cool fingertips. A surge of energy passed through her—did it pass through him, as well? It didn't matter because Hendrik wouldn't let it be explored. "Thank you," she said after a moment of silence passed between them. "I'll treasure it always."

Hendrik placed his other hand on top of hers. He dropped his gaze to their hands, nodded, then yanked his back.

She smiled. As sure as she was that only one path existed on a vector, she was sure he felt the energy, too. She cleared her throat, placed her hand on the touchpad, and dove into her comments on the slides. "I'll talk about the Abelian subgroups and the Greek letter mapping. You discuss the history and the Caesar shift." She flipped forward a few slides. "Your font is different on this slide, and you forgot an "alpha" right"—she jumped forward another two slides—"here." She pointed to the screen, waiting for Hendrik to catch up to speed. After a few moments of no response, she shifted her gaze from the screen back to him.

He stared, smiling. "Anna," he said, not shifting his gaze from hers, "it's good to have you back."

Being back was good…wasn't it?

****

Later that evening, inside her tiny apartment, Anna unpacked her suitcase—well, Anna Franklin's version of unpack. She flipped open her suitcase, removed the plastic bag of dirty clothes, tossed it atop the mound in the corner by the window, and left the remaining items in the suitcase. What was the sense of moving clothes from one holding place to another when she would wear them all within a week…maybe two? Okay, maybe a month. She sighed. Okay she should at least unpack the non-wearable items: her extra phone charger, the book on Ramanujan she read during the flight over, and Paws. She winced as she picked up the dog, drawing him to her chest. A hollowness seeped in. Memories of who-done-it debates, diorama boats, and pepperoni pizza sprang into her mind. Was it too much to ask that she and father finish something together? She gave the dog one last hug, feeling tears squeeze from her eyes. No, Father would always put Mother first, even if he didn't agree with her.

With a sigh, she placed the stuffed animal on the dresser next to the box from Hendrik. Opening it, she pulled out the smooth, silver bracelet inside. She traced her finger along the metal, the coolness seeping into her fingertip. The gift from Hendrik was so unexpected—so thoughtful. Perhaps he cared about her more than he let on? A roughness scratched her finger, and she ceased her trace. As she tilted the bracelet to catch the light, she squinted to see the hidden roughness beneath the curve. A tiny string of letters etched into the band: *Zomerschoon.* Anna furrowed her brow. Had Hendrik ordered the bracelet from a Dutch manufacturer?

The blood seeped from her face. Perhaps he bought the bracelet when last he was in the Netherlands for another girl who he failed to follow through with. With a brisk exhalation, Anna tossed the bracelet back into the box. As it settled to rest, she recalled his nervousness in giving her the gift—his shaken voice and his heat-seared cheeks. She let her head hang and her shoulders sag. She picked up the bracelet, shifting it side to side in her hand. No, Hendrik most definitely bought the bracelet specifically for her. The mobius band was a classic topology figure and also one of timelessness. She closed her hand around the bracelet, hiding it from view. No, just like Father, Hendrik was just another man in her life whose love she would never garner.

A chill rushed her spine. Did she want Hendrik Van der Aart's love? She opened her hand, examining the band—the beautiful eternal curve shimmered in silver. She would never have an eternal love, whether from Father or Hendrik. Something would always come between her and them: Mother, mathematics, or something as tangible as the Atlantic.

She slipped the bracelet back into the box and snapped closed the lid. Grabbing the Ramanujan biography from her backpack, Anna curled up on her bed. Unlike most mathematicians, Ramanujan received no formal training but learned from reading books on his own. A child prodigy, he didn't excel in school but rather let his imagination roam the world of numbers. He didn't let the expectations of society deter him from his passions: math, family, and the love of his life. Anna rested the book on her chest and closed her eyes. She revered this man for his devotion to his loves. Why couldn't Mother accept that academia wasn't the only path in life? Why couldn't Anna be a code-breaker without having to attend Quinton's dry lectures?

As she cast a glance across the room to the suitcase which would need to be repacked for the conference and then the box on the dresser, she let the memory of her first conversation about the conference percolate in her mind. "Lots of field reps will be at the conference,"

Hendrik had said.

Finding her phone, she quickly pulled up the conference website and scanned the page for the list of sponsors. Her breath caught. Hendrik was right. The NSA, FBI, MI6, and many others she'd never heard of topped the list. With a series of jabs to her screen, she learned each organization would have a table with representatives. Her heartrate accelerated. This conference could be the opportunity she needed to break free from Mother's demands and the ticket to a life Anna actually wanted.

Shoving clothes and books aside, Anna found her laptop. She raced her fingers across the keyboard. She needed a resume, a website, and updated social media profiles. Could she get it all done before the conference? She scoffed and rolled her eyes. Of course, she could! She didn't need a few days—only a few hours.

After brushing off her HTML and JAVA skills, the pages came to life: her success at MIT, her fluency in three languages—okay, her Spanish and Italian were a little rusty, but she'd bring them up to speed— and her accomplishments at Oxford.

Masters in Science, expected, she typed in. A tightness cinched her chest. What would Hendrik do if she left at the end of the year? And what about Cayley? A numbness washed over her fingers followed by a warmth in her right hand where Cayley had squeezed. Could she leave him like this...even if the perfect opportunity arose?

Chapter 15

A week later, in the city of the Dutch parliament, Anna stood with Hendrik at the front of a roaring crowd. Dressed in her most professional outfit, a slimline skirt and button-up shirt, she felt almost like a babbling professor with a pencil in her hair. Perhaps she might pass for one if she didn't have her phone stashed in her bra, rainbow laces in her combat boots, and purple-streaked hair with no pencil in sight. Some things, a girl couldn't change.

In an otherwise drab conference room of the convention center, mathematicians crammed the space—from bowties to bolo ties and fuzzy, Albert Einstein hair to crew cuts, Anna and Hendrik's presentation lured them all. Anna began the demonstration, explaining the history of the problem and abelian subgroups.

Hendrik rounded it off with the Caesar shift in two alphabets—giving all credit to Anna, as he should—and revealing the entire solution.

Most of the gaggle of mathematicians stood, applauding, while others raised their hands to ask questions. Others still elbowed their way to the front of the room, jostling for position in line to speak to Hendrik.

Who knew mathematicians were so rowdy? Removing her phone from beneath her shirt, Anna slinked into the shadows. First author or not, the credit *always* went to the more senior researcher. She was just a lowly, grad-student slave, at least in the eyes of the attendees.

Hendrik chatted with a man wearing a Harvard Math T-shirt. Dressed in gray suit pants, a dark blue shirt and matching tie, Hendrik gazed over at Anna. He smiled, cast his gaze to the dozen more nerds with business cards behind the Harvard man, and shrugged.

Take your time, Anna silently mouthed. On her phone, she pulled up the map of the conference tables and found the row of "classified" positions. While Hendrik networked his way into a tenure-track position, she might as well work on securing an operative one. Tucking her purple streak under her dark tufts, she slipped out the side door and made her way to the employer fair. Halfway to the FBI table, a voice stopped her.

"Miss Franklin," a man said.

His voice was quiet yet stern. Anna spun around.

Dressed in all black, the man leaned against a supporting post. He extended a business card.

Anna took it. *Mike Krueger. NSA*. She widened her eyes. Holy super prime number! This guy was legit. The card shook in her hand, and she fought against her mouth forming a wide grin.

"They call me Dr. K." He stepped away from the post, joining her.

"Nice to meet you." She attempted to match his laser-like gaze and steel-rod lips.

Dr. K tipped his chin, revealing a wire in his ear, and whispered something into his watch.

With the earpiece, perfectly pressed suit, and

rimless glasses, he looked more like a Secret Service Agent than a national security agent. But what did she know about NSA operatives aside from what she'd seen in the movies?

Dr. K lowered his wrist and lifted his gaze. "Have you ever considered serving your country?"

Her mind suddenly bee-lined to spy movie scenes—car chases, sky-diving, and martial arts-packed fights. "Would I get a gun?" She lifted a brow.

Dr. K squinted and scanned her up and down. "How about a taser and a fancy computer?"

Anna weighed the offer. The position didn't sound like Laura Croft or Jason Bourne but working for the NSA could be fun—intercepting messages of espionage, hacking into criminal's phones, and decoding secret commands. Maybe she could be a modern-day Lisbeth Salander? Anna squared her shoulders. "What color's the taser?"

The NSA agent furrowed his brows.

Anna grinned. Clearly this guy wasn't used to being toyed with. Maybe he didn't carry a gun but instead wore a pair of souped-up glasses that could see through lead and write code from his thoughts. "I just mean, if you're expecting me to carry around a pink taser or one with a blinged-out handle, you've got the wrong girl."

Dr. K cracked a smile but quickly straightened his mouth and resumed his Queen's Guard countenance. He tipped his head toward the card in Anna's hand. "I don't think there'll be any chance of that decoration. You know how to reach me." He nodded, stepped back, and then disappeared into the crowd.

She stared at the card in her hand. How likely was

she to secure this position? She hadn't even given them her resume yet, but clearly he knew of her credentials. Need she even consider the FBI or CIA? Every mathematician knew the NSA employed the whiz kids. But the NSA was based in Maryland. Could she work remotely? What about Cayley? What about Hendrik?

Her chest tightened. Shoot. Hendrik. How long had she been away? Was he done wading through his fan club? After stashing Dr. K's card in her boot, Anna dashed back to the conference room.

In front of no less than a dozen spectators, Hendrik stood.

His cheeks weren't flushed, and his hands didn't fidget with a pen. He seemed to take all this attention in stride. While Anna couldn't hear what he said, she could tell by his relaxed posture and smile, he was in his glory. He wouldn't miss her if she joined the NSA…would he?

Hendrik glanced over and widened his smile. He pointed at his watch and lifted his brows.

Anna smiled. At least he was concerned about wasting her time. She waved a hand, approving him to continue.

"Brilliant work." A woman with tight, blonde curls and dressed in a tweed suit extended her hand. "Emily Courtier, chair of the mathematics, Cambridge."

Cambridge? Talk about Oxford rival, especially when it came to mathematics. Anna shook the small, wrinkled hand and smiled. "Pleasure to meet you."

"You, as well. Might you be considering Cambridge for your post-doctoral studies? Or"—she raised a blonde brow above cat-eye glasses—"a tenureship?"

Anna scoffed. "I'm hardly near to receiving my degree." *If Quinton has anything to say about it, I never will.*

"Come, come." Ms. Courtier smiled and placed a hand on Anna's forearm. "Your contributions to Allerton are more than most tenured professors achieve in a lifetime. Surely, they warrant enough for a dissertation."

A dissertation? Anna jerked back her chin. She could get a Ph.D. just like that?

"Have you finished your coursework?" Ms. Courtier asked.

Anna flinched but quickly replaced it with a forced smile. "I will this year." *If I don't have to take Quinton next term.*

Ms. Courtier squeezed her hand. "Well, of course, you will. I hope you'll put Cambridge at the top of your list."

Anna nodded.

Ms. Courtier spun on her sling-back high heel and sauntered out of the room.

Bending down, Anna retrieved a piece of now-warm bubble gum from her right boot, unwrapped it, and popped it in her mouth. Of course, Cambridge wanted her. Statues of Turing and Littlewood decorated their halls, while Oxford memorialized their math geniuses with buildings named Penrose and Wiles. And, well known among the math nerds, was the fact that both schools one time had duked it out over acclaimed Hardy. Although Oxford seemed to take that claim to fame.

Anna blew a pink bubble. *Top of my list. Ha!* She popped the bubble with a snap and laughed as she chewed, molding it back into a sphere in her mouth. Since when did she make lists—let alone one that prolonged her existence in this academic hellhole? Besides, when Cayley found out—if he ever woke up— she considered Cambridge, it would surely kill him. Anna swallowed hard, nearly choking on her gum. She dropped her gaze to her left shoe where she'd stashed Dr. K's card. No, she was sure Cayley would much rather her go to NSA than take a position at Cambridge. Wouldn't he?

****

As the next presenters entered the room, Anna, Hendrik, and the flurry of attendees moved into the lobby. Anna separated herself from the crowd, finding a spot in front of a row of windows. Outside, striped, green awnings lined The Hague's central square. The sun danced on stone pavers. Much like the piazzas in Rome, people lounged around patio tables, enjoying food and conversation, only the Dutch called these pedestrian centers *pleins.* Here, during Netherland's winter, snow flurried at any moment, while in Rome, the sun still warmed her cheeks. Here no fountains decorated the square; rather the lake behind the parliamentary buildings sat icy in the distance.

"You want to catch some of the presentations?" a voice asked.

Anna turned to find Hendrik behind her. His entourage had dissipated, leaving a handful of conference attendees mingling in the lobby studying their conference booklets. Anna sighed. She and Hendrik had spent all morning in presentations—one about the remaining unsolved message on Kryptos and another about the implementation of Honey Encryption.

Neither kept her interest. She spent the three hours wiggling in her newly purchased dress-suit—one she wouldn't wear again anytime soon. Anna quirked a brow. "Any of them as good as ours?"

Hendrik laughed. "Doubt it."

Shifting her gaze back to the window, Anna surveyed the diners. What delicacies could she binge on here? Not pizza or gelato, but perhaps French fries or waffles. What masterpieces would they see in the museums? Not Botticellis or Da Vincis, but Vermeers or Rembrandts. And how would they travel to the different places? Not on a scooter or subway, but perhaps on a shiny, yellow bicycle. "How long are we *required* to stay here?" She faced him.

Hendrik sighed, rubbed his neck, and stared out the window. "I suppose we've fulfilled our obligations as presenters. The rest of the conference is more about shoulder rubbing and butt-kissing, anyway."

"Of which we don't need any." She snapped her gum. "Well, you don't need any, that is. You've got a regular Dr. Van der Aart fan club now. Shall we build you a website?"

Hendrik scoffed and raised his brows. "I'm just glad I have some viable employment options: Cambridge, the University of Amsterdam, and even Harvard. Although Mom will strangle me if I take a job out of Europe. She already had a fit when I moved across the Channel. She threatened to sell the farm and move over with me."

"That's pretty excessive."

Hendrik shrugged. "Weren't your parents upset when you left the States? What's it been…three years now?"

"Four and—" Her voice faltered. She cleared her throat and raised her chin. "No, they definitely didn't threaten to follow me here."

Hendrik stared down.

His amber eyes bored into hers, beckoning her to elaborate. Anna disconnected from his gaze. What should she say? That when she opted to take the job at St. Theresa's before going to grad school, they threatened her with other things—things nowhere in comparison to chasing her. In fact, they followed through with every one of their threats. After her move to Rome, Father turned her bedroom into his hobby room, and aside from paying for her airfare home, they hadn't given her a cent. They seemed to live by the old academic standard of publish or perish.

While similar to her parents in his motivation to further his career, Hendrik weighed the choice in schools for their location to his family. He gave the notion of blowing off the conference, too. Both things Mother never would do.

"I suppose we could check out the attractions. I did promise to take you to the Escher gallery."

"And cheese," Anna reminded him. "Don't forget the gouda and edam."

Hendrik laughed. "Trust me, I haven't."

Anna spent the afternoon with Hendrik, visiting The Hague's most sought-after sights: the *Mauritshuis'* collection of famed artworks, the Escher museum's mind-bending illusions, and the *Binnenhof*'s Hall of Knights. Sarah would be so jealous when Anna filled her in on her firsthand encounter with *The Girl with the Pearl Earring*. But, in truth, Escher's illusions intrigued Anna more than Vermeer's realism. Which way was up, anyway?

As evening approached, Anna's stomach growled, and her preppy outfit irritated her. With the tight fit of the jacket on her shoulders and the pencil skirt gripping her knees, she felt shoved inside a roll of paper towels.

"I'm starving." Hendrik turned the last corner of the sidewalk enclosing the *Binnenhof*'s lake. He reached for his breast pocket and started to remove his e-cig then stopped, leaving it inside. "Ready to try some classic Dutch food? Don't worry, we can skip the raw herring."

Anna grinned and shot her gaze at the main square. Their hotel stood a mere block beyond. "Totally! Well, as long as we skip the herring. But I can't eat in these clothes—or celebrate. We are drinking to your success, aren't we?"

Hendrik smiled so wide a small dimple appeared on his cheek. "Our success." He stepped in the direction of the hotel, calling over his shoulder, "I suppose we should."

Inside the hotel room, Anna squeezed into a pair of jeggings and daydreamed about a cone of thick-cut fries she spied during the outing. What was the gooey, yellow sauce on top? Cheese? Mustard? Whatever the substance, she wanted some. And those bags of fluffy clouds of dough she saw by the square. She wanted some of those, too. With extra powdered sugar, of course.

She squatted, testing the stretch of the pants— plenty of give. She could even opt for the ice cream on top of the fried dough, if she wanted. Sucking in her stomach, Anna gave her lower half a once-over in the mirror. Her butt still looked tight and lifted, and her stomach, while no longer concave, appeared flat and smooth. Confident in her choice of pants, she rummaged through her suitcase until she found the perfect shirt: a long sleeve, bright-purple midriff that showed off her belly-button ring. She might be a little cold, but why bother changing if she didn't look good? She slipped it over her shoulders.

"You almost ready?" she called through to Hendrik, whose room was adjacent to hers. "It's never too early to eat." Her stomach growled again. If she didn't eat soon, she wouldn't need to stretch her pants at all. In fact, they might just fall off.

The door connecting their rooms clicked, and Anna unlocked her side and pushed open the door.

On the other side, Hendrik stood, staring at his reflection in the dresser mirror as he combed his hair. Too long to spike up and too short to tuck behind his ear, his ginger strands refused to stay in place. Each time he swept the comb over them, the hairs just tumbled back into his face.

"Don't you have any hair gel?" Anna approached him.

"I guess I left it at home." He furrowed his brow and combed in a different direction. The change in part only succeeded in leaving his wisps standing on end.

Anna laughed. "May I?" She extended a hand.

Hendrik frowned and passed her the comb.

Comb in her hand, she sauntered to the bathroom sink, doused the comb with water, and returned. "It won't last all night, but long enough until we can get you some gel. Or, until you get your hair cut."

Hendrik ticked his brows. "That would be the practical thing to do, wouldn't it?" He extended his hand.

Anna hesitated, but then some urge inside propelled her forward, onto the tips of her toes so she could reach his floppy hair. Her face close to his, she could smell the cologne on his neck and could see the tinge of red erupting on his cheeks. The comb glided through his hair, and the water held it in place. "There, now you look more like Ewan McGregor than Ron Weasley." She lowered her heels and gave a light laugh.

Hendrik didn't laugh. He didn't speak, either.

In fact, based on the crimson of his cheeks, he wasn't even breathing. Staring up into his bright amber eyes that held fast to hers, time seemed to stand on end. It was as if the two of them stood alone on a mobius band—all paths led back to each other.

"Thank you." Hendrik released a shaky breath and raised a hand to her cheek.

His palm warm on her face, Anna melted under his touch.

He ran a thumb down the line of her jaw until it rested beneath her chin. Gently, he tilted up her face. "Thank you," he said again, just before bringing his lips to hers.

His kiss wasn't hungry like Butch's, nor stiff like Francisco's. Hendrik's kiss was like none she'd ever received before. A soft kiss, a gentle kiss, and a kiss so light and buoyant, she floated on water.

Hendrik paused, drawing his mouth inches away.

Anna hung mid-air, weightless and waiting. Dizziness overcame her. An excitement brewed inside. And in that split second that his fast breath met her cheeks, Anna feared his gentle kiss would be a friendly gesture only she wished would linger.

"Thank you," he said once more, and he kissed her again…then again.

Each kiss lengthened, and each tugged her deeper into the stratosphere. As she moved her mouth against his—her fingers finding the back of his neck, tugging him closer—she knew this kiss was anything but a friendly gesture. Her pulse quickened.

Hendrik shifted his hands to her waist.

Warm against her cool skin, his fingers wrapped around her stomach, gripping tightly as he lifted her onto the dresser.

He groaned as he leaned into her, opening his mouth and deepening the kiss.

Items on the dresser poked into her thighs—a wallet, a pen, and the comb. Anna shoved them off, and they hit the floor with thuds. She wrapped her legs around his midsection and drew him in until her back hit the wall and his torso pressed against hers.

"Anna," he said through kisses.

But his voice was in the distance now. She could only focus on kissing him and keeping his hands tight on her waist. She drew him closer.

"Anna," he said again, louder. He slowed his kiss.

"Sshh." She reengaged his mouth and ran her fingers down his chest.

Hendrik pulled back and stepped away from the dresser. He dropped his head and rubbed the back of his neck. "We can't," he whispered.

Headiness threatened, but a fire stormed her chest. To hell with what they couldn't do. She hadn't waited three months to kiss him to hear, "we can't." Anna flicked her gaze to beneath his belt. "Your physiology all seems to be working perfectly."

Hendrik frowned.

A twisted frown—almost one of pain. The burning in her chest simmered, and Anna jumped off the dresser and stepped close. "No one is here, Hendrik—only us." She ran her hands up his chest and leaned in to kiss him again.

Hendrik shivered and jerked his face to the side. "They'll know, Anna."

"How would they know?" She wanted to feel his mouth again and get lost in his embrace. She kissed his collarbone, then his neck, and then she reached for his face.

Keeping his head turned away, he tensed his jaw.

Anna froze. Her breath caught, and she stumbled back. "You don't trust me?" The question came out as more of a statement.

Hendrik whipped his head back and met her gaze. "No, no. That's not what I meant."

An urgency consumed his voice. Urgency for what? To keep her happy so she wouldn't blab about him making out with her? "The hell it isn't." She stomped farther away and glowered. No one else stood in the privacy of the room. Hell, no one else from Oxford even attended the conference. She flared her nostrils. No, Hendrik could only mean one thing. He thought she would use this against him somehow. His paranoia over jeopardizing his precious career made him push away what he wanted—what they both wanted. A pain pierced her chest as a lump swelled in her throat. Why did so many people in her life choose career over her? Squeezing her hands into fists, she swallowed hard. She wouldn't be put aside for career anymore. "Listen to me, hashtag narcissist, there's no take-backs on shoving your tongue down your advisee's throat." She jammed her fists into his chest.

Hendrik stumbled back, his eyes wide.

Anna ground her teeth. "I can't believe I let myself have feelings for you and your tenure-track heart. I thought you cared about me more than just your beloved Allerton puzzle, but I was wrong. I don't want to help you with your insipid codes. I don't want to travel to your home tomorrow. And I don't want your stupid cheese, either!" As her pulse raged between her ears, she stormed out of his room, slamming the door behind her.

How had she been so naïve to fall for him—not once but twice?

Chapter 16

Alone in her room, Anna stalked from bed to door and back again. Her heart still throbbing, she tried to force from her mind the feeling of Hendrik's lips on hers. Why had she let him kiss her? Why had she combed his hair?

A pounding on the door shook her from her thoughts.

"Anna!" Hendrik called through the door.

The door rattled. The knob wiggled. Thank goodness she locked it when she'd stormed out.

"Please, Anna. Open the door."

The pleading of his voice softened her rage, and she slowed her pace.

"I'm sorry." He lowered his voice. "I trust you it's…just…"

His voice sounded so sincere—so apologetic. Her pulse steadied, and she stopped in front of the door. "Just what, Mr. Van der Aart?" She reached for the doorknob, paused, steadying her breath, and then opened the door.

Hendrick stared for a split second before crossing the threshold into her room and wrapping his arms around her.

The warmth and firmness of his chest steadied her, and his cologne—a musky scent with hints of citrus— intoxicated her. The heady feeling of losing herself in his gravitational pull overwhelmed her again. She blinked her eyes. No. She wouldn't let him draw her in again until he explained himself. Reeling back, she forced steel into her gaze. "Just what, Hendrik?"

Hendrik opened his mouth, but nothing came out. Rubbing his temple, he crossed in front of her and took a seat on the edge of her bed.

Standing above him, Anna searched his gaze, and waited, just as she'd waited these past three months for him to say something about them.

He swallowed. "There's no doubt in my mind I want to be with you, but I don't want to mess up things. Not just for me but for you." He grabbed her hand. "I couldn't bear it if what happens between us blemishes your future."

Anna frowned and stepped closer. She rested her hands on his shoulders. "I still don't see how anyone would ever find out."

Hendrik laughed. "I'm not worried about you revealing our secret. I'm worried I will."

Anna furrowed her brows. "But why would—"

"Don't you see?" He grabbed her left hand and brought it to his lips. "The closer I get to you, the more I want you." He kissed her wrist. "And the happier I become when I have you."

A smile lit up his face, and his amber eyes glowed. Anna's doubts slipped away, and she leaned closer.

"It doesn't matter how hard I try to hide it, the whole department"—he kissed her nose—"hell, the whole university will see it written on my face. 'Hendrik Van der Aart is smitten.' "

Anna placed a hand on his pale cheek, cool like autumn's breeze, and lowered her lips to his. She kissed him softly but fully.

Hendrik wrapped his hands around her waist, letting his fingers climb her back, until they settled beneath her shoulders. "Can I stay with you tonight?"

Diamonds of goose bumps prickled her flesh, and she leaned back to gaze into his eyes. "But you just said—"

"I meant"—Hendrik sighed—"on the floor."

Anna frowned.

Hendrik kissed her lips again. "I know, I know. But we both know what will happen if I share your bed." He brought his forehead to rest against hers. "Can we wait? Please? Until I'm not your advisor anymore?"

Warmth flooded her chest. He really cared about her. He wasn't another Butch or Juan who merely wanted her bedroom performances. He cared for her. "Yes," she whispered.

Never before had she embarked on a relationship such as this—one which would certainly stretch well past her six-week max and one which didn't revolve around sex. Could she wait for him? Did she want to?

****

Anna awoke to Hendrik milling about the room, rustling packets of cheap coffee, and attempting to brew one in the plastic contraption labeled *koffiezetapparaat.* She rolled onto her elbow. "Sleep well?"

Hendrik frowned at the coffeemaker which wasn't dripping. "Oh yeah, that floor was like a pillow top."

"I did offer to share the bed."

"You don't need a Ph.D. to know that wouldn't have been a smart idea."

Anna sighed. She hadn't slept with a man since her souiree in Rome this past summer. If she stuck with

Hendrik's plan, she'd be abstinant until the end of Hilary term—maybe even Trinity—until the university assigned her a new advisor. Unless Cayley awoke... Warmth seized the hand he'd squeezed on her last visit, but a coolness breathed into her chest. She rested her hopes on him awakening for so many reasons—the least of which was her love life. Hendrik's tender kisses and stiff, outstretched arm, strewn from his position on the floor, would have to do for now.

Hendrik smacked the side of the coffeemaker. "The lack of sleep jostled a new problem for us."

"Oh yeah?" Anna stood, stretching her arms in the air.

Hendrik's eyes strayed to the band of skin revealed by her lifted shirt.

She smiled. If he kept eyeing her like a hungry animal, she definitely wouldn't have to wait two months for sex. He probably wouldn't last two weeks. She kept her arms extended a few moments longer than comfortable.

The coffeemaker gurgled, and a devient drop of hot coffee splashed his hand. Hendrik jumped back at the singe.

"Care to bring me up to speed?" Anna asked.

Hendrik shook his hand. "The Littlefield Sonnets. I think our next task should be breaking the fourth message."

"The sonnets?" Breaking the coded frippery had never been at the top of her list. Kryptos, the Voynich manuscript, yes, but the Littlefield Sonnets?

"Shouldn't you have attempted it long ago? Classic American sleuthing there."

What puzzle-solving nerd hadn't attempted it? The

hundred-year-old message remained a legend. The *San Francisco Examiner* still posted it every year to commemorate the first printing. The lure of another problem aside, the Littlefield Sonnets would mean more late nights working in Hendrik's office—perhaps his apartment, too. Maybe next time she stayed the night, it wouldn't be on his couch. Anna stepped up and grasped his hand. She kissed the red blotch which appeared on his skin. "You and me?"

He nodded.

"When do we start?"

Hendrik smiled. "I'll bring you up to speed on the ride to Lisse. But first…" He picked up the coffee cup and snarled at the substance inside. He slapped the cup on the counter. "First, I need a proper cup of coffee."

With two cups of coffee vibrating on the console, Anna rested in the passenger seat of a rental car. The ride out of central Hague was shorter than most cities Anna had visited, and the city and surrounding suburbs faded into countryside. The snow-covered fields sat as flat as the Cartesian plane—windmills dotted the quadrants, and frozen canals cracked the expansive domain. As they increased their distance from the town center, the fields changed to a rolling, checkered terrain. Upon closer inspection, the patches weren't squares at all, but stripes—row upon row of narrow trenches among snowy belts.

"We're in the southern end of *Bollenstreek*, the bulb region." Hendrik thumbed in the direction of the window. "In a few months, these fields will be a rainbow of tulips. Dutch, British, and the world alike will flock to see them."

Anna turned her attention from the window to

Hendrik. "Your family grows them?"

"For over three hundred years. Van der Aart means from the earth."

Anna blinked. Hendrik's family expectations ran far deeper than hers. Her grandparents hadn't earned doctorates. Educated, for sure, but they never considered careers in academia. "How'd they take your decision to leave the farm?"

Hendrik flicked his gaze in her direction and tilted his chin. "How about I fill you in on Littlefield, instead?"

"That well, huh?" Anna laughed. She could add overbearing parents to their list of things in common. "Sure, give me the short version, wizard code-breaker."

"Well, clearly the last sonnet is the hardest of the four as no one's cracked it."

"The same could be said of Allerton," Anna reminded him.

"Exactly, which is why we're the perfect team to solve this one. The first two were decoded with a Vigenere cipher. I solved the third with a transposition cipher. But I don't think the fourth will be so easy. I think it might be—"

"Don't say it." Anna pursed her lips. "Elliptic curves?"

Hendrik looked out of the the corner of his eye. "What?" he asked in an exaggerated shriek.

Not Hendrik's elliptic curves obsession again. If he was so bent on solving a code with them, he would need to write one himself. She patted his hand. "Elliptic curves weren't even suggested in the field until 1985, Hendrik. So, you're implying Littlefield was…" She paused to recollect when the messages were printed.

"Seventy-five years ahead of his contemporaries?"

"The man was a number theory genius."

Anna groaned. "Don't let your infatuation with curved beauties steer us toward another dead-end. You said the same thing about Allerton."

"You have any better ideas?"

"Well, we could start with the obvious—try a few transpositions and search for some abelian subgroups."

"There's no numbers, Anna."

Anna laughed. "I know, I know." But there must be an easier solution to the two-line message than elliptic curves. Except, if one existed, wouldn't someone have solved it before? She sighed. "I guess I should have paid more attention in number theory."

As he drove, Hendrik barked a laugh. "I think you could have paid more attention in most of your classes, wouldn't you say?"

Anna shot him a glare. The thought of sitting through another drool-inducing lecture was enough to make her gulp the rest of her coffee.

Hendrik placed a hand on her knee, rubbing lightly.

Warmth spread through Anna's thigh, and she stared at his fingers. Long and slender, yet strong— strong enough to lift her onto the dresser with ease and hold her tight from an awkward angle. What would his hands feel like caressing her flesh? Anna shivered.

Hendrik whisked away his hand.

But Anna caught it, returned it back to her thigh, and covered his hand with hers. "No more talk of classes. Whatever Littlefield used, we'll figure it out…together."

Hopefully, they'd figure out their little *personal* problem together, too.

****

As Anna stared out at a field ribboned with snow and grass, she heard the tires roll onto a gravel drive.

Hendrik parked in front of a boxy house.

Tattered whiteboards framed the windows. Weathered wood, faded from what appeared to have once been red, wrapped the sides. On the front porch, a wooden swing creaked as it rocked back and forth. The house was so different than any Anna had ever known—no bricks like Father's brownstone or modern intercom system at the front door that allowed Mother to screen visitors to her apartment.

"I forgot to recommend wearing boots." Hendrik had made his way to her side of the car and extended a hand.

Anna stepped out, and icy flakes stung her ankles. She definitely should have opted for the combat boots in lieu of the mary janes.

"You can borrow a pair of socks."

"I'm sure a pair of your tube socks will look stunning with my jeggings." Anna smirked.

Hendrik grinned. "Relax, you look great." He draped an arm over her shoulders. "You always look great."

Anna smiled as he pulled away and started toward the house. What was she worried about, anyway? She did always look good, and so what if his family disagreed? Yes, this was the closest she'd come to officially meeting a boyfriend's parents, but Hendrik wasn't her boyfriend—technically. Even so, she'd chosen her most conservative outfit—the jeggings paired with a T-shirt she'd picked up from the math conference with the phrase *Long + Live + Math* on it.

A teenage girl swung open the front door, bursting into the snow, slippers and all. "Henri!" she shouted.

Hendrik caught her in an all-consuming hug, lifting her off her feet. "Fleur," he replied before engaging in an exchange in Dutch.

Anna didn't catch any of the words. Dutch had so many darn consonants—not like Italian, where the vowels drew out like sticky syrup.

From inside the house, a voice screeched in Dutch.

Fleur scrunched a freckled nose. "Mama!" The girl stomped back inside, dragging Hendrik with her.

Context provided enough information for Anna. Clearly, a battle between a defiant teenager and reprimanding mother loomed. With her shoes slipping on the slush, Anna struggled to keep up.

Inside, the warm glow of a fireplace illuminated an otherwise dark room. Unlike the high-end department store choices in her father's home or the sleek, ultra-modern pieces in Sarah's and Eduardo's apartment, the Van der Aart home housed more modest furnishings. A frumpy, cloth couch that looked as old as Anna sat against the far wall. A chunky coffee table built from what appeared to be reclaimed pine boards stood in front of it. In the adjacent room, the kitchen, a pot bubbled on the stove, and a knotty, wood table dressed with six plates crowded the small space. Decorative plates hung along the wall.

Hendrik huddled with his family beside the table.

All boasted hair of various shades of red. Fleur a bright tangerine. The mother, a soft apricot streaked with white. A boy, a few inches shorter than Hendrik, was topped with a shade indeciperable from Hendrik's—a fiery orange like a shiny penny. One man among them didn't have red hair—Hendrik's father? But the limited sprinkle of hair on his head made it impossible to tell if the wisps were dark blond or brown. Hendrik's family was so close—not just in appearance, but sheer proximity. A hollowness filled Anna's chest. Had her mother ever held her so close? Ever smiled so genuinely?

Hendrik's mother planted a kiss on Hendrik's cheek.

Smiling, he freed himself from the family hug and extended a hand to Anna. "Mama, Papa, Fleur, Stijn, this is Anna, my…" His cheeks reddened, and he rubbed the back of his neck.

Fleur broke into a broad smile.

Stijn elbowed Hendrik's side, grinning.

Hendrik cleared his throat. "My advisee. We traveled to the conference together."

A tightness formed in Anna's chest. Advisee? Then why had she worn the blasted mary janes? She scowled.

Hendrik blinked rapidly, then fluttered his lips as he opened and closed his mouth.

As Anna held him steadfast in her scowl, she watched his Adam's apple climb higher in his throat.

He stepped beside Anna and placed a hand on her back. "Anna is also my friend and fellow researcher. Without her, I would never have finished my work on Allerton." Grabbing her hand, he squeezed and leaned his mouth to her ear. "Better?" he whispered.

Anna grinned and nodded.

His parents exchanged hushed words.

Fleur smirked. "Your advisee," she emphasized the word, "is *lekker.*" She whistled a catcall.

Hendrik blushed.

Stijn buckled with laughter.

Hendrik's mother clucked her tongue and stepped toward Fleur and Stijn. "Welcome to our home, Anna. Now, who's hungry?"

"*Mij!*" his siblings called.

"*Goed.* Fetch me some eggs from the coop, then. While you're at it, show Hendrik *Rups.* He's been sputtering lately." She swatted Stijn on his butt with a towel she'd had slung over her shoulder and shooed Fleur along with him.

"I'll be right back," Hendrik said to Anna. "And, FYI, my father's English is limited." He dashed after his siblings but stopped and leaned close. "And don't believe anything she"—he gestured with his eyes toward his mother—"says. Especially if it has to do with my love life or career choices."

Anna raised a brow. "I'll be sure to keep that in mind."

Hendrik, Fleur, and Stijn slipped out a side door, and Mr. Van der Aart took a seat on the couch by the fire. Mrs. Van der Aart resumed her position by the stove, stirring the pot. "*Rups* is a piece of farm equipment." Mrs. Van der Aart pointed to a large barn Hendrick and his siblings approached. "It means caterpillar."

Anna smiled and stepped closer to the stove. "Cute. And *lekker*?"

Mrs. Van der Aart paused her stirring and glanced right and left. "*Lekker* is a general term. It can be used for food or"—she scanned Anna up and down—"attractive women. The literal translation is vague—hot or tasty."

Anna laughed. She could think of far worse

descriptions for Fleur to have chosen.

"Actually, Fleur has a name for most everyone and everything. She calls *Rups de vernietiger*, the destroyer. The thing is a monster—scared Fleur half to death tearing through the fields, lopping off the blooms."

"That does sound frightening. Poor flowers." She stared out the window toward the barn, trying to get a glimpse of the machine, but she only caught sight of a bucket and shovel.

"You don't know much about bulb farming, do you?"

"About as much as I know about cooking."

Mrs. Van der Aart lifted her gaze from the pot and eyed her with a raised a brow.

The expression jabbed at Anna's belly, but she held up her chin, none the less. This was the twenty-first century. She was a codebreaker and not a homemaker. She returned his mother's expression with an equally crafted arch.

Hendrik's mother laughed lightly, then gestured with her chin out the window. "We don't sell the flowers. Only the farms with…how do call? Glass buildings?"

"Greenhouses?" Anna offered.

"Yes, greenhouses. The flowers you buy in the Netherlands are only grown in them. The fields are for bulb harvesting. *Rups* clears the blooms so the bulbs will flourish. He helps us dig the bulbs in the summer, too. But anyway, Fleur was so terrified of *de vernietiger* growing up, Henri invented the nickname. 'Looks more like a caterpillar to me,' he said. 'Green body. Yellow mustache of blades. I bet one winter he's gonna turn into a butterfly in the barn.' "

The firmness with which Anna held her body softened. Hendrik a storyteller? Two weeks ago, she wouldn't have thought Hendrik capable of imagining anything other than math annotations. The gift of the bracelet—Anna examined the mobius band on her wrist. His actions last night, and now *Rups* made Hendrik as foreign to her as the Dutch his family spoke.

Mrs. Van der Aart turned away from the stove. "May I offer you some cheese? You look like you might turn into a butterfly yourself and float away."

Anna grinned, nodded, and took a moment to examine the rest of Mrs. Van der Aart. Like her children, she was sturdy, not petite like Anna. With broad shoulders and narrow waist, she stood about as tall as Anna's father.

Mrs. Van der Aart retrieved a waxed wheel from the counter and cut off a wedge. "Edam, the name of a Dutch town." She handed it to Anna.

"That much I did know." Anna nibbled her cheese. The cheese was firm and mild in flavor; it melted in her mouth. As she savored it, she turned her attention to the painted plates on the wall. Each depicted a flower.

Mrs. Van der Aart returned to the stove. "Have you and Henri been friends long?"

Anna stopped in front of a purple flower—a tulip from its cupped shape, colored a deep violet. "A few months. We started working together after Cayley's illness."

"What a shame about Professor Cayley. Henri is still upset."

"Is he?" Anna stepped to the next plate. A yellow tea-cup and saucer. A daffodil. Anna scrunched her nose—they reminded her too much of a duck's beak.

"*Ja*. Called home three times in October. And Henri calls home about as frequently as he brings a girl to visit."

Her heart skipped a beat, and Anna flicked her gaze in Mrs. Van der Aart's direction.

"Not since his school days. I don't remember why she was here—probably needed help with her maths. That subject always fascinated him. I could never get him away from his books."

Anna giggled. Finally, something she didn't find surprising in the least.

Mrs. Van der Aart pointed to a plate nearest the door overlooking the fields. "That flower's Henri's favorite."

Anna crossed to it. A vibrant pink, with a base of creamy white that streaked the sides, the tulip stood out among the others on the wall. "It's beautiful. What is it called?"

"*Zomerschoon*."

Anna gasped and nearly dropped her cheese. "Come again?"

"*Zomerschoon*. Our most expensive bulb, and our most rare. Hendrik insists on keeping the blossoms, instead of crushing them like the others. We press them and make them into bookmarks, frame them…"

Mrs. Van der Aart rattled on, but Anna's thudding pulse drowned out her voice. She held up her wrist, turning it until the inscription came into view. She traced her finger over the letters, the word she'd meant to look up since Hendrik had given it to her, yet it had somehow slipped her mind.

Hendrik burst through the back door, his grease-stained hands holding a basket of chicken eggs. "We bring forth eggs!" He crossed to his mother and placed them on the table.

Anna stole one last glance at her bracelet before tucking her arm behind her and shifting her gaze toward Hendrik. *Zomerschoon*. Why had he engraved the bracelet with it? Had something about her reminded him of that flower?

Mrs. Van der Aart shooed the three kids like hens in a pen, doling each a task. Hendrik was charged with returning to the barn to tune up *Rups*. Stijl served as his assistant. Anna sighed. When could she ask him why he inscribed the name of the pink-flamed tulip onto his gift?

****

After dinner, empty bowls lined the kitchen table, and crumbs scattered over the tablecloth. Anna leaned back in her chair, satisfied with the warm beef stew and braised cabbage. Unlike any dish she'd enjoyed before, the meal suited the farming family. Thank goodness her jeggings had some stretch.

Fleur cleared the table, and Stijl approached, holding a long wooden board.

Anna tipped onto her elbows for a closer inspection. The long, glossy box spanned the length of the dining table and resembled a wooden shuffleboard.

"*Sjoelen*." Hendrik removed a handful of disks from the box. "You slide them into the slots. The great Dutch pastime."

"Like cornhole?" Anna asked.

Hendrik lifted a brow. "Cornhole?"

Mrs. Van der Aart brought steaming mugs of coffee and a plate of cookies. "Cornhole?" she repeated.

But the cookies already drew in Anna. With a

golden-brown finish, the cookies smelled of butter and sugar. Forget being full from the lumberjack dinner. Anna waved a hand in the air. "Just a silly game. Tell me about *Sjoelen.*" She snatched a cookie from the plate.

Hendrik explained the rules.

She downed three cookies while he talked. Thirty pucks. Four slots, each labeled one through four. Three turns to get all the pucks in. Highest score wins.

Mr. Van der Aart threw the first round.

Anna continued to savor the cookies. The flaky discs reminded her of Scottish shortbread, only better. "I need this recipe," Anna groaned.

"It's a family recipe." Mrs. Van der Aart smiled and picked up a cookie. "I'm sure Hendrik can make you some."

Anna gave Hendrik a sidelong glance.

He shifted his gaze, avoiding hers. "No crumbs on the board." He stood.

Anna stuck out her tongue.

Mr. Van der Aart passed the pucks to Hendrik.

Fleur sat next to Anna. "Don't mind, Henri. He's too afraid of losing to me." She gave Hendrik a shove just as the puck left his hand. It hit the rail and ricocheted to stop before making it through a slot.

"*Stront!*" Hendrik shot her a glare.

"Just giving Anna an edge."

Hendrik rolled his eyes.

Fleur turned her attention to Anna. "High score is one hundred forty-eight."

"One hundred forty-eight?" Even if she landed all thirty pucks into the four slots, she still would only manage one hundred twenty.

"Your score doubles for each complete set. You know, getting a puck into the one, two, three, and four. So instead of earning the face value of ten, you get twenty points."

"Ah. How nice of you to explain that part of the scoring, Hendrik." Anna nudged his elbow.

Hendrik grinned. "I figured you'd catch on."

Anna did a quick mental computation. "Seven complete sets scores one hundred forty. Land the remaining two pucks into the four slot and voila, one hundred forty-eight."

"Told you she would catch on." Hendrik depressed his grin.

"It's not Anna you have to worry about. You're rusty." Fleur rubbed together her palms. "It's time for your winning streak to end."

Hendrik collected his missed pucks for his final turn.

If Anna's skills in skeeball—or any other sport for that matter—were any prediction, she'd be of no help assisting in Hendrik's downfall. Unless…

Hendrik clutched the final puck in his hand.

"Watch this," she whispered in Fleur's ear, then stood.

Hendrik pulled back his arm.

Just as he flicked his hand forward, Anna leaned in and kissed his cheek.

Hendrik flinched, his cheeks burning bright, and faltered. The puck missed its target.

Fleur hooted.

Mr. and Mrs. Van der Aart roared with laughter.

And Hendrik sank back into his chair. "Thanks." He crossed his arms over his chest.

His tone was tight, but his lips flickered a smile.

He handed a stack of pucks to Fleur. "All right, missy. Why don't you show Anna how it's done?"

Fleur smiled and took the pucks.

Anna eased back in her chair, warmth spreading from her lifted cheeks to her full belly. Is this what quality time with family felt like? If only she could have it with her family. She dropped her gaze. No, that wasn't possible. Was it?

Chapter 17

Late that night, back in The Hague, Anna walked with Hendrik out of the rental car agency. Lights shimmered on the cobblestone streets, and her breath puffed in the frigid air. Anna rubbed together her hands and studied Hendrik's. Grease still tinged them. "I never knew you were a mechanic." She could add that to the growing list of things she'd learned about him that day—doting older brother, cookie baker, and undefeated *Sjoelen* player. Well, undefeated until her peck on the cheek opened the door for Fleur's victory.

Hendrik shrugged and shoved his hands in his pockets. "When you live on a farm, you need to be a lot of things."

She followed him in the direction of the hotel. "Close to your family seems also to be among them."

"A successful farm requires that tight bond."

Anna pursed her lips, knowing Hendrik's family interactions were about so much more than running a business. Their close hugs, ultra-competitive games, and even their food were all made with more love than Anna's mother had ever shown her. The Van der Aart affection seeped into Anna. She never felt so welcome and—she glanced at the bracelet on her wrist—never received such a thoughtful gift.

At the hotel, Hendrik opened the door.

She stepped inside and ran a finger over the cool

metal around her wrist. Now would be as good a time as any to ask him about the inscription. She intended to ask during the car ride back. But she asked so many other questions, instead. What was the difference betweeen gouda and edam? When would Hendrik make her some of those cookies? And would he take her back to see the tulips in the spring?

Of course, he answered all her questions, including a promise for cookies and a return visit. But somehow, she never brought up the bracelet. Perhaps she avoided the discussion because it might make his feelings for her real—feelings which could change. Or maybe she feared the inscription meant nothing more than a sentiment to his favorite flower.

"Long day." Hendrik yawned as they arrived at their rooms. "Early train ride tomorrow."

Anna nodded. Tomorrow they would head back to Oxford. Tomorrow they would be in the spotlight again—no more stolen kisses, and no more nights spent in each others' rooms. But they still had tonight. She dropped her hand and lifted one side of her mouth. "You want to give me a ride on your dresser again?"

Hendrik flushed as he scoffed. "Want and should have completely different meanings." Unlocking the door to his room, he opened it.

Anna snuck beneath his arm and ducked into the room before him. "What about a goodnight kiss?" She placed her hands on his chest. "How long will your dimples remain after one of those?"

As he entered the room, Hendrik chuckled and rubbed his chin. "That depends."

"On what? Who's giving the kiss or how good it is?"

Hendrik smiled. "Both."

Anna's pulse soared. Was this a challenge? Because she'd be damned if she ever passed up one of those. "Sit in the chair," she commanded.

Hendrik shook his head.

"What? You want a proper kiss, Mr. Six-Inches-Taller-Than-Me? Then sit. Or would you rather the bed?"

"No, no." Hendrik raised his hands. "The chair is fine." He eased onto the seat.

Anna approached, hovered over him, and cupped his cheek in a hand. She kissed him deeply, stroking his cheek with her thumb. She drew back. "How about that?" She smirked.

Hendrik smiled, revealing not one dimple, but two. "I said make me smile but not drive me to the cusps of insanity."

Anna burst with laughter.

He stood and kissed her forehead. "I'm not sure I can take another night on the floor." He rubbed the small of his back.

Anna lifted the side of her mouth. "I know a way to take care of that."

"Anna." He drew out her name.

She pursed her lips. "All right, all right. Waist up, I promise."

Hendrik stared down but then he wrapped his arms around her.

She clung to him, his arms enclosing her in an envelope of warmth. If only she could stay there forever. If only she could feel this love from him—from his family—forever.

****

The next morning, the train back to London zoomed out of the station. With the caffeine from the pit-stop coffee yet to kick in, Anna remained content in her dreamy state. As she sank into the *Eurostar* seat, she returned her mind to awakening in the hotel, warm in Hendrik's arms. She'd kept her promise, but they had made progress. Hendrik hadn't slept on the floor; he slept in the bed, his long, lean arms cradling her through the night. And now, he sat beside her with his smooth, shaven cheek just inches from hers.

Hendrik shifted in the seat beside her, pulling a notepad from his backpack. "So"—he scribbled on the pad with a black fountain pen—"Littlefield." Without referencing anything, Hendrik neatly wrote two lines of letters in box-print.

"You've been working on this too long." Anna leaned her head onto his upper arm. The scent of his cologne mixed with those of his family's home which remained on his shirt: butter cookies, soil, and beer. Anna closed her eyes and imagined herself in that home, playing *Sjoelen* with his family, baking cookies with his mother, and strolling through the tulip fields with Hendrik.

"Tell me what you see," Hendrik said.

Anna opened her eyes and stared at the text. Consonants. Vowels. The English alphabet. No symbols nor numbers, either—an oddity since the other three contained Sonnet references. Just as every other time she'd studied the bewildering message, nothing stood out. "It looks like someone sat on a keyboard."

Hendrik laughed.

His movement jostled her from the comfort of his support. "Exactly. I've stared at this text for more hours than you've studied at Oxford." He cleared his throat. "Bad choice of words. More hours than *most normal* grad students have studied at Oxford."

Anna jabbed an elbow into his side.

He laughed again. "But that's all I see, too."

His voice resumed a somber tone—a steady and uncertain tone. "What have you tried?" she asked.

Hendrik raised a brow. "The better question is what haven't I tried."

"We both know that answer."

Hendrik sighed.

Anna stared again at the text and pinched together her brows. "I know you have your heart set on cracking an elliptic-curve encryption. Why, I don't know. We're talking hours…no, months at a computer. And unless you've been hiding something, your comptuer skills aren't up to par. And as much as I might want to be Lizbeth Salander, I'm just a puzzle solver. And you are, too." She poked the paper in front of him. "And so was Littlefield. He didn't have a computer because they weren't even invented yet. So how could he have coded to one hundred twenty-eight-bit security?"

"We both know it can be done."

Anna swatted the air. "Littlefield was an algebraist, not a number theory man. To encrypt a message…even a teensie one like this, without a computer would have taken him half a lifetime. He had more pressing things to do—work on Jacobian matrices or Jordan Canonical forms. There must be something more to this message." She picked up the paper and stared intently. Maybe the solution would slap her in the face? Maybe she just needed time to pick up on a clue?

The train slowed, the wheels squealing as it

rounded a curve then lurched back to full speed. The light outside dimmed, then was gone.

They'd entered the tunnel.

Hendrik reached for the overhead light.

But Anna caught his wrist at the same time as she released an exaggerated yawn. "I think"—she placed the sheet of paper on her forehead, shielding her eyes from the light of nearby seats—"I'll try a little osmosis." She closed her eyes, seeing the jumble of letters in front of her—none of them making a bit of sense. "At the very least, a little nap won't hurt." Just before she nodded off, she heard Hendrik's gentle chuckle followed by his arm threading between her shoulders and the seat as he tucked her close.

When they reached Oxford, a snowy lull enveloped the town. Untouched white roofs sat above snow-covered porches gleaming in the afternoon sun. White-ribbon banisters, undisturbed by mittened hands, led the way into doorways brimmed with wreaths. The scene was as picturesque as the snowy waves of Netherland's countryside—as quiet, too. While excited tourists filled the shopping streets, the side streets, including the street where Anna lived, showed no signs of life. The students still remained away, visiting their families.

Anna pulled her jacket tighter as she and Hendrik approached her dingy doorway. The dust of undisturbed snow on her front steps indicated Conner must also be away.

Hendrik carried her bag inside. As he dropped it by the front door, he scanned the room.

"It's not as glamorous as your place," Anna said. "No desk in the kitchen. No whiteboard to stare at from the couch." She took a step into the living room, a space no larger than her father's master bathroom. "We do have a much-coveted TV." She waved a hand over the TV with a flick of the wrist. "No cable," she added. "But streaming service. Want to watch something?"

Hendrik smiled and drew close. "I should get back, unpack, and prepare for next term—all that stuff post-docs are supposed to do be doing."

"See you tomorrow? We could work on Littlefield. And visit Cayley."

"Sure." He shoved his hands in his pockets and dropped his gaze. "We should meet at my office."

Her heart lodged in her throat. "Okay." Her voice came out in a croak.

Hendrik grabbed his bag and turned to go.

A hollowness seeped into her chest. Were they back to just collegues again? Or not even that—teacher and student? Hendrik's sensibilities were practical—waiting for intimacy was the proper thing to do. And God forbid if they did anything to jeopardize his career. He was so close now. In two terms, he'd be free of Oxford, ready to begin a new journey somewhere she wouldn't be under his supervision. A surge of energy rushed down her arms to her wrists. Only, before they returned to their academic relationship, she needed to know one thing. Anna raised her hand, and the soft moonlight dipping through the window glinted off the bracelet. She placed a hand on his shoulder. "The inscription on my bracelet, *zomerschoon*." His shoulder tensed beneath her hand. "I've been meaning to ask you about it."

Hendrik took a deep breath, but he kept his body facing away. "*Zomerschoon* is one of the varieties of tulips we grow—a very rare and beautiful flower whose bulbs are highly sought after. The literal translation of the word *zomerschoon* is the beauty of summer."

"But why did you inscribe it on my braclet?"

He paused, keeping his gaze on the window. He blinked and gave a slow exhalation. "Because Anna, you are my *zomerschoon*—my beauty and beloved."

His voice was so quiet Anna held her breath for fear she might miss a word. Warmth brewed in her chest, but not just with stale breath, but because her heart felt like it would melt. Anna gripped his shoulder, spinning him around to face her. A pink as bright as the color she remembered on the *zomerschoon's* petals painted his cheeks. Anna tipped forward on her toes, placing a hand on his hot cheek, and kissed him on the lips—a gentle kiss, a soft kiss, like gulls' wings dipping in the ocean's froth. And even though he hardly returned her kiss, the sun lifted within her, rosy and warm, and her resolve not to tempt him broke. All her emotions crashed in her chest like a suffocating wave.

She shifted her hands to his chest and brought her forehead to his, resting her nose against his. His breath quickened and warmed her mouth which was still inches from his. "Stay with me." She'd meant the words as question; yet, they came out as more of a statement.

The muscles beneath her hands tightened. His breath clamped down, leaving only a raspy croak."Anna…please. We can't."

"I know we shouldn't." She fell back into the weightless atmosphere where everything was different. No judgment. No expectations. Only her and Hendrik. She kissed him, the headiness returning as she tasted the coffee on his breath and felt the softness of his full mouth. Then his hands on her arms, gently resisting her.

"Anna," he groaned through her kisses.

She drew back and stared. His amber eyes glistened with desire, but behind them rested something else—a caring and an innocence. "I love you," she whispered, the words spilling out without her even thinking them first.

Hendrik stared, his jaw slightly ajar and his eyes widened.

"I love you, Hendrik," she repeated louder—perhaps to prove it to him as much as to herself. She had no doubt in her voice, and no doubt in her mind, either. Whether she wanted to be in love or not, she knew it was true.

In an instant, Hendrik tugged her back and pressed his mouth against hers.

He kissed her with the same unrestraint showed in the hotel. Long and deep, his kiss seemed to lift her off her feet. And after a moment, she realized they actually had.

Hendrik lifted her and carried her to the couch. His hands roamed her body: her hips, her waist, and her arms.

The eagerness of his touch sent a rush of warmth coursing through her body. She clawed at his neck. She ran her fingers through his hair. She tore at his shirt.

He leaned back and lifted his shirt over his head.

She tugged him back, kissing his collarbone. She swept her nose over the notch beneath his neck. Her pulse quickened, and she let her hands roam. She traced a line over his shoulders.

Hendrik responded with a groan.

Yet, through his moans, Anna heard the whoosh of

air, the shuffle of feet, and the door snapping closed. She froze.

"I thought we agreed such activities would take place behind closed doors," Conner said.

Hendrick jerked away.

Anna sprung to her feet. "God damn it, Conner. I thought you—" The words stuck in her throat, because not only did Conner stand in the doorway, but a girl did, too. And even though Conner's lanky body hid her, the girl, with curly red hair and a scrawny frame, looked as much like Klara as Anna did Rapunzel. Anna smoothed her shirt, gritted her teeth, and flared her nostrils.

Conner laughed. "Don't get so uptight, Calculus. Your friend's nudity doesn't bother me."

Anna stepped forward and ticked a brow. "I can name a few people who'd be bothered to find out about yours."

Conner gasped, then glowered. "You wouldn't dare."

"Why wouldn't I? Klara is my friend. And she cares about you—really cares about you."

"Professor Van der Aaart?"

Anna and Conner both whipped their gaze to the side.

The girl stepped forward and stared into the room—not at Anna, but at Hendrik.

"Professor, eh?" Conner gave a mischievous grin.

Anna faced Hendrik, but he was already moving.

As he wrangled his shirt back on, he brushed past Anna, his gaze not meeting hers, grabbed his suitcase, and rushed out the door.

Anna hurried to catch up.

As she neared Conner, he grabbed her arm. "I won't tell if you don't," he whispered in her ear.

Anna shot him a glare, but she had no time to argue. The door had already slammed behind Hendrik.

Outside, Hendrik rushed down the stairs and charged down the street, one arm gripping his suitcase, his other yanking on his coat.

"Hendrik!" Anna shouted, increasing her fast walk to a jog.

He turned, let go of the suitcase handle, and fumbled with the zipper of his jacket.

His face hunkered down like a fist, his eyebrows scrunched, and his lips formed a scowl. And his eyes—his Indian ale eyes had darkened to a shade closer to burnt orange. "God dammit, Anna. I told you this would happen." He tore at the zipper, thrusting it up in a whipping movement. "Now all of bloody Oxford will know we're together before Hilary term has even started."

"No." Anna reached him, her breaths ragged. "They won't. I promise they won't." Her breathing slowed, and she stared at the clouds of their shaky breaths. What was she promising? What confidence with Klara would she have to break to keep Conner and the redhead temptress from spreading the rumor?

The cold air caught in her throat, its iciness jabbing at her neck like a knife; it burned her chest and suffocated her voice.

Hendrik didn't speak either. He just stared with his fiery eyes, unblinking—unwavering.

Suddenly, Anna felt the weightlessness return. Only this time, because she was going to fall, she reached for Hendrik.

But he stepped back.

Anna stumbled forward, and her hand caught a lightpost, dark and cold. Frozen, both in body and mind, she stared down the street.

Hendrik strode away.

Could she ever make things right?

Chapter 18

A quietness pervaded Cayley's hospital room. No nurses milled about. No attendants pushed creaky carts. Only Anna and Cayley occupied the room. A few Christmas cards lined the nightstand—one from the dean, another from *your friend, Charlie.* But no cards from family existed, that Anna could tell—nothing from a daughter, son, or wife, either.

Anna removed a box of toaster pastries from her backpack and added it to the stack of shortbread cookies that still remained. "From the US," she said. "A little on the sweet side, but I don't think you'll mind. Oh, and I tried some other cookies recently— *Boterkoek.* They're buttery and crisp, like the ones in the blue tin, only better. Perhaps I'll have Hen—" She caught herself. Hendrik wouldn't make butter cookies for her anytime soon, let alone Cayley. She strummed her fingers on the bed railing. "Well, maybe I'll bring you the blue tin, anyway. I'm sure they're not *that* much different."

She waited. Perhaps today would be the day he opened his eyes, lifted his fuzzy, white brows, and returned to being her advisor. Then everything would be as it should. She wouldn't have to worry about Hendrik or Conner, either. Anna cleared her throat and took Cayley's hand in hers. "The conference went well. I got an offer at the NSA, and Hendrik had a line of prospectives so long you would have thought he'd opened a hot dog stand." She squeezed his hand. Cold and stiff, his fingers didn't squeeze back. "But I don't think his family will be happy if he goes anywhere outside the Netherlands—maybe Belgium, but definitely not off mainland Europe."

Anna paused. She loosened her grip on his hand, and it limply settled back to the blanket. His chest raised and lowered in a legato rhythm.

Please wake up, Cayley. Hendrik needs you. I need you.

A machine beeped. The radiator hummed. But Cayley didn't move.

A coldness seeped into Anna's chest, and tears threatened to fall. Four months he'd lain here. Four months and the only sign of progress remained a tiny squeeze. Had she imagined it?

Squeezing his hand again, she blinked the tears from her eyes. "Hendrik and I are working on the Littlefield Sonnets now." Well, would be working on it whenever Hendrik decided to return her calls. "I bet we'll have it solved before the end of Hilary term. Won't that be something to wake up to? Not one, but two riddles solved?"

Anna waited for him to squeeze her hand…to smile…to do something. But only the soft whistle of his breath filled the room, and the coolness of his crinkled hand rested beneath hers. Anna released a heavy breath, leaned forward, kissing Cayley on the forehead, and then left. Did any hope remain in him awakening?

****

When Anna returned to her room, she found it as quiet as Cayley's. She'd been home two days, and her suitcase still remained unopened. Atop her bed, having needed a change of sheets, blankets piled high. She checked her phone for about the umpteenth-billion time that day and found no messages from Hendrik. There'd been no sign of Conner, either. His mystery siren hadn't reappeared, either.

She sighed, flopped onto the bed, and stared at the ceiling. Her mind filled with the arbitary letters of the Littlefield sonnet. Like an efficient machine, she shifted the letters mentally. She sorted them and swapped them. She searched for repititions and outliers. But she found nothing—just a random list of consonants and vowels strung together by a thread she couldn't see.

"Damn it!" She bolted up in bed. She'd been thinking about the seventy letters almost nonstop since Hendrik left. Attempting to crack the Littlefield code was about all she could do to keep her mind off him. And Conner. And…Klara.

But she was missing something, and the gnawing in her gut told her it had nothing to do with elliptic curves. Fishing through the pile of papers by her bed, she found the one with the other three Littlefield messages—the ones which had been decoded.

The first was printed August 1, 1912 in the *San Francisco Examiner*. The solution printed following week:

This bud of love, by summer's ripening breath, May prove a beauteous flower when next we meet. W.S. Romeo and Juliet, A2, S1, L46.

The second was printed exactly two weeks after the first. The solution found, again the following week:

Take all my love, my love, yea take them all; What has thou then more than thou hadst before? W.S. S40

Anna compared the messages to the fourth message, the undeciphered one:

Sdllkweroijc weon wefnd sdlfkdp weaprovn awekcvi aweanc awemc guyhiaf.

Both of the solved ones contained numbers, the act and scene numbers, or the sonnet. The fourth message didn't have a word with two letters nor an indication of numbers. Was the fourth message not from a work of Shakespeare? Maybe Wordsworth? No, he didn't write about love...did he? Robert Frost? No, no, no! Much too late. Anna hmphed. Why hadn't she paid more attention in literature class? She read the remaining message, again, from Shakespeare.

The third was printed October 1, 1912. The solution took longer to find, two weeks, which was understandable as this was the longest of the messages.

Shall I compare thee to a summer's day? Thou art more lovely and more temperate: Rough winds do shake the darling buds of May, And summer's lease hath all too short a date...So long as men can breathe or can see, So long lives this, and this gives life to thee. W.S. S18.

All contained the hallmark X.X. pattern in the encryped message. Why would Littlefield deviate from Shakespeare? Maybe the pattern became too obvious? Maybe the readers clamored for more? Or, maybe Littlefield tired of Shakespeare—God knew Anna had. Verses on love were the last thing she wanted to read right now.

She tossed the paper to the floor and stared back at the ceiling. The image of the *zomerschoon* engraving flashed in her mind: the gracefully brushed pink strokes, the curvy script of the letters beneath, and

Hendrik's whispered words, "rare and sought after—the beauty of summer." The words moved her more than Shakespeare's and touched her more than any she'd heard before. Her heartbeat fluttered, then lulled. Her eyes widened, then filled with tears. Would Hendrik still feel the same way about her? Would he still hold her so dear?

On the floor, her phone buzzed. Anna scrambled off the bed and snatched it up. But Hendrik wasn't on the line. "Hi, Dad," she said through a sigh. "Enjoying having your house back to yourself?"

"To some extent. I wouldn't mind having someone to share a pizza with."

The beginnings of a smile twitched her mouth, but Anna didn't let it take hold. Neither she nor her father finished the perfect New York-style pie.

Mother trashed the last piece and dumped the rest of the cola down the sink, too.

She sank back onto the bed, running a hand through her hair. Greasy at the scalp, her hair remained stiff at the ends. When was the last time she'd washed it? "I wouldn't mind having some company here, either." The words slipped out, and she paused her hands mid-comb, gripping a lock. When was the last time she'd been so candid with her father? She twirled the dry ends in her fingers, waiting for his response. Would he give her a fatherly response or a Mom-inspired lecture on the impacts of social life on her career?

He cleared his throat. "Anna, I'm calling to apologize."

Anna dropped the strands from her grasp. She expected him to ignore her grief, but to offer an apology? She swallowed hard. "For what?"

A heavy sigh rushed the line. "For Christmas, rather what should have been Christmas: for not taking you to the tree, for not finishing the thriller series, and for not building that boat."

His words cut through the wall she'd constructed around herself—the inpenetrable barrier that shielded her from her feelings with her parents, with Hendrik…with anyone. She sniffled and brushed the tears that began to fall down her cheeks.

"I'm sorry, Anna," he continued. "You came so far to spend Christmas, and our visit was more like a seance."

A small laugh escaped her lips. "Yeah, a seance to the research Gods. If left to Mother, I should start sacrificing small animals."

"Well, I know where you can get a stockpile of frogs."

"Do you think the research Gods would accept some toasty frogs? Maybe we should just burn down the whole lab."

Father laughed.

Although she couldn't see him, she imagined his smile would crinkle his brown eyes and dimple his cheeks.

"Only if you promise to hit my office, too. I can't believe we go back in a week. I'm still having nightmares of term papers from last semester."

"You sound about as eager as I do to get back to classes." Anna sat forward on her bed, resting her elbows on her knees, as she brought the phone closer to her ear. "Dad," she said, again surprising herself with her candor, "if you're tired of life at Northeastern, why don't you leave?"

"Where would I go?"

"You could retire," she suggested.

He laughed.

His laughter was so loud, her eardrum ached.

"And you think you're getting hounded by your mother? I can't even imagine the wrath she'd unleash if I even mentioned the "r" word."

Anna shook her head. Of course he'd throw the Mom-card, but the question still remained. "Seriously, Dad. Would you like to retire?"

His steady breath muffled the line. "I don't know, Anna. What would I do?"

"I'm sure you could think of something. There's always Swedish thrillers," she added.

"Well, I could build a boat—I mean, a real boat. Maybe take it out on the bay."

"Yes." The response was automatic, because her mind drifted off. Suddenly, she realized why her father had taken up the models. His father, her grandfather, built them, as well. And not just models, he'd sailed, too.

A fuzzy memory emerged in her mind. A sticky summer day on the Cape. Waves crashed in a frothy brine against the rocky coast. Gulls silently dove into the horizon, emerging with an unidentifiable plunder. Grandfather's boat rocked on the gentle waves, and her father tugged ropes, guiding the sails, as he drove his feet into the hull, leaning his back so close to the water it sprayed his face.

How old had she been? And where was Mother? All she remembered was Father's playful grin and the sails whipping in the wind.

"Anna?"

Father's voice jolted her back to the present. Her stomach dipped, as if she still sat on the bobbing sailboat. "Sorry…I…" She stumbled on her words. Should she bring up the memory? Would it make Father happy or only fester at old wounds?

"I should let you go," he said. "I know you're busy."

Anna hesitated, the memory of the sailing outing still tugging at her mind, then she numbly replied. "Yes."

Once they ended the call with their traditional "talk to you soons," Anna climbed off her bed, crossed to her dresser, and dug through the bottom drawer. Beneath her wrinkled clothes she found her scruffy carnival prize. As she hugged the dog close, a warmth blossomed in her chest. If only Father wasn't bound to Mother's ridiculous research rat race. She glanced at the pile of papers on the floor. If only Hendrik wasn't, either.

On the other side of the wall, something thudded. The dresser shook and the mirror, which leaned precariously against it, rattled.

" 'Love alters not with his brief hours and weeks,' " Conner's muffled voice resonated through the wall.

Anna released a low growl and shoved her back into the dresser. It slammed against the wall, sending the mirror crashing to the floor. "The walls aren't soundproof!"

A series of giggles followed, and then muted chatter. "No reason you should be listening," Conner called back.

A tightness replaced the mellowness in Anna's

chest. She grabbed the fallen mirror—at least it hadn't broken—and clutched the meager frame so hard she thought it would snap. Heaving raspy breaths, she stared at the wall. If she didn't get out of here soon, she'd make Conner the first man in history with a mirror for a backside.

Tossing the mirror on the bed, she kicked the pile of papers on the floor. Whether from Conner's mouth or Littlefield's pen, she'd suffered enough Shakespeare for one day. She grabbed her phone and rushed out the door.

Outside, the dimming light brought with it an air so frigid, it chilled Anna to the core. She hugged her arms, rubbing her shoulders and wishing she remembered to grab a coat on her way out the door. Her feet slid on the slippery cobblestone, but they didn't hesitate in their direction. Timber-framed storefronts held *closed* signs in their windows. As she passed New College, light glowed in the enclosed pedestrian bridge, The Bridge of Sighs. Another two blocks north and three east landed her on Hendrik's doorstep. A light shone through the window overlooking the street, and Anna hurried to the porch.

Cigarette butts overflowed the ashtray. A soda can served to collect the overflow. Smoke from a recently lit one drifted from the can, and the smell burned Anna's nose and stung her eyes. Hendrik hadn't smoked, at least in her presence, since they began working together. She had no doubt in her mind that she'd been the cause of his relapse. Anna slumped her shoulders as she raised a fist to the door and knocked. How could she make this right? How could she not compromise Hendrik's career without betraying her friend?

The door creaked open just wide enough for Hendrik to poke out his head.

His hair looked more disheveled than ever. Red stubble replaced his usual smooth cheeks. His eyes, absent of their usual gleam, looked tired…sad.

"Anna, you…you…" He narrowed the door's opening. "You shouldn't be here."

His voice was as gruff as his appearance. Anna placed a hand on the door, pushing against it.

But Hendrik held it firmly in place.

Her heart sank. "I'm sorry, Hendrik. I'm so sorry."

Hendrik sighed and dropped his head, resting it on the doorknob. "This situation is as much my fault as it is yours." His exhalation sent his smoky breath into the night. It fogged before dissappearing.

Anna shivered and wrapped herself tighter in her arms. "No, I should have waited—should have listened to you. Now everything is such a mess. I'm sorry." She stared at her shoes, waiting for him to respond, but only the buzz of the streetlamp filled her ears. She cast her gaze upward, but he only stared with his dull eyes. The coldness grew inside, and Anna inched forward into the threshold, drawing nearer to the warmth—nearer to him. "Hendrik, please, can I come in? Just to talk…or even to work on Littlefield."

He frowned, stepping back from the door. "We both know that's not a good idea. How many more people do you want to give cause for speculation? As it is, I've been racking my head how to keep Conner's and Laney's mouths shut."

"Don't worry about…Laney, you said it was? She was too drunk to remember much of anything. She probably won't even remember Conner. That's the way he likes 'em, sloppy and lusty. As for Conner…" She dropped her gaze. Did Hendrik even realize the predicament she was in? Had she mentioned Klara's one-sided relationship with Conner? Even if she had, Hendrik likely wouldn't understand the besties' obligiation to reveal Conner's cheating. Keeping the bargain with Conner, and not saying saying anything to Klara, was a BFF mortal sin. Shaking away the thought, Anna exhaled a tight breath. "Don't worry about him," she finally managed. "I'll take care of it." She held as confident a face as she could fake—chin up, eyebrows raised, and lips in a tight line.

Rubbing his scruffy chin, Hendrik held her gaze.

Anna's eyes burned from want of blinking, but she dared not look away.

Finally, Hendrik nodded. At the same time, he eased his hold on the door.

The deflation in her chest lifted, and Anna leaned forward, preparing for his invitation to enter.

"It's late," he said.

Every ounce of hope died with his words. Her insides sagged, like her organs would all start failing one by one. She'd be the youngest person in history to die and not have a single organ to harvest.

"Get yourself home before you freeze to death." He closed the door an inch. "Tomorrow, or maybe the next, we can start on Littlefield."

"Right." Anna forced a smile but knew it came off as a grimace. "G'night, Hendrik." She gave a perfuctory salute and spun on her heel. A whoosh of air from the closing door hit her back, sending shivers down her already frigid skin. She started down the road, not in the direction of her apartment—that was definitely out of the question. But to where, she wasn't sure.

Chapter 19

Anna awoke groggy. She rubbed her eyes and adjusted to the light. Her back ached, and her butt was sore like she'd been paddled. She wasn't hungover—thank God for that—but if she had to choose between a tempered headache and her body feeling like it'd been through a train wreck, she'd choose the former. Why in the hell did she feel like every muscle in her body had been pummeled?

She scanned the room. Cayley's dusty desk sat behind her. His whiteboard, pristine and clean, stood in front. She sat up, arched her back, and stretched her arms in the air. Apparently, at some time past midnight, crashing in his office as opposed to a chair in the common space seemed like a good idea. In theory, since no one occupied the office for the better part of four months, the room should be clean. Not so much. Stale cookie crumbs poked her back, and dust tickled her nose. Did housekeeping not believe in vacuuming?

She brushed off the crumbs and stood. At least she hadn't crammed herself into a chair all night—or worse, woken up in an unknown person's bed. The threat of such an encounter kept her clear of the bars last night. She'd gotten lucky with a paperclip on Cayley's lock. But the night away from Conner did nothing to help her predicament. She still had no idea how to tell Klara her boyfriend was a dirtbag without incriminating Hendrik. She yawned. Love might be helping her binge-drinking habit, but the same couldn't be true for her problem solving. Was being in love making her stupid?

Discarding the thought, she grabbed her phone. The battery had drained to six percent. Ugh. She definitely needed her charger. Would Conner be gone? She couldn't stand facing him without a plan of attack. She sighed. Maybe she could go to Hendrik's. No, he clearly said he would call her, and she didn't need to dig that hole any deeper. She scanned her messages finding none from him, but one from Klara.

—Coming back tomorrow. Can't wait to see you…and Conner!—

She finished the text with a kissing emoji. Bile rose to her mouth. She must tell Klara. But if the news came from her, Conner would blow the whistle on Hendrik. She tapped her index finger to her forehead. *This isn't elliptic curves, Anna. You can figure this out.*

But only thoughts of her bed and what she would eat for breakfast flitted in her mind. Not one lightbulb went off on how to nail Conner's coffin. Sighing, she stepped toward the door. Sleep, food, and a charged phone always helped in the past. Hopefully, they would now.

When she arrived back at her apartment, she found Conner's door was closed. Great. Conner usually left it open when he wasn't in—probably to air out the stench of body fluids. Anna snorted. Who was he kidding? Scouring every square inch of his room with bleach still wouldn't remove all the venereal diseases that lurked inside. What did Klara see in him? She shook her head. Poor Klara. Why did her first big-time crush have to be on the Don Giovanni of Oxford?

Finding her charger, Anna could think of only one person who could offer love advice: Sarah. With her phone tethered to a wall socket, Anna found the contact for her friend in Rome. Sarah's heart had been broken and healed more times than Hendrik's mother had cracked an egg. If anyone would know would to do, she would. She jabbed the green button.

"Uh oh," Sarah answered. "What turmoil happened in the Netherlands?"

"Can't a phone call deliver good news?" Anna crashed onto her bed.

"Not yours. Good news from you only comes in the form of emojis."

Anna laughed. "The Netherlands was charming, Hendrik included."

"Charming? It's about time you added that word to your vocabulary. I knew I would like this Van der Aart boy."

Anna fingered the bracelet on her wrist. *Zomerschoon*—the beauty of summer. A warmth blossomed in her chest. If only she could have stayed in *Bollenstreek*. She could have played *Sjoelen* and ate cookies for another week. Then after, she could have shown Hendrik how much his affection meant. She could have made love to him in the hotel where penis-for-a-brain Conner wouldn't have screwed up everything. "I wish I could dwell on him, but that's not why I'm calling. Because turmoil there was, but not until we reached Oxford."

Anna relayed the pieces of the story, each component a part of a complex equation she couldn't solve. She wished Sarah was with her—wished they were back at Al Forno's, the little restaurant near St. Theresa's, where Sarah ate caprese salad and sipped tea while Anna enjoyed a slice of pepperoni pizza and a bottle of beer. At least then the food and Sarah's eyes, always sincere in their gaze, comforted her. But now, as she told Sarah of her predicament, she only had the dim lighting of her room and the threat of inappropriate noises escaping Conner's room.

"What a misogynist son-of-a-biscuit!" Sarah pronounced when Anna had finished. "How are you going to make him squirm?"

"That's just it, I can't figure a way. It should be easy…just…"

"Just you feel like your heart and head are floating in the clouds?"

"Yes! Exactly."

"I know how you feel. Eduardo made me a total space cadet. I swear I'd never been such a ditz until I met him."

"I thought it was a blonde thing."

"Anna Franklin!"

"Kidding. You know I love you."

Sarah heaved a sigh. "You'll figure this out. You always do." In the background, a shrill cry echoed through the phone. "It sounds like Eduardo is testing another baby food concoction. Yesterday he tried figs and apricots. Today it's eggplant and cinnamon. He's determined his son will have a more diverse palate than his daughter. Poor Giac."

Anna huffed. She'd have put up with delicatessen baby food, if it meant having parents half as doting as Sarah and Eduardo. "You should go to him. And give him a kiss from his godmother."

"I will. But first, it seems the only way out of this pickle is for Klara to see Conner in action."

Anna perked up. "You mean, like set him up? Hmm. But it would need to be someone he doesn't connect with me."

"Does Hendrik have any friends?"

"No." Anna blurted the word. "Actually…" She pictured Hendrik sitting with the dark-skinned man in circle-rimmed glasses at the bar. Hadn't Rashaad mention he was married? Anna's heartrate accelerated, and her fingers twitched. She bolted to a stand, nearly yanking the phone charger from the wall. "Sarah, you're a lifesaver. I'll let you know how it feels to see Conner forget his lines."

Sarah laughed before clicking off the call.

Anna raced her thumbs across the screen as she phoned Hendrik. "Hendrik, it's Anna. Don't hang up. Your friend—the one from the bar."

"Rashaad?"

"Rashaad, exactly! Is his wife hot?"

"What?"

Hendrik's voice screeched. Clearly, he had no idea what she was talking about. "Just listen…" She explained her sting idea. Hopefully, it would work. It had to, because she had no other options.

****

The following night, Anna sat in the backseat of Rashaad's sedan and fiddled with her phone. Up front, Rashaad's wife, DeAndra, who was exceptionally hot, stared into the visor's mirror, applying a golden sheen to her lips.

Anna smirked and opened her tracking app. Thankfully, as a friend of Hendrik—and perhaps for a chance at a little nightlife—she jumped at the opportunity to play the part of seductress. DeAndra was all-in on operation Nail Conner Bloom.

Rashaad played the part of driver—both to Anna and DeAndra, as well as later to pickup Klara from the train station.

Somewhat out of the action, Hendrik stayed behind and babysat Rashaad and DeAndra's sleeping kid.

Rashaad cocked his head to the side. "Where's loverboy headed?"

Anna used her fingers to zoom in on a flashing blue dot which zipped down St. Michael's Street. "How predictable." She snorted. "He's approaching the Globe."

DeAndra laughed and smeared lipstick on her cheek. "I don't know which is funnier. You slipping a tracker in your roommate's shoes or that he, Mr. Shakespeare himself, frequents a bar called the Globe."

"I suppose we're both chasing our dreams, Secret Agent Wannabe and Playwrite Extraordinaire." Anna laughed but sank back into her seat. If things didn't go as planned tonight, she might be assisting a secret agent sooner than expected. Would Mike Krueger still offer her the position at NSA if she didn't finish out the year?

Up front, DeAndra rubbed at the smeared lipstick with her fingers, her nails flashing a matching glittery gold.

"What I find humorous is that my wife spent more time getting ready for tonight than she did the last time I took her out for a date." Rashaad tapped his fingers on the steering wheel and tipped his head in DeAndra's direction. "Hmmmmm?"

"I'm surprised you remember, given the last time

we went on a date was two years ago."

"Really? Has it been two years?" Rashaad blew out a breath. "Well, let's hope Hendrik does a good job tonight, then we'll have ourselves a regular babysitter."

"Oh, I'm sure he'll do a good job…destuffing my pillows and busting seams on my couch."

A twinge bit Anna's heart as she imagined Hendrik playing with Rashaad and DeAndra's son. He probably doted on him in the same way he did his siblings.

"Good help is hard to find." Rashaad winked at his wife.

The car turned onto St. Michael's Street, and the glow of The Globe's *open* sign came into eyesight. "I hate to cut into your marital therapy, but it's showtime."

DeAndra straightened her back, tucked a black strand of hair behind her ear, and zipped up her purse.

Anna slipped the hood of her shirt over her head and adjusted her wireless earbuds. "I'll be in the shadows, DeAndra. If anything goes wrong, just walk away. Rashaad, phone in as soon as you have Klara."

Rashaad nodded, pulling the car up to the curb.

DeAndra exited.

As soon as she saw DeAndra enter the bar, Anna scurried out and hid down a dark alley. She yanked out her phone and texted Hendrik.

—*Operation NCBA has commenced. How's it going?*—

As she waited, she spied a window a few feet above. She inched a nearby trashcan beneath it, hoisted herself on top, and peered through the grimy glass. A dark, blurry bar scene emerged.

Conner sat on a stool beside a lanky blonde. He

held a tankard in one hand and a feather in another.

Anna rolled her eyes as he ran it across the girl's bare shoulder. What trick didn't this guy have up his sleeve?

The blonde winced, bolted to her feet, and stomped off.

Conner frowned but then perked up.

DeAndra drew herself onto the girl's vacant stool, swept the feather from Conner's hand, and placed it behind her ear.

Anna grinned. This girl was good! Her phone chimed, and Anna lost her balance. She crashed to the pavement as the trashcan clinked and clanked. Okay, she might need to work on her stealthness before that NSA post. After brushing dust off her jeans, she found her phone.

—No explosions here on Baker Street—

Anna smiled. At least Hendrik seemed less angry about the situation. Her phone pinged.

—For now…can't wait for this mess to be over—

Anna's heart sank. Maybe she should have listened about waiting to be together, then his career wouldn't be in jeopardy. She straightened her spine and lifted her chin. But she would fix this. She peered up to the window. Well, DeAndra, Rashaad, and she would fix this.

Over the next two hours, Anna hovered in the shadows of the alley, the corners, and sometimes even the stalls of the bathroom. And whenever she glanced over at the bar, DeAndra still sat close enough to Conner to smell his cheap cologne.

Shortly after midnight, Rashaad texted that Klara arrived at the station.

Anna watched DeAndra closely. Her seductress friend checked her phone, then cast her gaze over the room, no doubt looking for Anna, and nodded. She stood, grabbing Conner's hand.

Even from across the bar, Anna could read DeAndra's lips.

"I'd love to hear some of your sonnets."

Conner grinned.

Anna slapped a hand over her mouth to keep herself from busting up.

The pair slipped out the door to St. Michael Street.

Her hands suddenly jittery, Anna waited. What if Conner saw her? What if Klara didn't see? What if—? *Cool it, Anna. Is this how Double-O-Prime would act under pressure?* After a few swift inhalations, Anna rehuddled under her hoodie and snuck to the entrance. She opened the door and gasped.

On the sidewalk, stood not only DeAndra and Conner, but Klara, too.

As Anna slammed closed the door, she barely made out Klara kneeing Conner in the crotch. Anna erupted in laughter, yanked out her phone, and texted Hendrik.

—We did it!—

But as she hit send a pit grew in her stomach. How could she cheer when poor Klara suffered? She poked her head out the door. Rashaad's car was gone—he must be in route to Klara's dorm—and DeAndra was nowhere in sight. She grabbed a cab as they'd planned. But farther down the sidewalk, Anna made out a tall figure—Conner. He swaggered slightly…or was he just favoring one side as he grabbed his crotch?

Anna snorted. The injury served the jerk right. To

217

think he was going to cheat on Klara and blackmail Hendrik. Stepping out into the cool, dark night, Anna started down the sidewalk to the bus stop. She'd catch one to Rashaad's house where the crew would celebrate their victory. As she neared the stop, her phone rang just as a text came in from Klara.

—*You up?*—

Anna's heart sank. How could she have neglected this part of the plan? Of course, her bestie needed consoling. She answered the call. "Hello?"

"We did it?" Hendrik's voice sounded cautiously optomistic. "Are you sure?"

Anna sighed. "As sure as a midnight phonecall to a friend warrants."

"Ohh. That bad, huh?"

Anna turned her back on the bus stop and headed toward the university. "You'll have to celebrate without me. I need to go see my friend." If only she was sure she'd want to be her friend after she learned what she'd done.

Chapter 20

Light from streetlamps sparkled on lead-paned glass; the tiny shimmers glowed in the blackened night. As Anna made her way to Klara's dorm, a few students crossed her path, most unsteady in their gait, their slurred speech filling the air. In this last weekend before the start of Hilary term, everyone got their last dose of fun before classes began. Anna should be among them, sipping beer with Hendrik and discussing Littlefield before returning to his place to nuzzle in his sheets.

Damn Conner. Not only was Anna miserable but Hendrik, too. And Klara…poor Klara. Anna shoved her hands into her pockets, kicked the gravel, and picked up her pace. Klara would hate her for putting her in this situation. But this wasn't just about saving Hendrik's butt. Her friend didn't need to lose her virginity to master-manipulator Conner. If only Klara believed her about Conner's behavior before, then Anna and DeAndra wouldn't have ripped out her BFF's heart. She winced at the thought.

Turning onto Longwall Street, Anna faced the New College fourth year dorms—among them the Sacher building. She hurried inside the building to the third floor. With a modern interior, the building stood out amongst the rest of Oxford's wizarding movie structures. Anna knocked quietly on Klara's door.

"It's open," Klara called back.

Anna stepped inside and found Klara curled up in her bed, and she rushed to her side. With flushed cheeks and strewn hair, Klara reminded Anna of Sarah. Only Sarah's turmoil ended in happiness. But not a chance in poetry purgatory existed that Klara would have a happily ever after with Conner—more like a Shakespeare tragedy. She settled in beside her friend. "Shhhh." As she drew out the soothing hush, a knot formed in her stomach. Should she tell Klara the whole story? Should she incriminate herself?

Klara whimpered.

The sound tugged at the rock in her belly. She wiped blonde strands from Klara's sticky cheeks. Klara was too upset and fragile to know everything tonight. She'd tell her soon. Taking a low, deep inhalation, Anna steadied herself. "What happened?"

"I...I..." Her voice shook, and she broke off into a sob. "I saw Conner with another girl." She looked up, revealing eyes wet with tears.

"I knew it! That jerk can't keep his poetry to himself. Does he...did you...?" Anna stumbled on the words. She couldn't reveal all she knew.

Klara pushed herself onto her elbow. "I don't see how kneeing him in the groin would be perceived any other way."

Anna widened her eyes. "You kneed his man junk?"

Klara nodded, her shoulders still slumped, and tears streamed down her cheeks.

But Anna couldn't contain her smile. If only she could have seen Conner's face, stricken with surprise and pain. Sadistic—yes, but oh so satisfying. Hendrik, Rashaad, and DeAndra must all be bursting with laughter and celebration right now. Anna slung an arm around Klara and squeezed. "You know what? You're the one with courage. And you deserve a man with some, too, which is more than can be said of Sonnet Pusher."

Sniffling, Klara buried her face deeper into Anna's shoulder. "I can't believe I was going to sleep with him."

"I can't believe it, either. That man is a walking venereal—"

Klara stiffened.

Anna cleared her throat. "I mean, you'll find the right person—someone with mutual respect for your body and feelings."

"I hope."

"You know, I certainly haven't had any luck with Englishmen. Maybe next time go for an Austrian."

Klara stuck out her tongue.

Okay, she didn't like men from her home country—another trait they shared. "All right, well I can vouch for Italians. And it appears the Dutch aren't half bad either."

Klara leered back, one eyebrow arched high, and narrowed her eyes. "What exactly happened at The Hague, Anna?"

Anna bit her tongue and stood. If Hendrik ever found out she told anyone—including Klara—about their weekend make-out sessions, she could kiss any chance of a repeat experience goodbye for good. As it was, Anna had to get by on drawn-out embraces. Anna averted her eyes from Klara's gaze. "Just some buttery shortbread and gooey cheese. You know I'm a sucker for food."

Klara lifted a brow higher.

Okay, she wasn't buying it. She drew in a deep breath, preparing to embark on the conversation, but the inhalation only incited a yawn. She lifted her brows against drooping eyelids, but the movement did nothing to help her tiredness. She'd fill in Klara once they resolved all this Conner stuff. "Let's focus on Italians. You should come with me next time I visit."

"Let's get through Hilary first, and grad school applications, and"—Klara sniffled—"the woes of a broken heart."

"Get in a few laps on the track, add a few pounds to your bench press, and you'll be ready to find another Romeo."

Klara twitched her lips into a smile.

While small, Klara's smile gave a glimmer of hope of her friend's happiness. Smiling, too, Anna strode to the closet, retrieved the extra blanket Klara kept inside, and bundled up on the floor.

Klara tossed down a pillow. "Thanks for coming."

"No place I'd rather be." She settled into the pillow. Even though the floor was hard and cold, it beat sleeping at home where Scumbag would undoubtedly have already arrived. Although, if he hobbled into the apartment with an icepack between his legs, Anna would have loved to be there. Smiling, Anna stared at the ceiling. Not thin like the walls at St. Theresa's or uneven like the ones in her current room, this Oxford dormitory felt like a boutique hotel suite in comparison to the places she lived the past three years. The large expansive room, with a fireplace, albeit not functioning, had windows that overlooked the New College chapel. Had Anna known the extra two hundred pounds a month afforded her such luxurious accommodations, she might not have chosen to live in an apartment. But then again, she hadn't missed the curfews, the sharing of a bathroom with four people, or the three flights of stairs.

She envisioned Hendrik's apartment with its equally meager offerings with a whiteboard instead of a television, and a desk instead of a kitchen table; Anna's place even surpassed its amenities. Yet, what wouldn't she give to be there right now, snuggled close to Hendrik's firm chest, or kissing away the cologne on the soft part beneath his chin. "Klara," Anna said softly. "Just remember, go for Dutch or Italian."

Anna stayed with Klara through breakfast where Klara rewarded her friendship with a plate full of New College's weekend brunch. While she preferred the American waffle doused in sweet syrup, the traditional English breakfast of cooked potatoes, eggs, and stewed tomatoes would keep her going for days. By the time she'd strolled back to her apartment, she experienced a renewed energy coursing through her veins. Hopefully, the threat of her and Hendrik's secret being exposed sat in the past. When she reached her apartment, she found Conner in the living room.

A frown etched his pasty face, and he sipped a cup of coffee while flipping through channels.

Anna glowered and stalked into the living room. "Still recovering from your bashing?"

Conner flicked his eyes in her direction but didn't move his head. He deepened his frown.

"I knew it would only be a matter of time before your disguise unraveled. Consider yourself lucky I wasn't with Klara when she found you. I would've made you a eunuch."

Conner flared his nostrils and rose. "You saved your friend's virginity, Calculus. So why are you still mad? Because your professor won't stroke yours anymore?"

Her pulse soared, sending the entire room into blackness...except Conner's face. She whipped her arm and smacked his bony cheek.

He jutted his chin with the movement. He slammed shut his eyes. He let out a groan.

"Get out," Anna spoke through gritted teeth. "I don't care what it costs to break our lease, I want you gone before the end of the week. Do you understand?"

Conner turned back with a raised fist.

Anna flinched and stumbled back.

He laughed. "Nothing would make me happier, Calculus."

His sinister chortle was anything but a playful Puck giggle. Anna raised her arms, preparing to thwart a blow.

Conner spun on his heel. He disappeared down the hall.

A flurry of thunks and whacks—a slammed dresser drawer, the clanking of hangers—echoed from his room.

Then Conner reemerged, a duffel bag overflowing with clothes slung over his shoulder. " '*Adieu! I have too grieved a heart to take a tedious leave*.' " Conner bent in a theatrical bow. He marched toward the door. "Merchant of Venice," he called over his shoulder. "And I'll take my five hundred pounds in cash. I'll collect it when I return for the rest of my things." He slammed the door behind him.

"I hope you meet a Hamlet ending!" Anna rushed to the door and smacked a hand against it. Snarky comeback or not, Conner secured the last victory in this war as the recipient of five hundred pounds. Ugh! Why hadn't the clause in the lease been two hundred pounds? She popped her knuckles as she stomped into the kitchen and grabbed a toaster pastry packet—her last box from her trip to Boston. She tore it open and trudged to her room. Trapped somewhere between kamikaze-level anger and tears, Anna yanked her stuffed dog from beneath her covers. Snuggling Paws to her chest, she did her best not to mess his already-matted fur with crumbs. Her eyes burned with tears, but Anna blinked them away and shoved the rest of her strawberry-filled sugar prism into her mouth. What upset her so much? Klara coped well, and Conner was gone—indefinitely. Except…

Anna scanned the room. The entire apartment sat still and quiet. Father hadn't called in days, Cayley remained incapacitated, and…Hendrik? Would they return to *just* colleagues again? She picked up her phone and texted Hendrik:

—*Littlefield tomorrow?*—

She munched on her lard pockets as she waited for his reply.

—*Sure. Up for a celebration? Rashaad invited us over*—

Anna smiled. A party with Rashaad and DeAndra didn't offer a private celebration at Hendrik's place, but the event wasn't an academic one, either. She flew her thumbs over the screen.

—*Yesssss!*—

Hopefully, all was well in the land of Hendrik and

Anna. She supposed she'd find out later that night.

****

Just north of city center, DeAndra and Rashaad greeted Anna and Hendrik at the door, each with a child attached—Rashaad with a squirmy toddler at his waist and DeAndra with a newborn cradled in her arms.

"Rashaad has a roast in the oven." DeAndra rocked the child as she spoke.

Roast—yum. First a New College smorgasbord, now a proper Sunday roast? If Anna stayed this well fed, she might actually break a hundred pounds.

"I brought cookies." Hendrik lifted a tin.

"Cookies?" A rumble attacked her stomach. Even with her Jupiter-sized portions for breakfast, sleeping through lunch depleted her reserves. "You were holding out on me?" Anna lunged for the tin.

Hendrik raised it high above her head, out of reach. "Hence why I stashed them in the front seat." He traded the tin for the toddler who eagerly latched onto Hendrik's hip. "I heard Father Christmas loaded you up, George. Anything good?"

George shook his head, and blond ringlets bounced around his chubby cheeks.

Hendrick bounded down the hall with the toddler, disappearing into the den.

Anna followed Rashaad and DeAndra into the kitchen.

"Anna!" Rashaad beamed. "I haven't had as much excitement as I did last night since Emma had the umbilical cord wrapped around her neck."

Anna tried not to look disgusted, but somehow the image of birthing children wasn't the least bit appetizing.

"God, Rashaad," DeAndra bit back. "How much whiskey have you had?" She rubbed her infant's back as she narrowed her eyes.

The dark circles of sleepless nights rimmed DeAndra's eyes—another unappealing aspect of childrearing. Except for the fact that Anna usually stayed up all night and slept half the day, so she pretty much ascribed to a newborn schedule, anyway.

"Whaaaat?" Rashaad picked up his glass, sloshing a bit of brown liquid over the side as he lifted it to his mouth. "Can't I celebrate my Sherlock moment? It's a 1977 vintage, by the way. You know how I love my single malt." He removed the roast from the oven.

DeAndra clucked her tongue. "Please, your sleuthing is more on the scale of Mrs. Bucket's shenanigans."

"It's pronounced 'bouquet,' darling." Rashaad swapped his whiskey glass for a knife and cut into the slab of meat.

"Let the meat rest, dear!" DeAndra rolled her eyes and started out of the kitchen.

"Don't mind Dee," Rashaad said in a lowered voice. "Aside from last night, she hasn't left the house since she popped out Emma."

Anna snorted a laugh. If Rashaad and Dee behaved any more like the characters from a classic British sitcom, they'd film a reality show in their kitchen tomorrow. But BBC shows were the last thing from her mind. Anna stepped closer to her accomplice. "So," she whispered. "Are you going to keep me in suspense? I want the lowdown, stat."

Rashaad grinned. "You should have seen Conner's face. He looked just like Mercutio when he discovered his wound. And when Klara kneed him in the groin, he dropped to his knees and keeled over like a tipped cow."

Anna buckled with laughter.

"When I drove off, he still lay there in the street, moaning." Rashaad laughed, spilling his drink.

Hendrik appeared in the doorway. "What's so funny?"

Anna tried to control herself.

"Just filling in Anna," Rashaad managed through laughter.

"Ah. So, he's told you about—"

A plastic building block flew through the air and smacked Hendrik square on the cheek.

"George!" Rashaad rubbed his fingers between his brows. "How many times do I have to tell you the blocks are for building, not chucking?"

George poked his head into the kitchen. "Unless I'm throwing them at Mum, right?" He grinned.

Hendrik laughed.

Rashaad flushed.

"Rashaaaaaad!" DeAndra called from somewhere in the house. "What in God's name are you teaching our son?"

Anna tightened the seal on her lips, but bits of laugher still broke through.

Rashaad grabbed George's shoulder. "I need another drink." He sighed as he dragged his son out of the kitchen.

At dinner, much to Rashaad's chagrin, George insisted on explaining the difference between the male and female anatomy.

DeAndra did her best to snuff the talk. "Not at the

dinner table," she chided. Or, "If you want dessert…"

Anna wasn't trying to encourage George, but giggles filled her ever since leaving the kitchen.

Even Hendrik couldn't keep a straight face. Muffled crack-ups interrupted his otherwise polite chewing of the somewhat tough beef.

"Devin says his uncle is getting his penis chopped off—says he's gonna change his name to Mary Lou, too," George announced with a straight face.

DeAndra dropped her fork, and it clattered against her plate.

Rashaad turned a new shade of red.

Anna laughed so hard, she exhaled beer through her nose. When had she last laughed so much? Or sat down to a proper dinner with her family? The pizza she enjoyed with Father came the closest. But aside from that meal, she held no fond memories of dinner-time exchanges. Even when the three of them sat down together, which only occurred on occasion with Mother's responsibilities in the lab, dinners consisted of mindless passing of microwaved peas and questions about Anna's progress in school. No laughter filled their conversations, certainly none which warranted snorts of beer.

"George," DeAndra said, once the laughter had settled, "why don't you clear the table?"

"But, Mum," George whined.

"No buts. If you want pudding, then you'll help clean up." DeAndra picked up Emma from the rocking bassinet which sat next to the table.

"Fine," George huffed. "But I want ice cream with mine. Uncle Henri's cookies taste like buttered blocks."

The seriousness in his expression made Anna think

perhaps he actually tasted a buttered building block.

He hopped up from the table. "Sorry, Uncle Henri."

"No offense taken." Hendrik patted George on the back, then smiled across the table at Anna.

She countered his expression with the lift of a brow. "Is that why you hid them during the ride over? Because they taste like buttered plastic?"

Hendrik held up his hands in surrender. "I said I *know* how to bake them—not that I can do it well."

Anna laughed lightly. Whatever the state of Hendrik's cookies, his attempt would better any she made.

With the two couples remaining in the dining room, DeAndra cooed Emma with a soothing hum.

Rashaad poured himself another drink. "So, has Cayley made any progress?"

Tension pinched her chest. Anna shook her head.

"That's too bad," DeAndra said. "I had Cayley for Freshman Calc way back when."

Hendrik cleared his throat. "Actually, when I visited him this past week, I could have sworn he squeezed my hand."

Anna practically sprung out of her seat. "He squeezed your hand? He squeezed mine as well a few weeks ago. When I told him about cracking Allerton."

"Really?" Hendrik pinched his brows. "That's amazing. I thought I was just imagining it. But I was telling him about Littlefield, that we were going to be working on it."

A broad smile spread over Anna's face. Her cheeks balled so high, they might pop. To think, Cayley awake soon, when they needed him most. Not just so she and

Hendrik could stop sneaking around, but so she could show him their work on Allerton and so he could help her decide what she should do next—apply to confer her masters, take her preliminary exams for the doctoral program, or take a position at the NSA.

"Well, that's fabulous," Rashaad said. "I'm sure the ol' chap will be up and running before Hilary's even in full swing."

Anna relaxed into her seat. She certainly hoped so.

****

Anna had never tasted a buttered block, but she had a sneaking suspicion they tasted identical to Hendrik's crisp-beyond-repair cookies. She followed George's lead and drowned them in vanilla ice cream. The effect mimicked the cookie butter ice cream she used to ask Dad to buy from the specialty store.

After dessert, Anna helped DeAndra clean up the dishes.

The boys escaped to the living room.

Anna wasn't sure whether to use the opportunity alone with DeAndra to pry about information on Hendrik or to hurry up with the washing—the quicker she and Hendrik could be alone. DeAndra didn't seem much of the talkative type, or perhaps that was just because she had a babe on her hip, and occasionally her boob. "So," Anna said, interrupting DeAndra's chittering over introducing formula into Emma's routine, "have you known Hendrik long?"

"Long enough to know that behind his brainy façade, he's really just a big kid." DeAndra slung a towel over her shoulder.

"Really?" Hendrik, the-all-work-and-no-play post doc? Well, he had skipped half of the conference—but

231

Anna chalked up that decision to being a come-on tactic. And there was the playful, albeit competitive, *Sjoelen* match. But big kid? That was a stretch.

"Yep, never a visit without him and George making a ruckus."

A crash boomed from the living.

DeAndra lifted her brows and sighed. "See what I mean?" She shifted Emma to her other hip and headed toward the exit. "Let me see what shenanigans they're up to now."

"No." Anna's word tumbled out before she considered the thought. She placed a hand on DeAndra's shoulder. "I mean, allow me." Smiling, she squeezed past DeAndra and the baby and found Hendrik and George in the thrall of a massive pillow fight.

Rashaad sat in an armchair in the corner, sipping another glass of whiskey.

A lamp—clearly the cause of the crash—lay on the floor, the bulb shattered. Anna crossed to it and swept the glass into her hand.

"Incoming!" George hurled himself onto the couch, where only a pair of feet was visible from beneath a pile of pillows.

A grunt, followed by muffled Dutch, drifted from beneath the pillows.

George climbed to standing atop Hendrik. "London Bridge is falling down!" He stomped on the pillows.

Each bounce produced a groan and more Dutch—cuss words, for sure.

From atop the pillows, George stared up at Anna and puckered his lips into a frown.

Anna should clean up the mess and tame the boys,

but when was the last time she'd partook in a pillow deathmatch? Had she ever participated in one? Her parents hadn't let her put her feet on the couch as a kid, let alone jump on it. She swept the bulb remnants into a pile under the table, upended the lamp, and then brought an index finger to her lips.

George grinned.

Rashaad chuckled.

A burst of energy jolted through her as Anna sprinted toward the couch, jumped, and landed on top of the pillows—and Hendrik.

"Ooof!" He groaned. "What in the hell…?"

George giggled and removed the pillow covering Hendrik's face.

Hendrik frowned, then narrowed his eyes.

Anna let a mischievous grin spread across her face. A spark of amber glinted in Hendrik's eyes.

He pushed himself up on his elbows. "New game." He smirked. "Boys versus girls—full tackle!"

"Charge!" George lunged toward Anna.

Anna shrieked and hopped off the couch, narrowly escaping the boy's fingers. She sprinted toward the door leading to the backyard.

Hendrik and George chased after.

By the time the battle ended, grass stains covered her jeans and mud lodged in the soles of her boots. But Anna left Rashaad's house with a smile wider than when she'd left the Van de Aarts'. Being a kid felt good.

Anna shared a cab with Hendrik, where they talked about the lighthearted events of the evening. They didn't mention Littlefield…Cayley…or even Conner—just whimsical musings of the evening's events. The cab approached Anna's flat, dark and empty, and she suddenly felt the same. How nice would it be to have some company for the rest of the evening? She turned to Hendrik. "Would you like to come in for a drink?"

Hendrik's smile faltered, and he sighed. "Driver," he called up to the front, "would you give us a minute?"

The cabbie nodded and stepped out of the car.

The chill of winter's evening rushed inside the car, sending a shiver down Anna's spine. Hadn't the victory over Conner been enough to secure his approval? What blow would he deliver now?

"Anna, you know I want to come in, but I can't. Not now, at least." He scanned the backseat, out the window, and even the empty driver side. He looked everywhere but at her. "Not until I'm no longer your advisor."

"And when do you suppose that will be?" Her tone was icy. She slid closer to the door and farther from him.

"I...I don't know. As you said, Cayley is making progress. Hopefully he'll recover soon."

"And if he doesn't?" She hugged her arms to her chest.

"Surely at the end of the year, they'll find a permanent replacement. By then, I might be finished with my post-doc. If not, I'll ask you to be reassigned."

"Then why not now, Hendrik? What's so wrong with requesting a reassignment now?"

"No." He nearly barked the reply. "We can't do that. That would draw attention—suspicion."

Anna's insides blackened. Attention? Suspicion? What was he afraid of? Tainting his career? She yanked the door handle. How could she have fallen for someone as career-obsessed as her mother?

"Anna, wait." Hendrik grabbed her arm and lurched toward her. He brushed his thumb over her cheek. "Please, Anna. This isn't just for me. It's for you—us." He kissed her.

His kiss was deep—a soul-searching kiss that shredded any doubt in Anna's mind that she didn't want to be with him.

He pulled back. "Please?" He kissed her again.

This kiss was softer and more distant—a kiss she knew would be the last for weeks…months. Anna let her head fall into a nod, a choice her body seemed to make without asking her mind.

He squeezed her hand, then shifted back to his side of the seat. "Tomorrow," he said, "we can work on Littlefield."

Anna slipped out of the car, the word "us" echoing in her mind. Would this sacrifice really bring them together? And was that even what she wanted?

Chapter 21

In her empty bedroom, Anna couldn't sleep. She could have blamed her awakening on the three cans of soda she drank while binge-watching a gruesome horror series, but neither fizzy burps nor nightmares kept her up. A jitteriness coursed through her veins when she remembered Hendrik's words. A warm glow tinged her cheeks as she relived his kiss.

Anna drew the cover close, hugging Paws tight. Whether he spoke the words or not, Hendrik loved her. Of that much, she was certain. She remembered the first boy who told her he loved her—a bony, scrappy Italian boy she met during her first week in Rome.

"Oh *mia Anna*," he'd cajoled. "*Ti amo.*"

Anna hadn't known whether to laugh or cry. She hadn't meant for any of the boys she picked up at the club to fall in love with her. But the harder she tried to keep an emotional distance, the harder they seemed to fall. Hendrik joined a long line of men who professed their love: Juan, Francisco, and someone else whose name escaped her…Antonio?

But this time the affection meant something more. His words didn't tumble off her like she'd just been asked if she wanted to upsize her value meal. No, Hendrik's words penetrated deep, like somewhere in her belly a small ember lit. For the first time ever, she returned the sentiment. As she closed her eyes, she let her mind dwell on his touch and his kiss.

A few hours of sleep later, Anna awoke and bounced into the kitchen and made a cup of coffee. She glanced at the clock. Wow was she peppy at only seven-thirty in the morning. The same energy that consumed her the previous night still held her captive. Hendrik's energy buzzed inside like a swarm of bees, and she itched to tell someone about it. Klara would be at the gym, but Sarah should be up with Giac. With shortbread between her teeth, Anna pranced into the bathroom, pulled out her makeup, and gave a cookie-muffled command to her phone to call her friend in Rome.

Sarah picked up on the second ring. "Another cataclysm?"

Anna grinned at her reflection and swept a thick line of black liner on her upper lids. "Quite the contrary. I'm in love." She spoke matter-of-factly.

"In love?"

"Yuuuuuup." Anna smacked her lips on the "p."

"Are you pulling my leg?"

"I'm entirely serious. Why else would I be calling?"

"Anna Franklin, I swear on Sister Maria's cross, if you're playing games with me, I will personally fly across the channel and strangle you."

Anna laughed. "Well, I think that's what this feeling is. I knew I loved him, and I even told him, but with the Conner fiasco, this is the first time I can revel in it. Last night he told me he wanted to wait to be together because it would be better for *us*. And that word—us—stirred something inside. Something like I've never experienced. And I'm so jittery...I can't sleep, and I have so much energy and—"

"Anna, slow down! And who is he? It's Hendrik, isn't it? Well, of course, it's Hendrik."

Anna widened her smile, smearing her lip gloss. She wiped it with the side of her finger. "Yes, it's Hendrik. But you're the only one who knows, and since you're not even in the country, I figured telling you is safe."

"Of course, I'm not going to tell anyone! Well, maybe Eduardo, but definitely not Lucia or Sister Maria. They'll just have to wait for the wedding."

"Wedding?" Anna dropped her mascara in the sink, black feathering the bowl.

Sarah laughed. "I'm the one teasing now. But seriously, it's well past your six-week max."

"Holy Fathers of Calculus. Just because I've been dating someone for a few months doesn't mean I'm shacking up with them."

"What about children? Do you think he'll want kids?"

Kids? She widened her eyes. "Sarah!"

Sarah burst with laughter. "I'm kidding."

Anna exhaled a shaky breath. Marriage. Kids. Who had time to think of such things? Littlefield still needed to be solved! With a wisp of setting powder, she finished her makeup. "Thanks for listening though, Sarah. You know I appreciate it. But now, I must rush off to meet the future father of my children." Anna laughed with Sarah, ended the call, and threw on her coat as she headed out the door.

When Anna reached Hendrik's office, she found him huddled over his desk. He feverishly inked a piece of paper. Anna smiled—at least his problem-solving techniques hadn't changed. She tossed her coat over the only other chair in the room—a stiff wooden one that made her butt hurt just looking at it. "Do we have to meet in your office?"

"My office is the least conspicuous place for an advisor and advisee to meet." Hendrik gazed up from his papers.

"Fine, Mr. Expert Pillow Fighter." Anna plopped into the chair with a harrumph.

Hendrik frowned. "Don't be such a sourpuss, Ms. Franklin. Or should I call you Bone-Crusher?" He pointed to his ribs. "I have bruises, you know."

Anna shrugged. "It was worth it, though, to see your and George's faces."

Hendrik chuckled. "George is a great kid."

Short, mouthy, and more energy than Anna on twelve shots of espresso, George was the typical kid-type. Anna couldn't say she usually was a "kid-person," but George brought out a side of Hendrik she'd never seen—his fatherly side. Her throat tightened. "Do you want kids?" The words fell out before she had a chance to process why she'd even thought them.

Hendrik's cheeks reddened.

She swallowed hard. The space between them suddenly seemed to shrink. Anna sank farther into the seat.

As Hendrik stood, he rubbed the back of his neck. "Kids? Well…I…I don't know." He lowered his head and strode to the whiteboard.

Anna considered his response. "Don't know" as in he couldn't consider the thought before he solidified his career or as in she'd caught him off guard? Except, shouldn't she, the product of the two most unlikely candidates for parents, be the one floundering? Maybe if she had a clue as to why her parents had birthed her, she would consider motherhood at some stage in her life.

"Do you?" Hendrik asked.

Anna fluttered her eyelids and gazed up.

He crossed back to his desk again where he held onto the chair, tapping the back.

Anna relaxed her shoulders enough to give a shrug. A coolness settled over her, and a numbness, as well. Was she even capable of being a mother? Sure, she loved the pillow fights and pizza, but being Peter Pan didn't qualify someone as maternal. The only people she knew to be good parents were ones who'd learned from their parents.

Hendrik released his grasp of the chair and squared his shoulders. "Actually, I do want kids. But I'm only twenty-six—you're only twenty-four. Kids seem a long way off for us, don't they?"

Her flesh warmed but clashed with rising goose bumps. Her heart leapt but also ached. He'd spoken so matter-of-factly, so sincerely his words had to be true, and the statement implied he wanted her to be the mother of his kids. Anna widened her eyes. Hendrik and her having a family? That change would mean…well…Responsibility. Love. Family. Pushing away her conflicted emotions, she nodded, stood, and picked up a dry erase marker. "So, Littlefield?"

Hendrik eked out a smile. "I thought you'd never ask." He took the marker from her and wrote on the board, $y^2 = x^3 + ax + b$

"Oh, come on, Hendrik." Anna rolled her eyes. "We've been over this. No Elliptic Curves."

"But why is that possibility so hard to believe?" He furrowed his brows. "Just because it took until the dawn of the Internet to utilize its greatness doesn't mean Littlefield didn't realize it."

Anna pursed her lips. What was she supposed to say? The proposition made absolutely no sense. Hendrik was chasing dreams again. "I never knew your fascination with phallic symbols was so great."

"What?" Hendrik practically shrieked.

Anna snatched the marker back and drew a sketch of a horizontally stretched elliptic curve on the board. "A penis, Hendrik." She tapped the board. "They look like penises! It's no wonder a man discovered them."

"Come on, Anna. We only plot the whole-number dots, anyway."

"Hmmf! If I connect your dots, I still get a penis." She tossed Hendrik the marker.

He bobbled it.

While he juggled the marker, she stole his seat at the desk. Scribbled equations and symmetric, penis-shaped curves inked the papers in front of her. "Even if it's an elliptic curve transcription, how far can we get without a computer? They're the worst trapdoors ever. We'll never break in."

"Un uh, no computers. I'm a mathematician, not a coder."

Anna sighed. She imagined he would say something of the sort. The man didn't own a television. His family probably had never even heard of a dishwasher. She swept aside his scribbled sheets until she came to one with the messages that had already been decoded.

This bud of love, by summer's ripening breath,

May prove a beauteous flower when next we meet. W.S. Romeo and Juliet, A2, S1, L46.

Take all my love, my, yea take them all; What has thou then more than thou hadst before? W.S. S40, L1.

Shall I compare thee to a summer's day? Thou art more lovely and more temperate: Rough winds do shake the darling buds of May, And summer's lease hath all too short a date…So long as men can breath or can see, So long lives this, and this gives life to thee. W.S. S18.

"Why Shakespeare? Why the *San Francisco Examiner*?" She squeezed together her brows.

"Does it really matter?"

"Sometimes these things give perspective—like Allerton and the Greek alphabet. Maybe if we knew more why he wrote the messages it would help us solve them."

"Maybe. But how are we going to figure out that reason? Littlefield was no Beautiful Mind. No one wrote a biography, and no one made a movie."

"What about children? Grandchildren? Maybe they have something with some clues."

"He never married—never had children."

"Oh." Anna stared at the sonnets. For such a romantic, that was surprising. No wonder he died so young—wait, had Littlefield died young? She didn't even know. But she could find out. She twiddled her thumbs over her phone's keyboard. Hendrik could keep himself busy for hours—hell, weeks—with his penis curves. She'd investigate other things.

Across the room, Hendrik held the marker between his teeth and stared at the board.

Clearly, the elliptic curves mesmerized him. She

shook her head. "Fine, we,"—*you*—"can look at the elliptic curves approach."

Hendrik grinned and stepped toward her.

Anna placed a hand out to stop him. "Until I can think of a better idea." She lowered her hand.

Hendrik beamed and kissed her cheek. "Perfect!" He turned back toward the board and scratched his unruly hair. "They do kind of look like penises, don't they?"

Anna laughed. "Yes, Hendrik. They most certainly do."

While Hendrik fiddled with his curves, Anna spent the next few hours researching Littlefield. He'd died at forty-three, only seven years after the publication of the last sonnet. And during those seven years, he didn't produce a lick of anything sensible—no publications, no presentations, no new theorems. He even lost his post at William and Mary.

She dug through virtual documents until she came across his obituary. *Died while in the care of Western State Lunatic Asylum.* Geeze. A shiver ran up her spine. Littlefield hadn't just lost his math mojo; he'd lost his marbles. Maybe this guy was another John Nash. Or, God forbid, an Alan Turing. They didn't commit people in the US for being homosexual, did they? Not wanting to know the answer, she closed the obituary and rubbed the bridge of her nose.

Hendrik stood beside her. "It's late, and you've got class in the morning."

"I do?"

Hendrik frowned.

Anna bit her lip. "Right, uh, yeah. Operator Theory with Lehman."

Hendrik took an exaggerated breath through his nose and shook his head. "Group Theory, Anna. With Professor Kunischzy."

"I knew that." She stood and ran her hands down her thighs. "I was just testing you." She started for the door.

"Uh huh." He followed. "You're lucky I care about you so much, Anna Franklin, or else I'd have to have you expelled."

Anna stopped before exiting the door. A warmth blossomed inside of her that even Hendrik's frigid hands couldn't erase. For the second day in a row, he'd declared his feelings for her, and the more he said it, the more truth it held. It became part of Anna's vocabulary, a fact like the Pythagorean Theorem. Anna faced him, grabbing his hand. "You know what you said about waiting?"

Hendrik jerked back his hand.

"Shhh." She gripped his hand, stroking the back with her fingers. "I'm not suggesting we do anything with *your* elliptic curve."

Red painted Hendrik's cheeks.

Anna laughed and stepped toward him, leaving one heel pressed into the bottom of the door. "Just a kiss." She leaned in, brushing her mouth against his. "One small kiss."

If only she could ensure someday soon she could have more.

Chapter 22

Over the next week, Anna fell back into the routine she assumed during the Michaelmas term: rolling in five minutes late to her classes, bumming lunches off Klara, and then working late into the evenings with Hendrik. While Klara threw herself into her studies and gym obsession, a dark cloud still hung over her friend—one Anna wished she could remove.

On the Friday of the first week, Anna sat with Klara on the quad, sharing lunch. Pristine rows of green striped the oval lawn. Set at the center of the original college buildings, large windows and spires surrounded the courtyard. Students and professors bustled past, en route to classes or perhaps a visit to the adjacent chapel.

Anna dunked her fried haddock in ketchup. "I tell ya, if there's one thing the British know how to do, it's fried fish." She took a bite, the breading crunching under her teeth before the warm, flaky fish melted on her tongue.

Klara ticked a brow. "It's pretty hard to mess up fried fish. But I'm over it. Fish every Friday for three years gets old."

Anna licked her fingers, then squeezed three packets of ketchup over her fries. "If someone feeds me—especially fried food—I'm not gonna complain."

From her cross-legged position, Klara picked up a French fry, examined it, and then dropped it back on her plate. She pushed it away.

She'd barely touched her food. "You've got to eat something. You're going to waste away to nothing." She examined Klara. Her face looked gaunt. Her long, lean arms hung like string beans.

Klara kept her gaze at the ground. "I wish I was still home. Christmas in Austria is just magical: holiday markets, fresh fir trees, and candles. Everywhere there are candles."

"It sounds lovely."

Klara smiled, and tears welled in her eyes. She shrugged. "Christmas still isn't the same without Mom. Dad can't roast a goose to save his life. And his cabbage is soggier than my socks. But he's trying to keep the family traditions going."

Family traditions. Klara had her Christmas Eve feast. Hendrik had shuffleboard. What did she have? Nothing. Absolutely nothing. The grease pit of a lunch twisted her insides.

"You're really lucky to have both your parents, and that you got to spend Christmas with them. I would give anything to have my mom around for just one more day—especially now. She always knew just the right thing to say about guys."

Anna squeezed Klara's hand. Klara told her in the past that she lost her mother to cancer and how the experience inspired her to study science. Anna couldn't imagine losing a loved one. A shiver rushed her spine. Did Mother even qualify as a loved one? When had she had a meaningful conversation with her? Lectures on career didn't count. What would Mother say if she asked her advice on Hendrik? Probably the same as she'd said about Cayley. Find a replacement, stat.

"Anna?"

Klara's voice floated into her thoughts. Anna blinked, and the quad drifted into focus. Their paper baskets of greasy food sat in front of them. Robed students milled around. And Klara sat across from her, her blue eyes questioning her. "Sorry?" Anna released her grasp on Klara's hand, which must have had the life squeezed out of it.

"I asked if you had any family traditions."

"Oh, you know, Santa Claus, Rudolph, and a Christmas tree." The last word caught in her throat. If only she and Dad visited Boston Common together. If only they'd finished the thriller series. If only Dad loved her enough to stand up to Mother. A weight formed in her chest, but Anna fought against it and rose to her feet. She extended a hand to Klara. "Let's go out for drinks tonight. I'm sure it'll cheer you up. Maybe we can even find you a hottie—a non-British hottie."

Klara rolled her eyes. "Oh yes. I'm sure plenty of foreign lovers roam Oxford's bars."

Anna winked. "Well, you won't know unless you go looking, now won't you?" If only her foreign object of affection could ignore his work long enough to be her lover.

****

After lunch, Anna caught up with Hendrik in his office. Elbow deep in inked papers, he chewed on a pen as he ran a hand through his unruly orange hair. He stared intently at his papers. Anna shut the door with an emphasized snap.

He didn't look up.

Anna sighed. "That bad?" She stepped behind him, placed her hands on his shoulders, and squeezed.

Hendrik mumbled about "x-cubed" and "a."

Anna couldn't make out the words. She peered over his knotted shoulders at the papers. The scribble was indecipherable. "Are you sure you don't want to bring in the programmers? Run this thing through some nifty software and presto-chango, bing-bang-boom, we'll have an answer in half the time it would take me to tame your hair."

Hendrik dropped his pen to the desk and sighed. "That's not how it works in math, Darling. We've got to lock ourselves in an attic with our problems and beat our heads against the wall until we find the solution."

"Turing used a computer."

Hendrik stood and faced her.

Smudges of black ink smeared his otherwise pale cheeks. "Turing invented the damn computer, Anna. Besides, he was a Cambridge man."

Anna raised a brow. He had a point there. She couldn't recall any accounts of Cambridge mathematicians locking themselves in an attic like Oxford's acclaimed Andrew Wiles had when he solved Fermat's last theorem. But that didn't mean they had to torture themselves. Besides, if she couldn't solve a problem in a week then either it couldn't be solved, or it wasn't worth the effort. She chewed her lip. Maybe that was her problem with graduate studies in math—she didn't have the stamina. Or maybe she just couldn't keep her focus. Maybe she just needed a break.

She grabbed his shirt collar and tugged Hendrik forward. "Why don't we take a break from Littlefield? A well-deserved break." She closed her mouth over his.

Hendrik didn't resist.

He hadn't refused her kiss for the past few days. As

soon as she clicked the lock on his door, he was comfortable with her touch—at least kissing. But with each passing day, Anna longed for more than just a kiss, more than his hands staying above her clothes. And she was sure Hendrik felt the same.

Hendrik broke the kiss, cursing in Dutch under his breath. "Kissing you is almost as frustrating as this problem."

Anna smiled, a warmth growing in her chest. He definitely felt the same way. "Soon we'll be together." But the fire within snuffed. She didn't believe the words, because soon wasn't in her hands—not in Hendrik's either. February had just begun meaning a good four months until the end of Trinity term and the end of the academic year. By then she would have a new advisor. She winced and suddenly longed for her fuzzy-browed, vending machine munching advisor. "We should visit Cayley." Hope simmered inside. "Maybe if we visit him together, it will help."

Hendrik nodded but didn't face her. "Tomorrow," he said. "Let's go tomorrow."

"Yes."

Hendrik returned to his desk, burying his head in his papers.

Anna found a comfortable position sitting cross-legged on the floor. At least the carpet was softer than the rickety wooden chair. Only the area rug in Hendrik's office matched the geometric pattern one in Cayley's. Images of her beloved advisor lying face-down flashed in her mind followed by a sharp pain in her chest. She rubbed at the spot—a quarter-sized wound above her heart. While Cayley wasn't dead, she had some inkling of an understanding of Klara's pain.

In many ways he was gone; only a shell of Cayley remained. *Please don't let me lose him forever.*

Squeezing back tears, Anna pushed away the thought and snatched Hendrik's laptop. With the flip of the top and a flurry of keystrokes, she resumed her Littlefield search.

Why the *San Francisco Examiner*? Why not the *Washington Post* or the *New York Times*? Why in a newspaper clear on the other side of the US from where Littlefield resided? Anna sifted through old copies of the paper, even found the photocopies of the original print of Littlefield's puzzles. Each one was printed on the third page of the Opinion section, but the solutions often made the front page. But in all her combing, she found no other puzzles and no indication of compensation to Littlefield for the messages.

So why create the goose eggs at all? To show off his coding brilliance? To have a publication—if an opinion column actually counted as one? To challenge his colleagues at…? Anna furrowed her brow. Which math contemporaries hailed from Northern California? Anna made a quick search of all the schools with strong mathematics programs in the area—Berkley being the most obvious choice. She cross-checked them all against Littlefield. But she found no joint papers and no joint presentations. None of the professors could be traced back to Littlefield. Another dead-end.

An idea rushed to her mind, and she straitened her posture. Wait, maybe one of these professors solved a puzzle. Flipping papers right and left, she unearthed the list of solutions and their authors. Alan D. Bliendide. Bennie A.D. Addille. Daniel Lee Bandid. She flew her fingers across the keyboard. But neither Alan, Bennie, nor Daniel taught at Berkeley…or Stanford…or UC Davis. Dang it all! Another endless loop. Anna slammed shut the laptop. Stupid Littlefield Sonnet. Who cared about solving it, anyway?

As she released a tight exhalation, Anna checked her watch. Still two hours remained until Klara would come. Anna flopped onto her belly, hiked up her elbows on the carpet, and sank her chin into her hands. Klara's talk of Christmas filled Anna's heart with a flurry of tiny snowflakes—cold yet beautiful. The irony matched that of their mothers' roles during the holiday. Klara missed her mother's presence when the only bright spot of Anna's Christmas occurred when her mother hadn't been around.

The pepperoni pizza. The donuts. The binge tv. Anna pouted her lip. She and Dad really should have built that model ship. A longing tugged at her heart, and Anna retrieved her phone from inside her back pocket. She pulled up Dad's contact, and a goofy picture of him she snapped before she left for Rome three years ago filled the top of the screen.

Wearing a crooked bowtie which matched his awkward smile, Dad stood in front of his rowhouse. His thinly covered head of blond and white hair was partially cut off from the picture.

Anna smiled, the warmth in her chest growing. While in appearance she and her father were as different as vanilla and chocolate, they got along as well as a twist cone—but never a Neapolitan. The comfort in her chest softened, a tightness forming. No, Mother never played the role of strawberry ice cream. She acted more like sour milk or hot sun—anything to ruin her and Dad's fun. Weren't the best memories of her father—heck, her family—when her mother had been absent? Winning the stuffed huskie. Watching the Swedish thriller. Sailing on her grandfather's boat.

As the memory of sailing rushed back, Anna's breath caught, and she smiled. Cape Cod's coast had looked like a tumbled mountain, the sails had snapped into full billow, and the salty air had whipped her hair. Even at six—or had she been eight?—her thick charcoal hair annoyed her. The errant strands flew into her face, blocking her view of Papa harnessing the rope. That trip prompted her to use the kitchen scissors to hack off her mane. Her hair hadn't grown past her shoulders since.

"Is it tight enough?" Father had grabbed the tails of her life preserver and gave them a tug.

Anna let out a shriek. "If it's any tighter, you won't have to worry about me drowning. I'll suffocate."

Dad handed her a peppermint patty, the wrapper already torn. "For the motion sickness." He winked. "But don't tell your mother."

Anna bit into the candy. Soft and sweet, yet with a stinging mint bite, the candy tasted like the wind picking up. She couldn't remember the last time she ate candy—the chocolate drops that decorated her birthday cake? The butterscotch candies she swiped from the front desk in Mother's office? "Where is Mother?"

Father's smile fell. "She's…um…"

His face soured like he suffered a bout of motion sickness. Anna stared up, waiting for an explanation.

He gazed over at his father.

Papa stopped reeling in the rope and stared at them.

Dad forced a smile and patted Anna's head. "Enjoy your treat. There's more where that came from." He stepped off the dock onto the boat and extended his hand.

Anna smiled and had slipped her hand into his.

A paper crumpled, tugging Anna from her daydream. She gazed across the room.

Hendrik balled the inked sheets from his desk and tossed them into the trash.

A disgruntled frown tarnished his face. Clearly, he got nowhere with his elliptic curves. If she thought his phallic attempts would get them somewhere, she'd offer to help him. Fortunately, she knew another way to boost his spirits because the sailing trip had prompted more than just chopping off her unruly mane. She also learned that day how well chocolate could pacify a wound. She hopped to her feet. "Want to split a candy bar?" Her stomach growled. "Actually, why split? I'll get two." Without waiting for his reply, Anna rushed to the door but stopped just shy of the handle. "Actually"—she wheeled around—"can I borrow two pounds? I drained my account evicting my roommate."

Hendrik chuckled and tossed her a coin.

By the time Anna returned to her quiet apartment later that evening, vending machine bloat set in. Hendrik hadn't helped her gut, either. He'd been so busy checking a = 2 that he'd only eaten one stick of his bar. Anna felt obliged to finish the rest.

Standing with her back to the kitchen, she faced the dimly lit living room. The couch and TV sat in shadow. The apartment was so quiet she could have heard a marker squeaking over a whiteboard. The place stood quieter than Dad's brownstone—probably not as quiet as Mother's apartment, not that she stayed home much. A coolness settled over Anna, and she shivered. She hurried into her bedroom. Thank goodness, she would meet Klara soon. Then she could escape this depressing apartment and enjoy the lights and noise of the city for the night.

Even though he wouldn't join them, Anna took care to pick something to wear Hendrik would approve—a pair of black leggings and an oversized tie-dyed shirt with holes strategically places on the lower back and right shoulder. Hendrik hadn't mentioned those parts of skin showing. Besides, she had no intention of picking up another Butch. She was content with Hendrik, even though his goodbye this evening had been nothing more than a meager kiss on the cheek before he asked her to exit before him.

As she slid on her thigh-high boots, the phone pinged. Anna sighed; Klara always arrived early. Anna still needed to smear on eyeliner and mascara. And her hair! She needed some major gel-action. She swept up her phone on her way to the bathroom and swiped the screen. Her heart skipped a beat. A message, not from Klara, but her mother appeared on the screen.

—Any news on a new advisor?—

Anna tightened her jaw. Did Mother always have to ruin her fun? The horror-show binge with Dad. The Christmas tree in Boston Common. She stomped to the bathroom. And Cayley was doing just fine—JUST FINE. He'd not only squeezed her hand but Hendrik's, too. Anna smashed her fingers into the screen.

—NO.—

Hmpf. With all caps, no less. After she slipped her phone into her bra-strap, she faced the mirror and applied her black liner and mascara. Too much time had passed since she and Klara had gone out...plus, she needed to show the new recruits how to hold down a pint. As she replaced the cap on her liner, her phone vibrated against her chest. Who called now? Only Sarah and—she yanked out her phone and groaned—her mother called.

Anna hesitated before answering. Shouldn't she at least let her liner dry? The phone vibrated in her palm, and Anna sighed. Mother really did choose the worst times to connect. Suddenly, Klara's words flooded back. "You're so lucky you still have your parents." A heaviness set into Anna's chest.

Annoying as Mother's interference was, maybe Mother's involvement in Anna's academic life was the way she showed her she cared. Maybe? She grasped the phone in her hand, staring at the austere, University staff photo of her mother. Her breath strained. Mother did care about her on some level, didn't she? Anna pressed the green button. "Hi, Mother."

"Anna, darling."

Her voice sounded overly sweet. Anna cringed against her souring stomach. This call wasn't about Mother caring, was it? She wanted something. Anna stepped back from the mirror. Did she dare ask?

"I can't believe you're still waiting on Cayley," Mother continued. "This minor speed bump could be a huge hurdle in your career."

Anna tightened her hand on the phone. "Mother, I told you, I'm doing just fine. Hendrik and I started another project, one even bigger than Allerton."

"Oh, now that does sound intriguing. Did the presentation go well?"

"Great, I ran into…" Anna trailed off. Should she mention the NSA guy? The professor from Harvard?

Hendrik's success? Anna bit her lip. If only she could ask her mother for advice on Hendrik—on love, on life. How did she get to twenty-four years old having never asked her mother a pointed question about any of her mother's relationships—including their own? She sat on the edge of the bathtub and fiddled with the zipper on her boots. "Mom, why are my studies so important?"

Silence hung on the line.

Anna squeezed her fingers over the hard metal clasp.

"What mother doesn't worry about their daughter's success?"

Anna flipped the clasp and watched it whirl. Her response was about as generic as the cereal Dad kept in his cupboard. She grasped the zipper again, her socks suddenly feeling lumpy, and pulled down. "What about Dad? Do you worry about him, too? He seems so lonely in the house without you. Why don't you spend more time there?"

"Anna, we've been through this. The commute was just too much. And your father and I, we…"

"You what?" Anna removed the boot and hastily rearranged the sock on her foot.

Mother didn't respond.

Anna tried to adjust the sock, tugging at the toes, smoothing the fabric around her heel, but no matter what she tried, it still felt uncomfortable. She yanked it off and chucked it across the room. "You didn't answer the question, Mother. If you weren't planning on living with him, why did you even marry him?"

Her mother's sigh rushed the line. "It's complicated, Anna."

"I doubt it's as complex as the problem I'm

working on." She scrunched the toes on her bare foot. She unzipped her other boot, that foot now also feeling suffocated.

"Your father was always kind, and his parents had connections at Northeastern. It seemed like the best thing—"

Connections? Anna scrunched her toes, and then kicked off the boot. "Are you saying you married Dad to land a job?"

"The arrangement wasn't *exactly* like that."

"Arrangement?" A sourness tainted her tone, but Anna made no attempt to conceal it. "Then what was it like, Mom? You pretended to be in love with him just long enough to get tenure?"

"God no!"

"Then what, Mom? Did Dad even know?" Anna bolted to her feet and paced the floor with one bare foot and another in just a sock.

"Your father is a smart man."

"Smart? Smart?! A lot of smart people overlook things when they're in love. Not that you'd ever know."

"Anna, please."

"Don't please me. Everything is starting to make sense now. Your absence in my childhood. You moving out. You never even wanted a family, did you?" The words shot out of her faster than the synapses firing in her head. Suddenly, the truth of her parents' relationship stood plainly in front of her...except for one detail, one tiny detail. Anna stopped pacing, her feet arched against the cold wood floor. "Why me?" she whispered. "Why did you even have me?" Her pulse pounded in her ears. Her breath rasped.

And Mother didn't say a word.

But she didn't need to because the pieces fit together so easily now. As the only grandchild on her father's side, the joy they'd exhibited with her, when they'd been alive, had been transparent. But her grandparents' love didn't serve as the only clue. Anna flipped through the index cards of dates in her mind: Mother's first publication, Mother's first position, and Mother's tenure award. The timing worked out near spot-on. Mother received tenure just months after Anna's birth. Quite convenient seeing as her mother hadn't been particularly productive, academically speaking, while pregnant.

Another bribe.

Every muscle in her body tightened, yet at the same time, the phone felt like it might slip from her grasp. "How could you?" Anna's voice tore out in a ghostly rasp—hollow like the feeling inside her chest.

"Anna, darling. You know the difficulty one faces to get ahead in the sciences, especially as a woman. Imagine how hard things were twenty years ago."

Anna didn't respond—couldn't respond. Her whole body shook. Her whole life, her whole existence, was a sham…a lie. Her whole world crashed in around her. The only thing she ever wanted in this life was a family, and this truth tore down the unstable foundation of the only family she ever knew.

"Anna, are you there? What about Cayley? What about…"

Mother's voice drifted off into the nightmare swirling in Anna's head. Anna lowered the phone from her ear. Was this the end of all her hopes to have a family? Or perhaps there had never been any hope at all.

Chapter 23

"Anna," a voice said.

From her bent position on the edge of the tub, Anna lifted her head.

With brows pressed together, Klara stood in the doorway of the bathroom. "We were supposed to meet at seven. I knocked…and called." She stepped into the room. "Your front door was open. Are you all right?"

The phone slid from Anna's fingers and thumped onto the floor. She shook her head. Everything was heavy. Her arms and legs were stiff and tight, like an overstuffed teddy bear but coarse gravel filled her limbs instead of fluffy cotton. Wet sand filled her lungs, making it difficult to breathe.

"Anna?" Klara stepped into the room.

The sand rose in her chest, and her breaths became ragged. Of course, she wasn't all right. Had she ever been? Her life, her existence, was a lie—just another part of her mother's meticulous plotting to get ahead.

Klara placed a hand on Anna's shoulder.

Anna slumped her shoulders and crumpled against Klara's chest. She struggled to find words. What was she supposed to say? That her mother was as dead to her as Klara's deceased mom? If words failed her, perhaps she could do something else—something she couldn't recall doing since Cayley's stroke. She could cry—for the mother she never had and never would have. She let go of the weight inside her body, the heavy stone in her arms, and the suffocating grains in her chest. She let her tears wash away the sand and gravel, her hopes, and her dreams. How appropriate that she shed her tears on Klara's shoulder, her kind friend who'd lost her mother, because as Anna rid herself of this pain, she knew, was to rid herself of any chance of having a mother.

****

The following morning, Anna met Hendrik at the front of Radcliffe Hospital. With bags under her eyes and yawns that came every few minutes, Anna hadn't felt this tired since the weekend she spent partying in Florence. But an all-night out didn't cause this exhaustion. As it turned out, spilling her guts about her mommy issues produced quite the brain-strain. Last night turned into a sob-fest in Anna's room that no amount of Klara's reassuring hugs or even snuggling Paws could alleviate. The conversation with her mother still replayed in Anna's mind. *His parents had connections at Northeastern* and *you know the difficulty one faces to get ahead in the sciences, especially as a woman*. Anna shuddered, and tears prickled her eyes.

"You, um, okay?" Hendrik handed her a cup of coffee.

Anna blinked away tears and shrugged. "Trouble sleeping." What could she say to the man whose family was like the Dutch version of the Cleavers? He wouldn't understand. She sipped the coffee—bitter and scalding, just like the feelings inside. She studied Hendrik. What if she was wrong about his ideas on family? What if his idea of a successful relationship matched Mother's? She sagged her face.

Hendrik frowned.

Anna took another sip, hoping to hide behind the paper cup. But the coffee singed her tongue, and she spit the coffee back inside.

Hendrik raised an eyebrow. "Are you sure you're okay?" He placed a hand on her shoulder.

"Fine." She shrugged him off and approached the entrance. "That coffee tastes like ground-up crayons. Not the good ones, either—like the generic ones that are all waxy and look gray instead of black."

"Okay." He drew out the word and rubbed his chin. "This is Britain, not Brazil."

Reaching the hospital's main entrance, Anna stepped inside. Brazil, huh? Now there was a thought. Lots of ex-operatives escaped to South America. Maybe she could hide out there, enjoy the sun, the sand, the tan dudes, and play under-cover agent? If helping Hendrik with Littlefield only served his and Mother's careers, what the hell was the point?

"I spoke to my mother yesterday. She sends her regards."

Anna reared to a stop and spun around so fast the coffee sloshed out of the cup.

Hendrik grinned.

He spoke about her with his mother now?

"I told her I baked you and Rashaad the most fabulous batch of *boterkoekjes* you'd ever tasted."

With the coffee cup in one hand, Anna planted the other on her hip; she pursed her lips. "Those burnt-to-a-crisp cookies make this coffee look good." She raised the cup to her nose and took a whiff. Okay, maybe his cookies weren't *that* bad.

"All right, all right." Laughing, he held up his

hands. "So I might not have mentioned the cookies. She did ask about you, though."

"Oh yeah?"

Hendrik leaned in. "Trust me," he whispered. "I'm sure she's already counting her dowry."

Anna froze, the cup of coffee still inches from her nose. Steam punched her face.

Shifting back, Hendrik laughed again. "I'm only joking." He rubbed her arm. "We're not gypsies. Besides, marriage is far, far down the road for me." He started toward the elevator.

Anna stared. If she was an oscillating trig wave, she couldn't have been more confused. On the one hand, he had spoken of kids—seemingly, with her. And now, a mention of marriage? Yet he would barely kiss her. And God forbid he request a different advisor for her so they could go public with their relationship. Heck, Klara didn't even know.

"You coming?"

Anna jerked back to the present.

Hendrik stood inside the elevator, one arm holding the door ajar.

With a shake of her head, Anna dashed to catch up, tossing the crayon coffee mixture into the trashcan along the way.

In Cayley's room, Hendrik pulled up a chair to the far side of the bed.

Anna stood nearer the door and clasped Cayley's hand. His skin was dry and rough. Patches of scales covered the back of his hand. Anna stroked them. Hadn't the nurses applied lotion? Was he getting bed sores, too?

Hendrik leaned across the bed and squeezed her

shoulder. "Hey, he's going to be okay."

Anna managed a smile.

"The conference went great," Hendrik said. "You better wake up before Cambridge steals your recruit." He winked at Anna. He shifted his hand from Anna's shoulder to Cayley's. With furrowed brows, he stared at their fragile advisor.

Anna relaxed her hold on Cayley's hand. *Please wake up, Cayley.*

Apart from the shallow rise of his chest with his shaky inhalations, Cayley stayed motionless.

She smoothed his cloud of hair and tucked the sheet under his chin. She kissed his forehead. *Please, Cayley, open your eyes.*

Winter's sun streamed through the window. The shuffle of feet drifted in from the hallway followed by the muffled voices of nurses and doctors. All around her, life buzzed…except in front of her. She grabbed Cayley's hand again and squeezed.

Hendrik cleared his throat. "Anything?"

Anna shook her head and gazed up to Hendrik. His brows furrowed above his amber eyes—the pain was evident.

He dropped his gaze to the bed and placed a hand atop Cayley's. "We've started another problem. The Littlefield Sonnets. And guess what? I think I might finally get use my elliptic curves. Of course, Anna agrees with you. She says it isn't possible. I'll show both of you. As soon as you wake up, you'll see." He lifted his gaze to Anna.

His stare strained like a hopeless puppet master desperately wishing life upon a doll. Cayley didn't squeeze his hand or open his eyes. He barely raised his chest with inhalations.

Cayley's stillness unsettled Anna. What if he grew worse but not better? Her heart sank. She couldn't take another letdown—not after last night. "Cayley"—Anna forced enthusiasm into her voice—"you won't believe it, but your stiff-lipped post-doc has THE biggest crush on me."

Hendrik's cheeks reddened.

Anna smiled. "But that's not even the surprising part. I told him I'd wait to be with him. Imagine six-week limit me holding out for months on end? Can you believe it?" She chuckled.

Beside her, a machine released a series of noxious beeps. The lines on the screen jumped like lightning in a pipe. The heart monitor whizzed to life. Anna's breath caught.

Cayley fluttered open his eyes.

His milky gaze settled on Anna. "Cayley!" Squeezing his hand, she leaned in close. "It's me, Anna. And Hendrik is here, too." She didn't dare take her eyes off Cayley.

Crust rimmed his eyes. He parted his lips as if he would speak, but only a shaky breath emerged.

"Cayley." Anna placed her hands on his chest. "Can you hear me? Can you see me?"

On the other side of the bed, Hendrik said something, too.

But the adrenaline rushing her ears drowned out everything else.

Cayley opened his mouth wider.

Anna focused every ounce of her being on him and what he might speak.

But his lids softened then lowered, drifting down

until the murky disks of his irises disappeared.

"Cayley!" Anna shook his shoulders.

Hendrik rushed to her side of the bed and grabbed her arms. Holding her in a tight embrace, he shushed her.

The machine's beeps released in machine-gun fire before an alarm blared.

A nurse rushed into the room, yelling on a walkie-talkie for a doctor.

Anna wriggled free from Hendrik. "He was awake. He opened his eyes. He was going to tell me something." With each word, the exasperation in her voice grew. A shakiness seized her arms, and her legs trembled. She reached for Cayley again. If she could just get close, she might be able to wake him.

Hendrik pulled her back. Holding onto her, he shifted on his feet in a soothing, rhythmic motion. "It's going to be okay." He kissed her forehead. "The doctors will know what to do."

More nurses and doctors entered the room, and alarms continued to blare.

Anna quivered in Hendrik's embrace. This couldn't be happening. Cayley had looked at her…had tried to speak. He had to be all right…didn't he?

****

The two-mile walk back to the mathematical building seemed longer than usual. The punters on the river seemed to linger as they thrust their poles into the shallow depths. The athletes tossing a rugby ball and tackling each other moved as if coated with syrup. And the clouds hovering above Oxford's famed spires stood as if wind had never touched them.

Turning off the grassy field and onto Parks Road, a

265

wind whipped up the path, and Anna sank into her Rome hoodie, just as she'd done thirty minutes ago when the doctor, who as it turned out was a complete imbecile, visited Cayley's room.

"If he woke up once, it's likely he'll wake again." The doctor tucked his light into his breast pocket.

His easy demeanor gave the impression that Cayley had just fallen asleep on the couch after Sunday football, not being stuck in a coma-induced slumber for four months. Tension crept up Anna's shoulders into her neck. "Any idea when?" She strained to keep her tone from becoming condescending.

The doctor shrugged. "Hard to say." With his gaze glued to a clipboard, he sauntered out.

Anna tugged her hood over her head, balled her fists, and stalked to the corner of the room. She slammed a fist into the ledge of the window. Damn these medical doctors! Their crackpot science was never as definitive as a mathematical proof or a deciphered codex. Her fast breaths fogged the window and had obscured her view of the city…of her world.

"What's this six-week limit?"

Hendrik's voice drew her back to the bustling street leading to the mathematical building. Huddled under her hood, Anna wasn't sure if she'd rather talk about relationships or Cayley. Both made her stomach feel like it might spew her vending machine breakfast. "Pre-Hendrik rules." She sighed and stole a peek in his direction.

Hendrik beamed.

"What about the delayed marriage thing? You have a certain number of publications you want to put on the table before you tie the knot? Two? Three?"

Hendrik dropped his grin to a frown.

"Okay, you don't want a prime number. Four?"

"Anna!" Hendrik careened to a stop. "As if you want to get married."

Anna sank farther into her hood, letting it drop over her brows and obscure her sight. Hendrik was right. Why badger him? Because she wanted a committed relationship or because she didn't like the idea of him not dropping to his knees and begging her to be with him like every other guy she dated? She scuffed her boot against the sidewalk and sighed. "So maybe you're right that I'm not eager to be tied down. Not that I'm a loose cannon or that being married to you would feel like a restraint. Just marriage in general."

"Riiiight." Hendrik drew his gaze away and sagged his jaw.

A pain pierced her heart, emulating the discomfort Hendrik showed on his face. She placed a hand on his elbow.

He turned, lowering his gaze.

His amber eyes bored into hers, and suddenly a lump welled in her throat. "What I mean is, I've had some experience with, um, people—yes, people—choosing their career over relationships."

Hendrik frowned, then sighed. Then he lifted his hand, brushing her face as he eased the hood off her head. "You care to elaborate?"

He held her in a deep gaze, and the eyes of the world seemed to fall on her. The taxi driver who honked his horn as he zipped through a light just turned red. The mother pushing her sleeping baby in a stroller. But most of all, Hendrik. What would he say about her mother's choice? Would he agree with her decision? Would he be disgusted at her family's lack of love?

"It's okay. If you don't want to talk about him I—"

"No." She shook her head. "It's not a him—it's my mother. She told me…" She bit her lip.

"Yes?" Hendrik softened his voice.

"She told me *yesterday* that she only married my father to garner a position at her University."

"*Stront*." Hendrik ran a hand through his hair.

"And, although she didn't outright admit to it, she made it pretty clear my birth was a sort of payoff for securing her tenure."

"What?" Hendrik widened his eyes. "God, Anna." He grabbed her to his chest. "What a heartless woman." He stiffened. "I mean, not that I want to say anything against your mother, but…"

Anna smiled and nuzzled into his warm chest. "It's okay. She is heartless. I guess I was just holding out hope all these years my wicked witch of a mother might somehow morph into the fairy godmother."

Hendrik laughed and snuggled her closer, smoothing his hands down her back.

His spicy cologne filled her nose. His warmth radiated through her. She could stay here forever—so warm and so safe. "But you're not heartless," she whispered. "You won't put your career before those you love."

"No, I wouldn't." Placing his hands on her upper arms, he stepped back. "I love you, Anna. And I promise as soon as Cayley wakes up, we'll be together."

A numbness prickled her lips. This proclamation of love was like no other she'd received—not from Juan, not from Francisco, not from that drunk guy she made out with in the club on Via Corleone. Lifting her heels off the ground, she let her excitement propel her toward his lips.

Hendrik tightened his grip on her arms, halting her. His gaze scanned the street.

Anna lowered her heels to the ground, the excitement inside simmering at his refusal.

He removed his hands from her arms and stepped in the direction of the mathematical building. "I should head back to my office."

Anna nodded and followed. For someone in love, he showed so much restraint. But that was just a testament to his devotion to what he believed in…wasn't it?

Chapter 24

All through the afternoon, Anna stayed with Hendrik in his office. As he settled into his elliptic curve tail-chase, Anna stared dreamy-eyed at the whiteboard. Could it be that everything would fall into place? Cayley restored. She and Hendrik together. Which meant...she stole a glance at him. His long slender fingers, already stained with ink, tangled in his hair. His angular jawline tightened as he chewed on the end of a pen. Anna twisted the bracelet on her wrist, with the metal cool against her skin. Soon she could be with Hendrik, actually *be* with him—not this dark corners, hasty kisses thing. She would lie against his pale cool flesh and not worry about Cayley, about her mother, about—she glanced up at the board again— Littlefield's insipid sonnets.

Perhaps this feeling was what Father experienced when he married Mother? Perhaps Mother made him promises—not like Hendrik's, of course. He was a man of his word. But her mother? She invited Anna home on the pretense of family time together when she really wanted no more than to badger Anna about her advisor. Why? So Mother could brag about it at Harvard? So Mother could use Anna's position as leverage when she asked for her next grant? She wouldn't put it past the woman who used her commute as an excuse to move out.

Dad remained in stupid love with her. Why else did he put up with her rudeness? Why else would he let her toss the last slice of pizza? Let her ruin their streaming marathon? Why else would he put Mother before her?

"Anna?"

Anna snapped her gaze upward.

Hendrik stared. "You, um"—he dropped his gaze to her hands then back up—"okay?"

Anna realized her hands gripped her thighs so tightly her nails pierced through the thin fabric of her leggings. She softened her claws, her thighs throbbing, and smiled. Hendrik looked unnerved. Perhaps because of Cayley or because he worried about her after she unloaded all her mom-drama. She crossed to him and planted a kiss on his unruly hair. "I'm fine." She rubbed his shoulder. "Any progress?"

"Not unless emptying another pen counts for anything." He tossed a pen across the desk. It skittered before falling on the floor. He placed a hand over hers and tilted his head, glancing up. "You?"

Anna searched the papers scattered over the floor: Littlefield's obituary, an illegible medical file from the mental hospital, and a list of all known mathematicians residing in the state of California from 1900 to 1920. "I cross-checked all the California professors with Littlefield's publication and presentation list, and zilch, nada, *niet*—nothing there." She chewed her lip. "Maybe I should see if any of them attended the same conferences? No, back then they probably held only one big conference a year. They'd all be together anyway. That wouldn't tell us—"

"Anna." Hendrik pursed his lips.

A bit of steel tinged his voice, and he sounded like

when he scolded his little brother Stijn for sneaking that extra turn in *Sjoelen*. "You were supposed to be checking a equals two." He narrowed his eyes. "Remember?"

"Oh…um…right." She bit her lip and turned her back to him. "How could I forget? I'll get started now." Back at her mountain of strewn papers, Anna dropped into a cross-legged position and scribbled on a half-used sheet. The computations came easily—the variables and constants painting the page in some sort of Jackson Pollack homage. But the effort was futile. Looking for an elliptic curve deciphering in the sonnets was about as pointless as asking her mother whether she'd been joking when she said she married for tenure. Glancing over her shoulder, Anna placed the page of figures in Hendrik's line of sight then picked up another sheet and bent over it so he couldn't see her work. She wrote,

—Call Dad—

He'd been on her mind since her phone call with Mother. Should she tell him she knew about their arrangement? Did he already know?

—Text Sarah—

Or should she call? Her boyfriend saying the "L-word" probably justified a call.

—Cookies, soda, chocolate—

Ugh, how she needed some chocolate! Ooh, and how had she'd forgotten those shortbread cookies with chocolate medallions on top? If those didn't wake Cayley from his slumber, she didn't know what would. She was definitely picking up a package of those.

Anna added chocolate cookies to her list, folded the paper, and shoved it into her bra strap. She paused, her hand still inside her shirt. One more thing begged to be added to the list. She unfolded the paper, flattened it on the floor, and added, in all caps *HACK MOM'S EMAIL*. Sending one teensy email to Mother's boss dropping the F-bomb couldn't damage her career too much, could it? Grinning, Anna slid the sheet back into her bra. Maybe the email would hurt just enough to make Anna not feel so awful about herself. Maybe…

****

Late that night, alone in her quiet apartment, Anna camped out on her couch. Without the threat of Conner barging in with a plastered first-year at his side, and the long since passed amusement of the email exchange between Mother and her dean explaining her email had been hacked, Anna stared at the *are you still watching this*? message on her TV. The laughter of drunken students drifted in from the street, and Anna slumped her shoulders. Why wasn't she among them? When had she morphed from unruly undergrad to taciturn TA? With a huff, she flipped off the TV and snatched her phone from the coffee table. She knew the answer to that question. Everything changed when Cayley suffered his stroke, when Hendrik appeared in her life, and when her parents butted their heads into her academic choices.

She pulled up Dad's contact but hesitated. If she called now, Dad would harp on her for being awake at three a.m. Dad's lectures she could take—they were brief, even toned, not even any raised eyebrows. But could she take it if he acknowledged the truth about his marriage and her birth? Her stomach dropped. Could she take it if he also was a part in this plan for Mother to gain tenure? What if he also hadn't wanted a child but went along with whatever Mother wanted to do?

The phone slipped through her grasp and clattered to the floor. She lowered her head, feeling a deep knife slice through her chest. Why couldn't she have a normal family? Like Hendrik's or Sarah's or Klara's? Why did she have jacked-up, academic-on-steroids parents? Why? Why!

A jolt of energy rushed through her veins, and she clenched her fists. Jumping to her feet, she stomped into the kitchen and yanked the chocolate shortbread cookies from the plastic bag on the table. She shoved two into her mouth. To hell with her parents. She didn't need them, anyway. She applied for the job at St. Theresa's, and she lived on her own in Rome for two years. She DID NOT need them.

From the fridge, she found a half-empty container of soda and popped the top. She washed down the cookie crumbs, guzzling the flat soda until nothing remained. As she tossed the bottle into the trashcan, she surveyed the room. Now, what was she going to do with herself? Hopped up on sugar and caffeine, she certainly couldn't go to bed. Klara was still asleep, and Sarah wouldn't be up with Giac for another two hours. She let her gaze stray to the glass on her front door, and a buzz of excitement tempted her. She turned her back on the door. No, no, no. She certainly couldn't go gallivanting in the clubs, where she wouldn't leave alone on the same night as Hendrik revealed he loved her. She should do something more practical…more meaningful.

An idea sparked. She'd spend tonight as she had so many at MIT—solving a complex problem. Crossing back to the living room, she rustled through the disarray of papers on her coffee table—a phone bill, a late topology assignment, and, at last, the Littlefield Sonnets. With the paper clutched in her hands, she returned to the couch and curled her knees under her. She would make progress on this problem, even if it meant sacrificing the last candy bar on earth. She reread the verses.

This bud of love, by summer's ripening breath, May prove a beauteous flower when next we meet. W.S. Romeo and Juliet, A2, S1, L46.

Take all my love, my, yea take them all; What has thou then more than thou hadst before? W.S. S40, L1

Shall I compare thee to a summer's day? Thou art more lovely and more temperate: Rough winds do shake the darling buds of May, And summer's lease hath all too short a date…So long as men can breath or can see, So long lives this, and this gives life to thee. W.S. S18.

Anna gasped. She sat up and grabbed the sheet. Of course! Why hadn't she seen it before? She'd looked too closely—had narrowed into the center when she needed to see the whole shape. Littlefield wasn't just a Shakespeare aficianado. He was a lovestruck Shakespeare nut. And the messages weren't meant to find the next Isaac Newton. They weren't to show off Littlefield's genius coding, either. The messages were meant for someone special—a Juliet, a Lady Macbeth, or a Titania. Goose bumps rushed Anna's flesh as a wave of adrenaline coursed through her. If he wrote the verses for his lover, maybe that person had solved them. Anna dropped to the floor and sifted through the papers. She struggled to grasp them with her shaking hands. Her breaths came rapidly and lightly as the sheets of paper drifted through the air. Then she found it, the paper with the names of each person who decoded one of the sonnets:

Alan D. Bliendide
Bennie A.D. Addille
Daniel Lee Bandid

Her heart thudded. The commonality of the letters set stared her in the face, and she knew at once they were anagrams. The letters shifted in her mind as one common name emerged from the jumble—a name she recognized from her research on the mathematics professors at Berkley. This name, the recipient of Littlefield's messages, Anna should have soon before, but at least she saw it now. Annie D. Biddle.

One small piece of the Littlefield puzzle joined together in that moment. How would it inform the rest of the mystery?

****

By the time Anna stumbled up the stairs to Hendrik's flat, she felt her whole body shake with excitement. As she banged on the door, she clenched her teeth to stop them chattering and she reached for her hoodie and found only her bare arms. She pounded the door with her fists and bounced on her toes, hoping to send warmth through her body. How had she left without a jacket? Right. *Annie D. Biddle.* She smacked her thigh, the blow sending a sting through her already blistering cold legs. How had she missed the easiest code of them all? Even now as she transposed the letters in her mind, the anagram seemed obvious. How had no one else noticed it before, either? How had Hendrik missed it?

Her breath clouding in front of her, Anna stared at

the peeling paint on Hendrik's door. Why did Hendrik have to silence his phone at night? No wonder she shivered—her fingers, her knees, and even her teeth chattered. She banged on the door again. Come on, Hendrik. If he didn't get his butt out of bed, he'd need to thaw her out with a hair dryer.

The door creaked open, revealing Hendrik, dressed only in plaid pajama bottoms.

His smooth, pale skin shimmered in the porch light. Her heart leapt to her throat. A warmth replaced the coolness of the winter night.

"Anna...you..." His gaze scanned the street. "You shouldn't be here."

Anna scowled. Of all things, he worried about getting into trouble. No, 'are you all right?' No, 'let's get you inside from the cold.' As she crossed her arms, she stepped into his flat, brushing his torso as she plowed through.

Hendrik winced and stepped back. He widened his eyes, then narrowed them, sweeping his gaze over her. With a furrowed brow, he closed the spaced between them. "You're freezing." He shut the door, then wrapped his arms around her. "What are you doing here?"

The warmth of his chest seeped into her, and his musky scent filled her nose. Anna placed her hands on his back. Smooth and hot, his skin seared her frigid fingers and matched the heat growing inside. Around them, darkness filled the room. The only light dipped in through the window over the couch—the couch where they'd shared their first discovery and where she'd now show him her next. Taking one last inhalation of his dreamy scent, Anna stepped back and toward the living room. "I found something." She rushed to the whiteboard and wiped away Hendrik's scrawling.

"Hey, I was on to something there."

Anna ticked a brow and tilted her head in the direction of the couch.

He assumed a spot on the couch and ran his hands through his hair.

The shag of red remained hopelessly out of place, and she longed to tame it. But not now. They had a bigger obstacle to conquer. Anna took a swift inhalation, turned back to the board, and wrote the three names on the board.

Alan D. Bliendide
Bennie A.D. Addille
Daniel Lee Bandid

She stepped back. "What do you see?"

"This is what you woke me for at"—he searched the room and stopped when his gaze landed on a clock teetering on the walls—"Two-thirty?"

Anna wrinkled her nose. "What do you see?" She darkened her tone and emphasized each word.

Hendrik sighed. "The names of the solvers."

"Nothing else?"

"All men. All have middle initials. All have B's, D's, A's, and…" His voice trailed off. Hendrik studied the board. He scratched his head and cocked his chin. Then he froze. "The letters." His eyes flicked from the board to Anna, then back. "They're anagrams."

Anna gave a slow nod, a smile creeping to her face. "Annie D. Biddle."

Hendrik stood. "The mathematician?"

"No, smarty-pants. Annie Biddle the lady cowboy. Yes, the mathematician. One of the first women

Ph.Ds."

"First awarded in California. Berkley, right?" Hendrik jumped to his feet and paced the narrow opening between the couch and coffee table.

"Very good. You're a quick study."

With a scowl on his face, Hendrik reared to a stop. "So what?"

"So what?" Anna jabbed the dry-erase marker into the board. "So what if Annie D. Biddle solved all the puzzles? So what if Littlefield wrote all the sonnets for her? So what if she didn't solve the last one because—" She tapped the board, and a cluster of black dots formed around the three names. *Why didn't she solve the last message?* She exhaled a tight breath. "Because, I don't know, but it's a lead, and we should follow it."

Hendrik tightened his jaw and his shoulders. "This doesn't tell us anything."

A fire brewed in her belly, and Anna flared her nostrils. "To hell it doesn't. It's closer than we're going to get chasing your penis curves."

As his face burned red, he tightened his lips so hard wrinkles formed above his lips. "This isn't working."

His voice was a gravelly whisper. His face shone like a bright red balloon, ready to pop. Anna stared as a coldness crept down her hands. "What isn't working?"

Hendrik turned his back. His shoulders raised and lowered with his breaths. Even his ears, which poked through the scraggle of his hair, burned red.

Anna held her breath and massaged her palms, but they remained as icy as the feeling in her chest.

With head hung low, Hendrik faced her but kept his gaze on the floor. "I'm your advisor, Anna. I'm supposed to lead our research. I'm supposed to be the one making the breakthrough discoveries. But working with you, even though I love you more than any woman I've ever known, is—" He lifted his gaze to meet hers.

She welcomed the fluttering in her stomach—the quickening of her heart. Finally, he'd spoken the words. He loved her. But…his amber eyes held more than just truth. They held pain. While some of the iciness in her chest melted, and she still gripped her hands. Did his love not bring him happiness?

"Working with you makes me feel like a complete imbecile."

His words tugged at her heart. "No." Anna grabbed his hand. "You're not stupid. You're just not looking in the right places. You're just—"

"Not as brilliant as you?" He yanked away his hand.

Anna reached to pull it back. He must know their relationship hinged on more than research—that he was the only man who truly understood her. She thought he loved her genius. Would he now reject her because of it?

Hendrik avoided her grasp, running his hand through his hair before resting his fingers on his forehead. "I don't know how to fix this." He massaged his temple.

"Fix what, Hendrik?" A steeliness bit her words.

Hendrik winced but kept rubbing his temple and staring at the floor.

Anna's breath shook, and her pulse soared. "Fix this or us?"

Hendrik lifted his gaze, furrowed his brows, and dropped his shoulders.

The look of pain returned in his eyes—the pain of

letting someone go and breaking someone's heart. His expression answered her question without an utterance of a word. If she waited to hear confirmation, she worried her heart might explode with anger…with rage…with sorrow. She dropped her hands to her sides and lowered her head. If he wanted to fix *this…them…*she knew of only one way, and his silence told her he felt the same way. He couldn't work with her anymore.

She placed the marker on the ledge and sulked past Hendrik, past his makeshift kitchen table, and out the door. As the biting cold hit her face, only one question remained: could he work with her in his life at all, or was this the end of them?

Chapter 25

The wind thrashed her face, changing the trajectory of her tears. With frigid fingers, she swatted away the tears. She wouldn't cry for him. She was done crying over those who put their career before her. She was a human being. She had feelings. She wasn't a line on a CV.

Tucking her chin to avoid the wind, Anna turned a corner, and then another until the lights from bars dripped onto the cobblestone. Co-eds in robes staggered onto the sidewalk, their laughter drifting down the street. A shiver rushed Anna's spine, and she folded her arms over her chest and glanced down at her watch. Three a.m. She scanned her outfit. Her black leggings and an oversized tank looked about as flattering as one of Klara's clunky gym outfits. She sighed. What did it matter? She wasn't here to pick up a guy…was she? She stiffened her shoulders.

"I don't know how to fix this." Hendrik's words echoed in her mind, and she clenched her jaw. So what if she went home with someone else? Hendrik sure as hell wouldn't be. Toes now frozen, she hobbled toward the Coat and Arms and shouldered open the door. Warmth breathed out from inside along with blaring music and the scent of sweat and beer. Anna relaxed her shoulders. The atmosphere offered something comforting—a familiar place without judgment and expectations. This place wouldn't tell her what time to arrive for class or what problems to solve.

Shoving through a crowd, Anna found a space by the bar. "Whatever pale ale you have on draft." She slid onto a stool.

The bartender nodded.

Across the bar, two men sat. One wore a bowtie, and the other a faded tee shirt with a stretched-out collar. Anna's heart sank. The pair could easily pass for Rashaad and Hendrik. "Actually, make that a whiskey. A double, please."

The bartender glanced up and furrowed his brow. He nodded and swapped the pint glass in his hand for a tumbler on the counter. He poured the amber liquid and slid it down the bar.

After throwing two bills onto the counter, Anna held the whiskey in her hand and turned toward the open area. With her back against the bar, she surveyed the males. A tall, skinny blond who looked barely old enough to be legal stood by the TV. No thank you. She didn't need any potential students in her bed. By the dartboard stood a husky man with a ginger beard. With a tweed vest and circular glasses, this guy definitely wasn't an undergrad. But she also wasn't keen to bed Watson, either. She'd take Sherlock any day, though. Releasing a tight exhalation, she raised the glass to her lips and sipped. Smooth, smokey, and…whoa—strong! The liquid burned from the back of her throat halfway down her sternum.

As she blinked, Anna returned to the counter and slapped the glass atop it. Wow, she really was turning into Sarah. She used to throw back anything without feeling a thing. But since she started working with

Hendrik, she left her partying days behind. A twinge of pain attacked her belly, and Anna struggled to hold back tears. She'd given up so much for him. She scanned the bar. Who wouldn't give up *all this* for the chance…to be loved? Tears sprang to her eyes, and she squeezed shut her eyes to mask them. She gulped another mouthful of her drink and checked her phone.

Still no messages from Hendrik, and no missed calls, either. Clearly, he wasn't going to be the one to love her. And she doubted she'd find someone to love her in a place like this. She took another sip of her drink. Who were the people who truly loved her—who'd always been there for her when she needed them most? Sister Maria. Sarah. Klara. Her friends—her confidantes. Screw her family, and screw Hendrik. Who she needed right now weren't those who would use her as a pawn in their career track. Who she needed right now was a friend. She checked her watch: just past four a.m. If she hurried, she could intercept Klara on her way to the gym. She just wasn't sure she wanted her friend's advice on Hendrik.

****

Anna entered the quad just as Klara exited the building.

Dressed in blue leggings and a matching long-sleeved shirt, her friend trotted down the front steps as she swept her hair into a ponytail.

"Going for a run?"

Klara jumped and dropped hold of her hair. Blonde waves fell to her shoulders, and she squinted into the darkness. "*Schessie*, Anna! What on Newton's grave are you doing up at this hour?"

Anna shoved her hands into her pockets. "Late

night out." She kicked an imaginary stone. "I thought I'd stop by on my way home."

Klara drew back her hair again and secured it with a hair tie. She frowned.

After a long pause, Anna heaved a sigh. Okay, so her friend wasn't buying it. That's what best friends did—saw right through lame excuses. "And Hendrick might have just broken up with me."

"What?" Klara shrieked.

Anna shushed her. "Do you want to wake up all of New College?"

With a shake of her head, Klara trotted down the steps, crossed the courtyard, and embraced Anna in a tight hug. "I'm so confused. You didn't even tell me you two were together." She shifted back and gazed down at Anna.

"Yeah, well he sort of made me keep it a secret. I mean, after the whole Conner blackmail situation, things took a—"

"Whoa, whoa, whoa." Klara squeezed Anna's arms. "Conner blackmailed you?"

Ugh. First a break-up, and now she needed to go through this revelation with Klara, too? She didn't have the energy for all this drama.

Klara furrowed her brows.

"Can we talk about this over breakfast? I'm starving. If I have to survive on vending machine food for another day, I'll keel over."

Laughing, Klara shook her head. "I can't eat before a run." She broke away from Anna's side and jogged in place. "Will you be okay?"

Anna nodded. "I'm fine. I realized I don't need him or my mother."

"You don't?" Klara jogged down the path leading out of the courtyard.

Anna followed. "Nope. I've got my friends who are always here for me. You, Sarah, and all the other friends I'll make along the way."

Klara smiled.

"But I do need food. How far are you going?"

"Just ten kilometers."

Anna reeled back. Ten kilometers! If she walked any farther than two, she'd be rolled up in a ditch.

"Back in forty-five minutes. I expect a full report on Conner." Klara picked up her pace. "And Hendrik!" she called as she rounded a corner.

Dang, Little Miss Marathon sure got over Conner fast. Two weeks ago, she would have chased Anna for ten kilometers for a chance at reconciliation. Now, she barely cared when Anna dropped the blackmailing reference. At least this boded well for revealing her mission. But forty-five minutes? Ugh. What would she do until then, gnaw on her fist? Dropping her head, Anna stalked over to the stairs and plopped down on the second step. She tapped her foot. She chewed her nails. Finally, she yanked out her phone. Battery at fifteen-percent. Just enough remaining to catch up on news, social media, and conveniently ignore any messages from family and Hendrik.

Yet as she sifted through the day's headlines and scrolled through her friends' posts, her stomach soured. Because she could tell by the absent number above her message icon, as well as above her phone icon, she'd received no communication from Mother, Father, or Hendrik. She pressed the side of the phone, and the screen darkened. *You don't need them, Anna. Forget about them. All you need is right here.*

Anna scanned the courtyard. Unlike the courtyard at St. Theresa's, no fountain sat in the middle and no fig tree stood outside the window farthest from the stairs. Was she really where she needed to be? Cayley remained dead to the world, her research with Hendrik was dead, and everyone knew British food tasted worse than any state penitentiary. But if she didn't stay here, where should she go? Not back to Boston, surely. She could go somewhere new, of course. But should she go somewhere comforting while she figured the next step?

Ragged breaths and thunking footsteps echoed through the air. Anna looked up to see Klara standing in front of her.

With hands on her hips, Klara's chest raised and lowered with quick breaths. "All right." She sucked air. "I ran." She swallowed. "Fast so." She inhaled again. "We could go."

Laughing, Anna stood and pocketed her phone. Klara's cheeks burned so red she could garner employment as a clown. "Oh, Klara, whatever would I do without you?"

Klara wiped sweat from her forehead. "I don't know…starve?"

"Most probably." Anna hopped down the steps and looped an arm through Klara's. Sweat undoubtably transferred from her friend's arm to her, but who cared? At least she had a dear friend by her side and—her stomach grumbled—a mammoth-sized English breakfast on the horizon. If only she could see past breakfast.

****

With a full stomach, a clear conscience, and a

quasi-clear head—as clear as possible on three hours sleep—Anna left Klara at her dormitory and headed… Where exactly was she headed? She checked her phone—still nothing from Hendrik, and he always got up before eight. Always. Anna sighed. Had he given Littlefield any more thought? Had her breakthrough sparked an idea in him?

Forget Hendrik. She let out a groan. Screw effing Hendrik! And screw Littlefield, too. If he hadn't made the last sonnet one his lover could decipher, then why bother writing it at all? Anna stopped in her tracks. Had Annie D. Biddle really been Littlefield's lover? She stared up at the spires where a bird perched at the apex. Another flew by, and the settled bird joined it in flight. They fluttered off into the distance. Biddle and Littlefield must have been lovers—well perhaps just in love. The sonnets must have been a game lovers play.

A memory of Hendrik whizzing pucks down the *Sjoelen* board flooded her mind. She smiled but then winced. A pain struck her chest, as if a thousand *Sjoelen* pucks crammed inside; the pressure threatened to burst her wide open. "Dammit." Anna clenched her hand around her phone. *Stop thinking about him. Stop thinking about his blasted problem, too*!

Releasing a tight exhalation, Anna lifted the phone and commanded it to call the only person who could possibly understand, the only person who could possibly offer some advice, and the only person who would pin her for heartbroken the moment she answered the phone.

"Anna, no. Please say it isn't Cayley."

Anna winced at the pain in Sarah's voice. She heaved a sigh. "No, he's still alive." She slumped her shoulders. "For now."

An exhalation rushed the line. "Well, thank goodness for modern medicine. But…Anna…oh, Anna, it's Hendrik?"

The disappointment in her friend's voice matched that inside Anna. She nodded, momentarily forgetting she didn't stand beside her friend and that she wasn't about to binge on pizza and beer and gelato and forget about men for a while. "Yeah," the word nearly stuck in her throat.

"Well, shoot, Anna, I thought better of him. I mean, this is the first guy you've ever dated who didn't want to marry you upon first sight. He must be flawed. Maybe he's out of touch with his feelings. Wouldn't you say most mathematicians are out of touch with their feelings?"

"Sarah, I'm a mathematician."

"Oh, right. There I go again with my inability to construct a logical argument."

"It's all right. I'm tired of logic. I'm tired of hospitals. And I never thought I'd say it, but I'm tired of boys!"

Nearby on the sidewalk, a pimply-faced boy lifted an eyebrow.

Anna sneered and mouthed, *what are you looking at?*

He huddled under his robes and scuttled down the sidewalk out of view.

"I wish you were here. I'd take you to Al Forno's and—"

"And get me plastered?"

"Exactly! Then we could find a quiet spot and swear off men, well, except Eduardo and Giac, until

Sister Maria called lights out."

"And then we'd still chat the night away, you with earl grey and me with prosecco, and spoons knee-deep in a bottle of choctella."

"Yes!"

Anna smiled. If she were in Rome right now, she could have some proper pizza and ice cream.

"I wish you were here," Sarah said.

So do I.

"But you'll be fine—just fine. Screw that Dutch boy. Who wants to wear orange, anyway?"

Anna released a tiny chuckle. Sarah had a point there. No one looked good in orange—not even any boys with matching orange hair. "Thanks, Sarah. Give Giac a kiss for me."

After she ended the call, Anna scanned her surroundings. Clearly, she hadn't walked aimlessly at all because in front of her stood the Mathematical Institute. She checked her watch—ten minutes until Kunischzy's class. She hadn't showered. She hadn't slept. She really didn't feel like going, so why had her feet led her here?

"Ms. Franklin," a male voice sounded.

Anna looked up.

Dean Bugger stood near the entry waving. He jogged across the pavement. "I'm glad I ran into you." He scanned her and raised a brow. "You're a hard one to track down."

Anna shrugged. "As long as I fulfill my duties, I see no need to spend my life here."

He tapped his index finger to his lip. "True. And Dr. Van der Aart tells me the two of you are making fine progress on Littlefield."

Heat shot through her arms. "Hendrik told you this?"

"Yes, I just came from speaking with him about what I want to tell you."

"And what is that?"

He pinched his lips. "Well, there's no easy way to say this but with Cayley still incapacitated, we will have to replace him. I'm afraid you'll have a new advisor, after all."

Joy and despair clashed inside. Was this the answer to her and Hendrik's dilemma? Could Cayley's replacement fix "this"? She let her gaze drift to the stairwell and the path to Cayley's office, and she shuddered. But what about finishing her thesis with Cayley? What about seeing the fuzzy-haired professor hood her at graduation?

"Things won't be too different for you." He patted her shoulder. "I've asked Dr. Van de Aart to apply for the post, and between you and me, I can't imagine how he wouldn't get it."

The blood drained from her face. "You…asked…him to apply for the position?" Her voice sounded confused. "What…what did he say?"

Dean Bugger beamed a smile. "Why, yes, of course. He said he would be honored."

Honored? Honored! A queasiness seized her gut, and Anna suddenly wished she hadn't consumed two servings of sausages because she was quite sure she might hurl at least one of them on the dean's loafers. If only the dean's shoddy shoes were Hendrik's face. How could he do this? No other cryptography posts existed at the university. She either had to finish her work with Hendrik or leave. Bile rose in her throat, and she stepped back from the dean. "Excuse me, I just remembered I left my protractor at home."

The dean cocked his head and crinkled a smile.

Normally, Anna would stay to observe the bewildered expressions of one of her stiff professors morph into realization that she was joking. But not today. She couldn't get away from the mathematical institute fast enough.

Clutching her stomach, she raced through the doors and down the steps. Why was Hendrik pushing her away like this? What had she done to make him go from professing his love to getting rid of her...overnight?

Chapter 26

Anna's chest heaved with rage and sorrow and all the other emotions she had yet to experience as a newly heartbroken woman. She slammed shut the door to her flat and stomped into her bedroom. She ripped off her bracelet and threw it on her dresser. From the closet, she yanked out her suitcase and haphazardly jammed items inside. She needed to get away from Hendrik, hell from Oxford, and she could think of only one place she'd feel welcome. As she continued to pack, she texted.

To Sarah, she typed:

—I'm getting out of here for a while. Okay if I stay with you?—

Into the suitcase, she stuffed socks, two pairs of leggings, and her leather jacket.

To Klara, she typed:

—I've decided to go to Rome for a few days...or weeks...or maybe forever.—

Anna found her hoodie under her pillow and added it, too. She gathered shampoo, toothpaste, and her toothbrush, and added those to the pile. But Paws was nowhere to be found. Her phone dinged. Klara. She swiped to answer, leaving the phone on speaker.

"You're going to Rome?"

Anna scanned the top of the dresser for her stuffed dog. "Yup." No Paws. Darn it. She needed her stuffie.

"Did you buy your tickets?"

"Nope." Anna dropped to her knees and searched the floor: under the pile of dirty underwear, behind the stack of books, and in the basket of overdue library books. No Paws.

"Do you think they'll be expensive?"

"Expensive?" Anna stood on her knees and sighed. "Heck, Klara, I don't care if they cost me a whole trimester's stipend. I am not staying in this town a second longer than I have to."

"Not for you…I mean, for me."

"You?"

"Yeah, I just thought…"

Klara kept talking, but an incoming call masked her voice. Hendrik's contact shone on the screen. Anna's breath caught. Now he's calling me. Now? That excuse for a man probably wanted a letter of reference. She watched the phone, her heartbeat bouncing in her head, until the contact faded. She missed the call.

"So what do you think?"

"Ummmm." Anna lowered herself to the floor, flattening her body against the carpet until she could see under the bed. Voila! Paws. She grabbed her fuzzy stuffed friend and tossed him into the suitcase. "Sure. Sounds like fun."

"Great! I'll be right there."

Klara ended the call.

Anna stared into space, wondering exactly why and how but at least she knew where. She shrugged. It didn't matter why Klara wanted to come to Rome. It just mattered that Anna was getting out of the UK. Retrieving her phone, she swiped through the missed messages from Sarah. Yes, of course she would let her stay there. But Hendrik had left no voicemail nor written a message. Should she call him back? Anna chewed her lip, then pulled up his contact, swiped the phone, and jammed her thumb into the words *block caller*. She didn't need to talk to him while she stayed in Rome. Maybe she didn't need to talk to him ever again.

****

Eduardo and Sarah's penthouse hadn't changed, but the same couldn't be said of Lucia and Giac. Lucia bounded with grace and smiles and fortunately still silliness. Gone were the days of light-up shoes. She now wore knee-high boots and mini-skirts. Anna looked down at her own outfit which matched her friend's daughter's. Hopefully, Sarah wouldn't blame her for Lucia's fashion choice. And Giac walked and talked—and Anna thought Lehman's lectures made her head spin. Try kids!

Anna settled into the guest room with Klara. On the flight over, she tore out the reason Klara wanted to join for the weekend. Yes, she wanted to be there for Anna, but it didn't hurt that the Austrian soccer team played Italy that weekend. Klara itched to scalp a ticket.

Anna spent two days catching up with Sarah, tickling Giac's toes, and showing Lucia how to keep her socks in place in her boots. But on Sunday, Anna knew where she had to go and who she had to see. She found Sister Maria in her office. Her old boss stood at the window overlooking the fig tree and the fountain in the courtyard beyond. Anna knocked on the ajar door.

"*Entra, Anna.*" Sister Maria kept her back to Anna.

She must have seen me through the window. Or…she's just using her divine foresight again. Anna took a seat.

Sister Maria turned and smiled. "It's good to see you, my child. We have missed you." She lowered herself into her seat and spiked a brow. "But I'm not giving you your job back."

Anna dropped her jaw. How in the world did the old dog know the thought crossed her mind?

"I'm not giving it to you because I don't need you, nor because I don't want you, but because it's not what you want."

Anna stared. How could Sister Maria know what she wanted when she didn't know what she wanted?

"I don't know what you want."

Anna popped her eyes. Holy super prime numbers, she really needed to start thinking about taking up the faith.

"But I know it's not this school. You want to be challenged intellectually. You want to be stimulated creatively. And"—she lifted a hand to her chest—"you want to be loved."

A pang surged through her chest. But she was loved here...only here. Hendrik, her father, and her mother didn't love her the way these people did.

"You reached for your dreams by coming here, Anna, and by going to Oxford. Keep reaching. You'll find your way, and your heart will be full, I promise."

My heart will be full of sawdust. Anna sighed. Where was she supposed to reach? Should she go back to Cayley? Should she go to her father in Boston? Should she start a new life at the NSA? Sister Maria meant well with all her philosophical chatter, but would it be too much to ask for some guidance as clear-cut as the quadratic equation? Anna lifted her gaze to her old boss.

Sister Maria stared back.

Her serene, gray eyes displayed a calmness within Anna yearned for—a peace with the people in her life and the choices she made. Anna dropped her gaze and stood, thanking the nun. She knew Sister Maria would say no more. The rest she'd have to figure out for herself. How she'd do that, she wasn't sure.

****

Back at the penthouse, Anna gathered around the table with the others for one of Eduardo's famous roast dinners.

"Just a heads-up"—Anna nudged Klara's side—"this dinner is about a gazillion courses."

Klara furrowed her brow.

"Just think a Polish wedding reception."

"Ah." Klara laughed and fixed her gaze across the table. "And who's MI6 over there?"

Anna laughed. "Matteo is definitely no secret agent—far from it. He's a lawyer in Eduardo's firm. But from the way he's been eyeing you tonight, I don't blame you for taking him for a spy. Only a spy would be more subtle with his prey."

Klara flushed, fluttered open her napkin, and laid it on her lap. "Well, I wasn't implying I—"

"Oh, whatever, he's hot."

"Anna!"

Matteo and the rest of the table looked over at Klara.

Klara gave a tight smile and straightened her spine.

Anna giggled. If only Matteo were a spy. Now that would be a guy she'd be interested in. Secret missions. Black tuxedos. Fast cars. A jolt rushed Anna's spine.

Maybe this was a sign of what she wanted—action and adventure. Her heart pounded, and her thoughts raced. She knew exactly what move to make next. She needed to call Mike Krueger—now. Anna jumped up from her seat.

Everyone at the table looked up.

"Just one second," she called as she rushed from the room. "I forgot to make a phone call."

Chairs squealed in the background, and voices called, but Anna focused her attention on one thing: finding Mike Krueger's business card. She hurled items out of her suitcase until she found her steel-toed boots. From the right boot, she retrieved the card. Her breath became ragged. Did she really have a shot at a job with the NSA? Oxford hadn't even conferred her master's degree yet...might not even confer it. *Screw it.* Sister Maria said to reach for her dreams, and what did she have to lose? Nothing.

She thumbed the numbers on the screen, and the strange tones of an international call filled her ear, and then silence followed. Anna yanked the phone from her ear, checking to make sure she hadn't inadvertently disconnected. The call's timer continued to climb. She replaced the phone to her ear. "Hello?"

"Good evening, Miss Franklin. I was wondering how long it would take you to call."

Anna gulped. Did everyone have hard wiring into her feelings except her? "I was calling about the position...a position."

"Yes, we still have something in mind for you."

Anna smiled but bit her lip. Outside her window, a scooter zipped by. She leaned forward, furrowing her brow as she took in the cobblestoned street. A block away, a couple entered a quiet café. A few feet beyond, a *gelataria* flicked on its neon sign. And in the distance, the clouds perched above St. Peter's Basilica. Did the suburbs of mid-Atlantic United States house all of the NSA's positions? Or could she work from anywhere like Rome or Paris or Marrakesh? She shrugged. No harm asking that, either. "Do you have any remote positions—perhaps something I could do abroad?"

Krueger cleared his throat. "For a woman of your capabilities, we might be able to make that happen."

Anna bounced on her toes. "That's lit." She bit her lip. "I mean, I'd love to discuss that possibility."

Krueger laughed. "Why don't you finish up your Littlefield problem, Miss Franklin, and then we'll talk specifics?"

Anna cocked her head to the side. Had she mentioned she was working on Littlefield? And working on Littlefield meant working with…she gritted her teeth.

"We'll speak soon," Krueger said.

A click announced the end of the call, and Anna released the stale breath she realized she'd been holding. Littlefield? Littlefield! She chucked her phone across the room. She could not get away from Hendrik and his stupid problems, could she?

"Miss Franklin?" a voice said.

Anna jumped and looked up.

Across the room, Lucia stood in the doorway. "Mom wants to know if you're coming back to the table or if should just bring you a glass of wine?"

"Better make that the whole bottle of wine, Lucia. And no glass needed."

Lucia widened her eyes and took a step back.

Anna laughed. "I'm teasing, Lucia. Tell your mother, I'll be right there, please."

Lucia smiled and turned.

Quiet footsteps informed Anna Lucia trotted down the hall. "And tell her I expect that bottle when I return!" she called after the girl. Anna dropped the shade on her window, tucked Mike Krueger's card inside the boot, and retrieved her phone from the floor. Should she text Hendrik? Had he told Krueger about the Littlefield project? Had Hendrik made any progress? She turned the phone over in her hand. She tossed it from one hand to another. She even pulled up Hendrik's contact and gave considerable thought to unblocking him. "*Zomerschoon,*" she heard him say. *Zomerschoon.* In her mind, she pictured the inscription on her bracelet. The familiar feeling of loss and longing lodged in her throat, and she shoved the phone back into her bra strap. She definitely needed that wine and straight away.

Later that night, after Giac stopped crying and the teenie-bopper shows stopped blaring, Anna lay on the floor beside Klara's bed. As her friend slept soundly, Anna sleuthed. She decided over dinner, she most definitely would not call Hendrik for help on this problem. She would figure this out on her own without him. If she wanted to be Special Agent Franklin, then dammit, she would! She flipped open her laptop and searched Annie D. Biddle. The mathematician and solver of the first three riddles held some clue to the last message, she was sure of it.

For hours she read of Annie's life, of her contributions to the field of mathematics, and her dedication to her students. Biddle had married—not

Littlefield—but another man after the sonnets. This gave Anna some pause. Was her theory about a Littlefield and Biddle love affair wrong? Had Littlefield just been toying with Biddle? Were the messages some sort of test, like the one she was under now? Anna shook her head. No, the sonnets were too personal—too sentimental. The skin on her wrist lay bare where her bracelet would have been. Hadn't she thought *zomerschoon* was personal? Hadn't she thought the message was sentimental? Anna squeezed closed her eyes, forcing the burning tears away. She would think of Hendrik no more. He chose his career over Anna just like Mother had. They both made their choice, and Anna was making hers.

A choice. Anna gasped as a spark fired inside. Perhaps Littlefield made a choice when he wrote the last codex? Perhaps Annie hadn't had a choice in who she married? Yes, yes! This was it—this was the solution! Anna just needed to be sure…

With a click here, and a scroll of the mouse there, Anna searched for the missing information. In front of her, she ordered the dates of all the sonnets and added in the date of Annie D. Biddle's marriage. She married someone other than Littlefield the same day of the last codex. That definitely wasn't a coincidence. A shiver rushed Anna's spine. The pieces of the Littlefield Sonnet finally fit together.

The reason Anna hadn't cracked the last sonnet, the reason Hendrik nor Annie nor anyone else could, was because the message couldn't be solved. The message was gibberish—the message was nothing. Because once Annie married someone else, Littlefield had no one to write his sonnets for. He wanted her to know—wanted the world to know—that without her, his puzzles held no more meaning. Hell, from the history of the rest of his days, it seemed his life held no more meaning, either.

A numbness crept into to Anna's lips, and she snapped closed her computer. Solving this problem held no joy. Instead, an emptiness filled her chest, and a hollowness gripped her heart, because if she thought hard about it, was her plight really that different than Littlefield's?

Chapter 27

Anna saw Klara off to the airport the next day. Well, Anna and Matteo. He insisted on driving them. Anna overheard him ask Klara for her number, but Klara's sternly arched brow told her that exchange hadn't happened. Anna shook her head. Maybe Klara still wasn't over Conner, after all…or maybe she could spot a player now.

She asked Matteo to drop her off along *Corso del Rinascimento,* a stone's throw from her favorite square in Rome, the *Piazza Navona.* Water danced around Neptune, and tourists lounged along the side, catching the spray and enjoying the street performers. Anna strolled the square, perhaps in search of her former friends, but she knew she wouldn't find Francisco or Marco or Adriana. She knew them two years ago. They'd moved on—gone to school or gotten better jobs.

Anna stared down at her outfit, a deliberately mismatched pairing of a mini-skirt and a midriff sweater. Her taste in clothes certainly hadn't changed in the last two years, and neither had her circumstances. She had no new degree and no new job. And how could she get either if she had to explain to Mr. Krueger that the Littlefield problem had no solution but was a product of star-crossed lovers? She was stuck like too much choctella on the roof of her mouth kind of stuck. At least she could find plenty of food to ease her sorrows here.

Moping, Anna surveyed the local *ristorantes* for the cheapest slice of pizza. As she scrounged menus, her phone dinged. Her father. Her heart ached for yet another person she loved who didn't love her back. "Hi," she sighed into the receiver. Why pretend she was excited to talk to him when he probably just wanted to convince her to help her mother's career in some way.

"Hey, kiddo. I hear you're in Rome."

Anna stopped so fast she nearly dropped the phone from her hand. Kiddo? Hear I'm in Rome? She looked at the receiver. Yep, Dad's number all right, but the person on the other end didn't sound like Dad at all.

"I'm sorry you're having a rough time. I hope what I have to tell you will cheer you up."

Anna scoffed. "Cheer me up? Unless you're going to tell me my birth wasn't payment to promote my mother's career or that my boyfriend didn't dump me because I'm too smart or that you aren't going to sell-out to Mom anymore and actually be there for me, then I don't think you have anything to say that would cheer me up."

Silence reverberated on the line.

Around her, a customer looked up from their plate of food and frowned. A server, busy filling a glass with water, sloshed it over the cup. Anna crossed her arms over her chest. Hadn't they heard a woman go off before? Hell, if she had spoken in Italian, she might have caused a scene. She turned her back on the restaurant and stalked away, still waiting for Father to answer.

"Your...um...mother told you?"

"Heck yeah, she told me." She raised a hand and

splayed her fingers. "Why, Dad? Why didn't you tell me? Why did you let me go on trying to win her love when she has no love in her to give?"

Dad stumbled over words, and a smattering of consonants sputtered through the line.

Anna marched back to the fountain and stared up at Neptune. He stood tall. He stood strong. She lifted her chest and flared her nostrils. "Why, Dad?"

"I guess for the same reason I haven't been there for you all these years. Because I thought she might love me, too."

A wave of understanding washed over her, and her body, as well as her heart, softened. A sudden longing to reach through the phone and hug him rushed to her mind. "Oh, Dad." Anna dipped her hand in the water, and the coolness bit her fingertips. "I'm so sorry."

"Don't be sorry. I'm the one who's sorry. I should've been the better parent, instead of better husband. I should've spent more time with you—taken you to Boston Common to see that tree and bought you more donuts and toaster pastries."

A warmth filled Anna's chest and rose to her cheeks, blossoming into a smile. "I want that, too, Dad. I want to build a sailboat. I want to watch the rest of that thriller series. I want to finish that heart-attack-on-a-plate pepperoni pizza!"

Dad laughed.

Now the people around the square stared. But Anna didn't care. She didn't have her mother. She didn't have Hendrik, but she had her father's love, and she wasn't going to let it go. "I miss you, Dad."

"I miss you, too, Anna." He didn't hesitate in responding. "I want to come visit you—soon. Maybe in a few weeks. But first, I need you to do something for me."

The coolness from her fingertips ran up her arm and replaced the fire in her chest. Do something? Please tell me he doesn't want me to do something for Mom. Please tell me this wasn't all some cruel joke.

"I need to you to go buy an Italy daily."

"What?" Anna reared back.

"*Il Giornale d'Italia.*" He stumbled on the Italian. "A newspaper. I need you to read the classifieds."

"O-Okay." Anna fought against literally scratching her head.

"You promise?"

Anna was already searching the square for the nearest vendor. Curiosity alone lured her in. "Yes, Dad." On the far side of the piazza, near a juggler, Anna spied a newspaper stand. Only as she walked toward it, did she notice the annoying tone in her ear. She'd been so engrossed in curiosity she didn't notice Dad had hung up.

As she moved toward the stand, the whole world seemed to rotate as if someone had changed the increments on a parametric equation—everything slowed. Perhaps because she suspected her father didn't play the mastermind behind this game. Who did? Mike Krueger? Or…could it be Hendrik? Her breath caught as she placed a coin on the stand, picked up the paper, and flipped the pages. Her heart tumbled in her chest, because somehow, she knew what she would find before she even saw the jumble of letters mid-way through the page.

He didn't. She shifted the letters in her mind. Two places left. Five places right. *Did he?* She rearranged the letters forward. Then backward. A smile danced on her lips. He made this challenging for her, didn't he? Paper in hand, Anna careened past a restaurant, swiped a pen from the hostess station, and scribbled as she walked. Not a Caesar shift. Not a block cypher. Aha! She poked her pen into the newspaper. Greek. He mapped to Greek and then shifted. She widened her smile. He encrypted the message just like Allerton, the first puzzle they solved together. On the page, from the scrambled letters emerged a message:

Meet me at the Pantheon.

Her heart slammed against her chest as she dashed down the Piazza and hung a left and two rights. In front of her stood Rome's perfect dome, and beneath its columns stood one very imperfect Dutch mathematician in need of a haircut. Anna rushed to him.

Hendrik lifted his head, and pink illuminated his freckled cheeks. "Took you longer than I thought."

Anna smacked his arm with the newspaper. "Took you long enough to call."

"I called you like five hours after you left my place." He stepped closer. "How is that long?"

Anna shrugged. "It's long if you're counting in nanoseconds."

Smiling, Hendrik shook his head. He stiffened his shoulders, and then his jaw, before releasing a tight breath. "I'm sorry, Anna. I'm so sorry." He placed a hand on her arm.

His hand, so strong and so firm, secured her in place. His eyes, like a meteor shower in a dark night, sent sparks through her chest. "I'm sorry, too," she whispered. "I shouldn't have blocked you."

Hendrik jerked back his hand. "Hold up. Are you

saying you were never going to talk to me again? Like again, again?"

"Well…"

With the flick of his hand, he grasped her arm and pulled her close.

His musky aftershave filled her nose, and the warmth of his chest filled her bosom. If this wasn't love, she wouldn't know it if it smacked her in the face.

"I deserved it. I'm still getting used to having a genius for a girlfriend." He kissed her nose. "But I promise I'll learn to live with the fact that you're smarter." Tilting his head, he leaned in to kiss her mouth.

Anna reared back. "But what about Cayley's post? Are you really going to take it?"

Releasing a slow exhalation, he stared down at her. "I want to do what's best for us—for you and me."

A giddiness rushed through her. "Really?"

"Really. I love you, Anna Franklin, and if you don't hightail your butt back to the UK this instant, not even Newton himself can save you from flunking out."

Anna laughed.

He leaned in, pressing his lips against hers.

Soft and moist, everything about his kiss was everything she ever wanted and everything she ever needed. Well, aside from a challenging problem in need of solving. She drifted back from his kiss, clearing her throat. "There's just one thing."

Hendrik lifted a brow.

"I kinda solved the Littlefield problem."

Hendrik widened his eyes, and he opened his mouth to speak.

"Shhh." She covered his mouth with her fingertips,

then tipped onto her toes to kiss him. She'd fill him in on the details of her discovery later. First, she wanted a close-up inspection of his elliptic curve.

Epilogue

Winter's shadow had lifted, and spring's warm, yellow rays streamed over Oxford's spires and domes. On the first day of Trinity term, Anna tucked her hand into Hendrik's and climbed the stairs once more to John Radcliffe Hospital.

Inside, Hendrik headed straight for the elevator.

"Just a sec." Anna slipped her hand from his and ducked into the hallway hidden between the flower shop and reception—the vending machine station. After popping a coin into the machine, Anna retrieved her sweets and jogged back to Hendrik.

He lifted a brow. "I thought you'd sworn off vending machine breakfasts?"

"I did. These are for Cayley, of course." She jammed a thumb into the elevator's button and waited for the doors to slide open.

"Sure." He drew out the word.

Anna shot him a glare but said no more. Could she really fault him for being right?

Two floors up, Anna followed the familiar path to Cayley's room—around the nurses' station, past the linen closet, and turned two corners. How many times had she visited these past six months? Her heart sank. Not many more visits remained now.

"Cayley," Hendrik boomed as he entered the room. He placed a strong hand on Cayley's shoulder. "Your advisee and I have come with great news. Won't you awaken to hear it?"

Anna stared at the white puffs of hair on Cayley's head. Hadn't anyone bothered to trim his hair or clip his brows? And how she wished she could make those brows move now—make his eyes flutter open as they had just after Christmas. She joined Hendrik by her advisor's side and placed a hand near Hendrik's. "We cracked Littlefield." She cast her glance up at Hendrik. "Well, we learned it cannot be broken."

"Anna learned." He placed a hand over hers. "I just, erm, supervised." He squeezed her hand, then stepped away from the bed. "The other news is I've accepted a post in the Netherlands. I'll be leaving at the end of term. And…" He gazed up at Anna.

His eyes pleaded with her—asked her to say the words which would be the hardest for Cayley to accept. Anna bit her lip. "And I'll be joining him. We, Hendrik and I, will be going together."

Suddenly, beneath her hand, Cayley's chest raised with a swift inhalation. The whoosh of his exhalation filled the air at the same time as his eyes popped open. "The Netherlands?"

The words came out in a warble. The left side of his face sagged. Anna gave a little jump. "Cayley, you're…you're awake." She leaned over him, and he wrapped his right arm around her. Even while recognizing his impairment, excitement soared through her.

"How long have I been asleep?"

"About six months, sir," Hendrik said.

"Six months?" He sat up with a start.

The motion knocked Anna off balance, and she

tumbled back.

"And what's this about going to the Netherlands. You"—he lifted his head in Hendrik's direction—"I can understand, but why Anna? She hasn't even earned her Master's yet."

Hendrik's cheeks reddened, and he rubbed the back of his neck.

Anna smirked. "Well, it's funny you should ask that." She sauntered over to Hendrik.

His cheeks burned brighter. "Well…I…"

"Hendrik asked me to accompany him because he thinks I'm the most intelligent and beautiful woman on the planet. Isn't that right, Hendrik?"

He furrowed his brows, cocked his head to the side, and sighed before nodding.

"Don't worry, we made sure everything was okay with the dean first." She squeezed Hendrik's hand.

Cayley blinked his eyes and stared from Hendrik to Anna, then back to Hendrik. "Can someone please tell me what in the bloody hell is going on here?"

In her pocket, Anna's phone dinged—not her personal phone, but the phone Mike Krueger delivered via a man dressed all in black. Anna jumped. "Oooh! I gotta take this!" She rushed to Cayley's side and kissed his cheek. "Don't worry," she whispered in his ear. "I'll be able to travel. I'll come see you every other weekend."

Cayley scrunched his brows and raised a finger. He opened his mouth to speak.

Anna swiveled on her foot and dashed out the door, pressing her thumb into the screen as soon as she was out of earshot of Cayley. "This is Agent Prime."

"Agent Prime," said a computer-altered voice, "we

are sending an encrypted file. Are you in a secure location?"

Anna bounced on her toes. An encrypted file? Yes, her first official case! And how awesome was it they let her go with the Agent Prime name? She scanned the corridor, spied a broom closet, and snuck inside. She dropped her voice to a whisper. "I'm locked and loaded."

A word about the author…

Wendi Dass is a math professor and author from Charlottesville, Virginia. Her writing interests include literary short stories, flash fiction, and novel-length women's fiction and romance. When she's not devising deceptively delicious problems for her students, she can be found in her office drafting her latest story. https://wendidass.com/

Another title by this author
Bella Cigna, Foreign Endearments book 1

Thank you for purchasing
this publication of The Wild Rose Press, Inc.

For questions or more information
contact us at
info@thewildrosepress.com.

The Wild Rose Press, Inc.
www.thewildrosepress.com